THREE MEN ON A PLANE

THREE MEN ON A PLANE

Mavis Cheek

Thorndike Press
Waterville, Maine USA

-L
F
CHE

This Large Print edition is published by Thorndike Press, USA.

Published in 2002 in the U.S. by arrangement with Harold Ober Associates, Inc.

U.S. Softcover ISBN 0–7862–3961–1 (General Series Edition)

The text of this Large Print edition is unabridged.
Other aspects of the book may vary from the original edition.

Set in 16 pt. New Times Roman.

Printed in Great Britain on acid-free paper.

Library of Congress Cataloging-in-Publication Data

Cheek, Mavis.
    Three men on a plane / Mavis Cheek.
       p. cm.
   ISBN 0–7862–3961–1 (lg. print : sc : alk. paper)
   1. Middle aged women—Fiction. 2. Divorced women—Fiction.
3. Large type books. I. Title.
PR6053.H4334 T47 2002
823'.914—dc21   2001054070

For my mother

Especial thanks are due in the boffin department to Dave and Dennis the Disk Doctors, Jan Holzhauer and Hugh Gilbert, without whose computer wizardry I would have remained, as so many of my sisters before me, terminally corrupted, degraded and with a very nasty virus. And this book would have been published posthumously. For their time, their calmness and their kindness during a spell of computer madness, grateful thanks.

Think carefully and often what you are,
what you were, what you will be.

St Aelred of Rievaulx, *The Mirror of Love*

CHAPTER ONE

'You've got a ladder in your tights,' said The Girlfriend, quite without emotion.

Since conversation with The Girlfriend was as rare as contentment in a bikini, Pamela Pryor did not rise but took it, gratefully, as a conversational gambit. Accordingly she began to burble.

'It's my nails,' she said. 'Always were weak and splitty. Never managed to grow them.' She stared at the ten offenders as if for confirmation, gave The Girlfriend an apologetic smile, and ended in a rush with the highly philosophical confidence that she always forgot to eat a square of jelly a day.

More silence.

The Girlfriend looked at her blankly.

Pamela shrugged and gave what she hoped was a girl-talk smile. She was twenty-seven years older than this ladderspotter, so she ought to be able to cope. 'Gelatin,' she added sagely, as if pronouncing a great truth. 'Gelatin.'

More silence.

Twenty-seven years made no difference after all. The Girlfriend was a superior being and ever would be. Pamela moved her leg surreptitiously to hide the disgrace.

'As a matter of fact,' she said with spirit,

1

'they are stockings.'

Despite feeling like a trussed turkey in them, stockings and suspenders reminded her that somewhere underneath it all, she could still display a mean and womanly thigh top. Stockings were sexy and functional as opposed to just functional. She nearly added this to the conversational package when she realized that it was not the kind of thing one said in front of one's departing son and his Girlfriend. Apart from anything else, she did not think The Girlfriend needed any help in that department. If her skirt got any shorter and her top got any smaller, she'd be naked.

The train began to whirr.

Pamela jumped and gave a bright smile. She was close to tears. Hard enough to lose a son; harder still to feel this combination of sadness and liberation. It reminded her of the time she had her plaits cut off in the name of growing up. She had cried for a week and felt blissfully happy. Life did not seem to have moved on much since then in terms of clarification.

Margie would say that it was psychological, the turning up at the station with a rip in her hose. Margie would say it was *deeply* psychological. Margie said everything was psychological, even what you put in the bloody salad. 'Watercress? Ho ho, Pam—' Which she pointedly ignored. Margie also said it was psychological when she decided not to open another bottle of wine at two a.m. and packed her friend off to bed in the spare room. Psychological, Pam, she would say, sinking into the duvet and falling instantly asleep. Until now Pam had thought it was daft, but maybe it was true? She was going to have time to ponder things like that from now on. The thought was supposed to be celebratory.

The train continued to whirr.

'Oh, where *is* Peter?' she said, not so much enquiring as desperate.

She looked around her at the high echoing roofs and the trolleys of ragged packages, as if hoping that the father of Daniel would suddenly appear from some hideaway and swoop down to rescue them all. That she should think this now, she thought sourly, when he had never done such a thing in his life, showed the measure of her turmoil. Of course he would not. As ever, she reminded herself, where Daniel is concerned, you are on your own. So she sighed, merrily, she hoped, and moved the one leg a little further in front of the other, thinking it probably was very psychological indeed.

'Oh, *Mum*,' said Daniel.

He said it in the same voice he had used when she once asked him the rules of football. He had been twelve then, twenty-two now. A lot of water had flowed since. She swallowed very hard at the thought. Life, she told Margie, on the telephone last night, is beckoning. Margie agreed. 'Great,' she said.

But since life had only beckoned Margie as far as a little cottage near Newbury and the teaching of drama to juniors, it seemed rather a fulsome response. 'Get out there and give it to them,' she also said, as if Pamela were some kind of trainee boxer.

She watched a draggled pigeon crap benignly. At least it hadn't hit her. Small comfort. She felt like offering it a thank you. Nothing felt right now, standing here. The beckon did not seem quite so encouraging. More like a finger wagging at her and reminding her, All That Glisters . . .

Euston Station certainly made the whole experience rather brisk. Pamela Pryor, mother of Daniel, now dared to look at her son and he looked back.

'Oh, Mum,' he repeated softly. But made no move towards her.

Behind him the train to Liverpool whirred again and began to make a few acceleration noises as if it were practising for the off. She could do nothing beyond continue to stand there, at least a foot and a half away from her son. The Girlfriend had her arm tucked so securely through Daniel's that even had Pamela dared to embrace him, she would have got all tangled up and ended by entwining and hugging both and probably kissing the wrong one. The Girlfriend would then have rolled her eyes and added this to her private list of Pamela's madnesses.

4

Oh, nothing was ever said, of course, but it was just a fact that a twenty-one-year-old beauty who was tall, blonde and skinny enough to have stepped off the catwalk, would naturally think her boyfriend's forty-eight-year-old not-entirely-gazelle-like mother was a well-meaning idiot. A well-meaning and ancient idiot, who knew nothing whatsoever about anything of importance. Neither of fashion nor sounds, neither of love nor sex. Especially, Pamela felt sure, the latter.

Pamela knew this because one evening when they were all watching television together and the programme on Cuba showed clips of Che Guevara, she told them how she used to fantasize about being naked in the jungle with him. Just to shock a little. The Girlfriend had eaten her way through an entire box of chocolates while Pamela had only dared eat two, so Pamela was feeling a bit uppish. The Girlfriend gave a polite smile of total disbelief. 'But he's dishy,' she said simply, as if that closed any likelihood of Pam knowing what she was talking about. Thinking of her only as The Girlfriend was a small but necessary compensation.

The train whirred harder. The last passengers began hurrying along the platform. Pamela shrugged and gave a little smile. And Danny did the same. And then Pamela leaned forward, put her hand on the bony shoulder (would she feed him? would she?) and kissed

5

his cheek.

He bore it. At least he bore it. Even if he did look acutely embarrassed. The Girlfriend just looked bored.

'Dad isn't coming,' he said shortly. 'He rang this morning. Biked me over this.'

He held up a mobile telephone. Stars shone out of his eyes. Pamela nearly grabbed the thing and tossed it under the train. 'How lovely,' she said. 'What a lovely thought.'

Daniel was pressing bits of the little dark creature and making it beep.

'Cool,' he said.

'Let's go,' said The Girlfriend. And with a definite look of kindness, she turned to Pamela. 'Bye,' she said, through her sweetly youthful mouth.

And suddenly they were on the train.

'Only three hours,' said Pam, as they leaned out at her through the open door. 'And you'll be there.'

'Less,' said Daniel. 'We'll be there in two and three quarters.'

Pamela had an urge to shake him. It was exactly what his father would say. What was a ruddy quarter of an hour when he was her son and they had spent twenty-three years together, not counting the nine months in the womb, and it was about to end?

'Even better,' she said brightly. And then she handed him a £20 note and said, 'You must have a proper lunch on the train. It'll be

6

something to do.'

Both Danny and The Girlfriend looked at her as if she were mad then. She had forgotten, of course, that when you are young and in love you have no need of things like cheese and pickle sandwiches to help you pass the time. She supposed they were in love. They never seemed to show it. Or say it. Just for a moment she remembered how it felt to be in love and envied them. You did not need youth to be romantically inured to the pleasures of an Intercity buffet. Love could hit you at any time. No point in telling them. Her stockings and suspender belt bore silent, historical and bravely laddered witness to that. Any time. Douglas, she remembered, for a little whisper of time, but she quickly dismissed the thought. That was the past. Before her was the future. The future *seulement*. And she would not, really, choose to be young like them, or crazily in love, as she had been at forty, ever again. Just at that moment and having forgotten her breakfast, she would have settled for the cheese and pickle sandwich.

'Thanks,' said Danny. He pushed the note casually into his jacket pocket, where it fluttered precariously, which made Pamela blench, but she did not say, Put it somewhere safe. He also drew out from that same pocket, in wonder, as if he had forgotten its existence, a crumpled cheque. He stared at it for a moment. And then he smiled a smile of such

7

crystalline beauty and lightness that her heart turned over. 'Dad's cheque,' he said, waving it around. 'Be able to get a car now.'

'Put it somewhere safe,' she said, hating herself. But she went on smiling. 'That was kind of him, too, wasn't it?'

Peter, she thought. Father Christmas. It still rankled. Of course Margie, childless but nevertheless self-appointed fount of all knowledge, warned her about it all those years ago when she was first divorced, and the warning had proved true. It never ceased to hurt that Peter could afford to swan in with largesse while she swanned in with refusals of the second Liverpool kit that season, but nevertheless, today, she could begrudge her son nothing in his happiness. If only he was happy. It was always so difficult to tell.

Emotions. Muddled emotions. Suddenly she wished Peter were here. If Peter were here, she would have sobbed into his shoulder, she was sure. He used to be very good at holding her in the old days. Or she would have had a cathartically furious row with him. Something he was not at all good at in the old days. Instead she must bear this alone. Today was the celebration of the first day of her life (thank you, Margie). But twenty-two years, not including the nine months in the womb, and her son could appreciate a sodding mobile phone and a car so much more! He couldn't even put his arms around her in front of The

Girlfriend. Let alone say anything of an emotional nature. Dear God, what had she bred? And what, in the name of pigeon shit, was she doing wishing *Peter* were here? Suddenly, after all these years? It didn't bear thinking about and was clearly some form of maternal dementia.

The train jolted and jerked. It was going to move. Danny stared at his phone dumbly, then at his mother. The world suddenly seemed to stand quite still. Breathing stopped. Now or never, said the air around them. A pigeon flapped. A guard called. Then Daniel leaned out as far as he could, put his arms around her neck and nearly choked her. Or something did. A large grapefruit seemed to have lodged itself among her tonsils. And then he was gone. Waving and waving, even The Girlfriend was waving, as if waving was the release of everything they had so carefully held back. Wave, wave, wave all the way down the line— and then—it was over.

Everything suddenly seemed very small. Except the ladder in her stockings, which grew larger and larger as she stared at it. Of all the crazy memories, she thought again, dropping tears all over the platform—of all the crazy and inappropriate memories—Douglas. Douglas and how he loved to hook his little finger into a ladder and rip the whole nylon to shreds. She was appalled to remember it at a solemn time like this. It was like laughing at a

9

funeral. Peter? *And* Douglas? And why not little Dean Close, too? just to be completely absurd.

The past is another country. She sniffed, swallowed and tried to be brave. She felt so alone. She looked back at the empty track, washed and hazy with her tears, and thought in a thoroughly pleasurable rush of pathos that she was alone, entirely and completely alone, and that there was no one, now, to offer his chest for the dampening of, or stick his finger in her hole and pull, or smile at her with complete incomprehension because of the age gap. All she really wished, feeling so small and silly standing there, was that she had taken Jennifer's sensible advice and booked a facial and a massage. It would have been very nice to be touched by someone in that gentle and intimate way. Even if she spent the entire hour sobbing into the couch.

This is not really me, she thought. This is temporary emotion. It will pass. I will be fine. She turned and walked back up the platform. More trapped pigeons flapped in amongst the girders of the roof. She tried not to think about their futilities. Any minute now, she thought, and it will overwhelm me. I shall then be found tearing my hair, beating my breast, and wandering the Marylebone Road.

So she straightened her back, clenched her hands, and decided that she would go home and take Margie's advice instead. Drink to

Freedom. But, unlike Margie, it would only be one glass. She had a couple of clients to visit that afternoon. In that respect she was not entirely without understanding of Peter's absence. After all, they had both done the same degree at design college, met there, in fact. She was in the business, too. Though now, of course, while he did the grand projects in the grand manner and lived in almost theatrically cool elegance in Bayswater, she had a small interior design shop in West London where people liked curtains and new lamps to express their change of mood—not the raising, in designer terms, of Lazarus.

*   *   *

Not until the following weekend, on a muggy August morning, did she have time to experience both her loss and her gain. In no hurry for anything, having declined Jennifer's invitation to dinner and Margie's to drive down to Hampshire for drinks and bring the dinner, Pamela, mother of Daniel, patrolled her territory.

She opened the airing cupboard. Where once the neat stack of sheets and pillowcases and towels had filled the shelves, now there was space. She dosed the doors, sighed, pursed her lips and went and stood in front of a closed door. I have fitted out their marriage bed, she thought (not that they seemed to be interested

11

in marriage). What more can a mother do? A faded, half-peeled transfer on the door's outside panel said BEWARE and a half-remaining Batman sticker, fist rampant, made the point. She pulled this off determinedly.

Inside the room, if ever she had needed it, was the final proof. Nothing of the techno-world remained—not even the clock radio. Computer, stereo, television, electric keyboard—all gone, leaving only dusty marks on the benches, pits in the Coca-Cola stained carpet, vaguely human smells about the room. Orphaned posters hung limp or flapped from the black and red walls, and the wardrobe, when she swung it open, contained a few bent metal hangers and lifeless, unfashionable garments.

She let the ritual sadness do its work, touched a school blazer, much worn at the collar, a striped tie still in its knot, some threadbare trousers and an old check shirt almost too faded to proclaim Levis across the breast pocket. There, still, were the pristine, non-U jeans she once bought him in Kensington Market. She had been so delighted to find stonewashed.

'Mum. *How could* you?'And the inevitable rolling eyes.

She let the door swing shut and sat on the end of the narrow bed looking at the red blind he demanded she make him. Which he had then slashed and pinned and festooned with

12

chains. Secretly she was rather admiring of it. She stroked the single black duvet cover and heard him—positive, pompous.

'I *ought* to have a double bed.'

'No shoulds, no oughts, Danny.'

'I want, then.'

'Can't have.'

He might never have gone if she had given in to that. Ambiguous thought. She began to wish that she had.

Remembering the cats she had kept over the years helped. Remembering how they carefully nurtured their kittens for the allotted time and then suddenly, one day, wham—they batted them around the earhole and sent them on their way. I have given you as much as I can and now it is up to you. It made it a little easier knowing that this was as right in nature as it was in a Victorian semi in Disraeli Road. That any other route was false and stultifying. That economics did not make it right. That those who could not leave home because they could not afford it were doubly damned.

She did not feel quite so certain now, despite the woman at number thirty-nine who had recently got her divorced son back after fourteen years of marriage. She was washing shirts again, like a tired washerwoman in a Brueghel, just as she had got her husband pensioned off and only wearing three a week. And Pam had read that somewhere in Italy a son had sued his mother for throwing him out.

He was thirty-four. Pause for thought all right. She put her hands in her lap. Alone. It was an odd word. Challenging. Frightening. Margie called it Enhancing.

She would. But Margie never called it Enhancing when discussing, late at night and over a bottle or two, her own Alone.

She caught sight of herself in the long mirror, cheeks pink, eyes blue-bright and misty, fifteen per cent grey hair flying all over the place and, strangely, at nearly ten o'clock in the morning, still in her Japan-Air Happy Jacket. Looking, she decided, every one of her forty-eight years. She refused to acknowledge that she also, at that moment, looked remarkably like her mother. The stage, she knew with alarm, before being *like* her mother.

Danny had gone. *Really* gone. He would never come back, except as a visitor. Not like the university days. University had been a temporary respite, punctuated by weekend visits with dirty washing and long vacations of loafing about or intermittent employment. Getting a flat and a job in Liverpool, and selecting a mate, was for ever.

She eyed the horrible black and red walls. It had been a long time coming. And she was not altogether sure it was what she wanted. She tried a few bars of 'The best is yet to come . . .' And hoped it was true. She also hoped that Age brought Wisdom. The understanding that you could only go on for so long travelling in hope. One day you had to realize that this, really, was it. You had already, probably, had the best.

She shook her head. In Daniel's mirror she eyed the greyness sprouting through her curls. Well, overdue at the hairdresser. Time to take herself in hand again. Had the best of what? she asked herself. Maybe the best of her body, which was a bit saggy, maybe the best of her hair, which was a bit grey-ey, maybe the best of her brain where ideas about design were concerned. But not in every department, surely? Oh, no. She held on to Margie's admonition. Life beckons, it *beckons*. '. . . and, babe, won't it be fine . . . ,' she trilled. She could not remember the next line. Did the song writer say it would or it wouldn't?

She went out, shutting the door firmly. On the landing she looked in the washing basket. One silk shirt, hers; two brassieres; and four pairs of knickers. Now that was more like it. No Mrs Brueghel for her. She was untrammelled, free. She tried the next line again but it still would not come. So she whistled it. And wondered, as she went back down to the silent kitchen, if she was not perhaps whistling in the dark?

15

CHAPTER TWO

Peter Pryor sat in the cool, white loft space and waited for the cafetière to brew. He liked delayed gratification and would not open his post until the coffee was ready. He enjoyed being aesthetic. Among the post was a letter from Daniel, so he felt quite impatient. What car had the boy bought? He looked at his watch. Another two minutes before aromatic perfection.

To pass the time he drew delicate doodles on a plain white pad set exactly square to the shiny white German table top. He doodled curlicues and devices and decorative conceits—an acanthus leaf surrounded by a swan's neck, an initial P intertwined with another P by means of a rose garland—the baroque designs he used to play around with when he first graduated. Before he became an ardent minimalist and sold himself to his future clients as plain, plain, plain.

He looked up with pleasure at the flat white-painted canvas he had just purchased. Smooth as a baby's bottom. Just the odd flaw here and there in the smoothness to show the painter's hand. Saatchi bought the others. He smiled more broadly. Good company to keep. He poured the coffee, which was almost black, into a white cup and added no sugar, though he craved it. He took the first sip. And then he turned to the pile of post. He had to hold the envelopes some way away from his face now, to focus. A change that he did not like. He made a note to see his oculist.

He poured more coffee. Something showed pink among all the whiteness reflected in the metal of the cafetière. He peered and was upset to discover it was his eyeballs. He had been rubbing them again. Damn. He opened Danny's letter. It was simply a photograph of a small red sports car, with black tonneau, out of which popped that girlfriend's self-consciously smiling head. Written on the back was, 'Thanks, Dad. Only six years old and goes like a bomb.' Which he took to refer to the car.

He wondered for a moment how Pamela was bearing up. Badly, he expected. She always did wear her emotions on her sleeve. Whereas, now that Danny had moved from London and got a job, got a flat, got a girl, he felt pleasantly adrift. Like a smooth white iceberg. As he said to those few who knew of his fatherhood and who enquired, it was appropriate that Danny had moved to Liverpool. He could always combine his visits to him with a visit to the Tate.

He opened another envelope using a bone-handled paper knife. Danny had brought it back from a Portobello junk stall when he was just fourteen and when Peter had first moved out of the house to here. At that point he wondered if the boy was going to follow in his footsteps and 'have an eye', but he did not. He followed no one, embraced red and black, drank a lot of lager straight from the bottle, did a degree in business studies and went into computers.

'Wise up and surf the net, Dad,' was a lastingly unpleasant aural memory. Only made worse when Danny decided to refer to his father in company as *Pete*. Apart from the ugliness of the shortening, it also made him feel like a sack of something bought in a garden centre. If Danny really wanted to break down the barriers of parental authority, surely Peter was fine? It was Pamela, of course, who encouraged it. When he asked *her* to suggest that Danny should call him Peter in future, she just said, 'Oh, bollocks.' Once they separated, he had no control over her any more, except in the matter of Danny's maintenance money, which he found irritating.

From the envelope he removed the payment for one of his accounts. The Swedish heiress who wanted a cubic home. No doorknobs, no skirtings, no nothing. Easy money. He had created that environment in one form or another for the last ten years. Even to designing the extension to the Shoreditch Gallery in the same way. Caused quite a fuss when no one was sure how to get in or out of the lavatories. But they learned. He could almost do the design sleeping nowadays. In

18

fact, sometimes it felt as if he *were* sleeping. To Simplify Your Environment is to Simplify Your Life was his philosophy. Pamela, who had once been so admiring of him, said 'Oh, bollocks' to that, too. He opened another envelope, took out another cheque, this time from a delighted American couple. You had to peer quite hard to find the doors in their house, too.

Sometimes he thought that if he could harness the sky and the trees he could make even the houses themselves disappear. Like a Rachel Whiteread in reverse: a conjuring trick for the cognoscenti. The Peter Pryor philosophy. He had designed everything from museums to a pop star's barge on the same principal, though, truth to tell, he was just the tiniest bit tired of it now. The thought of doing anything so grandiloquent as harnessing nature made him feel quite weak.

He first conceived the Design of Absence years ago. While Pam graduated and took a post with a fabric designer, he began his professional journey towards a creative philosophy to herald the ebbing of the age. A profound journey. One that reflected the damage man had already wrought on the world. It took many years. On the way he made a name for himself. And then, one day, he was ready. He made an announcement about it during a particularly targeted, select gathering at his then home.

Which was when his then wife, Pamela,

pulled one of her funny faces and said, 'Don't be so silly. Think of children, pets, grubby finger-marks. What would you do? Make everyone wash their hands before coming indoors?'

Later, a glass or two down the road, she had added the familially famous 'Oh, bollocks'. He was shocked then, still shocked when he thought about it now. It was the beginning of the end. She was for colour, of course, bright colours, often vulgar colours. And destined to be unambitiously domestic. He then reminded her, and the gathering, that Corbusier had done just that. Put a washbasin in the hall. Put washing facilities in every conceivable part of the house. Made washing an integral part of living. Pamela laughed, also reminding the gathering that the despairing Mrs Corbusier said enough was enough and knitted a cheerful cosy for the bedroom bidet by way of rebellion.

That was the trouble with having a wife who had been educated in the same discipline as you but who took diametrically opposing views. No respect. She served red wine at their parties, too, which splashed on to the polished stone floor. Since he went she had actually covered those lovely German Furtzwanger flagstones in *carpet*. Royal blue carpet. And where once there had been white Japanese blinds she had now put sweeping sky-blue curtains. And she *still* had not hemmed them.

He wondered what she would think if he

20

told her that recently he had begun to miss her. *He* still did not know what to think about that. It took him completely by surprise. They had seen rather a lot of each other during the run-up to Daniel's leaving and got on rather well. He wondered if he could forgive her for the offensive cry of Oh, bollocks. If he could, he might consider living with her again. The calm-as-an-iceberg-adrift philosophy was wearing strangely thin. He dared not think the unthinkable, that he was lonely . . . He turned to the final envelope a little sadly. An invitation to give a talk at the Dublin Arts Festival in the New Year. Bill Viola was showing. A favourite artist of his, Bill Viola, cool, measured. He might go. But it was a long time ahead.

On the pad, on a separate page from the conceits and curlicues, and the note about the oculist, he wrote 'Call travel agent: Dublin.' And then he looked around the room a little anxiously. Given the tonal qualities of matching whiteness and his fifty-one-year-old eyesight, he was forever losing the phone.

CHAPTER THREE

In little terraced number twelve Hadley Rise, several streets away from the Victorian villas of semi-detached Disraeli Road, and with a row of hand-to-mouth shops in between, Miss Phoebe Glen picked up the brown envelope from her hall carpet, stared at it for some moments, and then, holding it gingerly, took it into the living room.

She switched on the electric fire—two bars seemed appropriate, though it was but September—and went to the sideboard, an item which was the crowning ignominy of the room: deal pretending to oak, carved with the machine precision and profound insensitivity of poor Utility, a junk shop purchase, made by the landlord. So were the chairs, so was the carpet, so were the entire contents of the shabby little house. It was rented by Miss Phoebe's mother during the war, but not by her father, who ran off with a clippie. After her mother's death the tenancy passed to her. Now the ownership, in its remorseless way, had passed to the landlord's son. It made Miss Phoebe's blood run cold to think of it.

She opened the left-hand cupboard of the sideboard, in which she still kept her mother's white damask table-cloth, square-cut Woolworth's cruet and the doilies, and took out a bottle of sherry and a glass. The postman came later and later these mornings, thought Miss Phoebe Glen, as she removed the cork and poured. She would go to the newsagent's at the end of the road and get her usual paper in a minute. But for now she would just wet her lips before opening the envelope. She was

22

fairly sure she knew what it contained.

*　　　*　　　*

Ani Patel put up a sign, spelled out for her by her son Ari, who was known to be something of a wag in the sixth form, saying, 'One pound a week and you may advertise in our widow.'

Having fixed it neatly with Sellotape, she peered out, through the clutter of advertising stickers and cigarette motifs, to watch her son as he walked off down the road. She wished he still wore his school uniform. He was a good boy and it hurt to see him in a T-shirt and jeans. The morning was not all that warm. Autumn term, first day back, final year of the A-levels, and he was doing so well.

She felt a burst of pride, which quickly evaporated, replaced by a cold fear that clutched at her heart. Oh, my god, Daddy, she thought, putting a hand to her mouth, Oh, my god. For her son, her only son, Ari, had just placed his arm around a girl. One with very long white legs and a very short skirt and with only half of her blouse buttons done up. Ani Patel tried to make out which girl it was, but they all looked the same to her.

She shook her head. Just as well that Ari's waggishness contained truth. Daddy had died five years ago. Widow she was. Looking at the way the girl swung her body at her son, Mrs Patel counted her blessings: she would never have heard the last of it. Oh, Daddy, she repeated under her breath, and returned to her duties.

The cheap sweets were in disarray after the morning school rush. As she tidied she marvelled again at the amount of sugar each individual child bought and consumed every day, twice a day, with money given to them by parents for that very purpose. Ani Patel considered that the purchase and consuming of these sweets and fizzy drinks served two strange uses. It filled their mouths so they did not have to speak, and it represented the sweetness of love, making them feel cared for instead of fat and rotten-toothed. Ari's teeth were pure, like white tombstones, despite living above the shop. Yet she had served very small children who paid for their purchases with a £10 note. It was unfathomable. But it was very good—she went back behind the counter to wait for the day's regular customers—it was very, very good for business. And it was the business that would see Ari through.

In a shop like this, if you worked hard and gave good value and supplied the services the people needed, then you did well enough. Window advertising was just the latest little idea—no money in it for her, of course—but a necessary and useful service all the same. Well might Ari mock. But he was never without shoes or books, was he? When she thought of

24

her father's tales of the dusty fields around Karachi and how he had carried stones on his head to build the airport instead of attending school, she felt that no burden, no burden at all, could ever compare. If you had a friendly word to say to people, a little help and advice here and there, it smoothed the oily wheels.

CHAPTER FOUR

Pamela was pampering. And the bath was almost too full for her to move without splashing scented water over the sides. It was that Zen moment of rightness. The silent emptiness of the house was real and in many ways beneficial. Even down to the freedom to leave the bathroom door open without fear of shocking Daniel or his friends. It was more than a month since she had stood at Euston waving. And she was just beginning to feel the benefits of liberation. There were sad moments, of course, but she did not want to think about those now.

She surprised herself by not going into the shop that morning. It was such a rare event that Jennifer, her partner, assumed she was ill. Pamela smiled to herself and decided that youth was wasted on the young. If she had said, 'It is because I feel liberated . . .' Jennifer would have told everyone she was being brave, and privately put it down to the menopause. Jennifer, at thirty-six, had done all her research in readiness. Terms such as natural progesterone and yam extract fell from her youthful lips and she was fond of saying that the future held no fear. Pamela wanted to say that she felt the same way but she would not have believed her. Jenny would get a nanny for her own children when the time came. Jenny had made up her mind that Pamela was a brave, determined, successful role model of a woman in business, but sadly domestically downtrodden out of it. You wait, Pamela said, lying there luxuriating. You wait until you have children. Nannies won't be armour enough against them. One day, Jennifer my girl, you'll *know*.

She pushed herself right under the water, leaving only her eyes and nose free. The telephone rang. Indistinctly she heard her partner's voice leaving a message on the answerphone. Something about the Wilkinsons' curtains not being ready. 'I wouldn't bother you but she says it is terribly urgent. Her daughter's wedding is at the weekend and she needs to get them hung. Could you ring back?'

'Urgent?' mouthed Paula, reimmersing herself. 'How can curtains be *urgent?*'

It was not *exactly* the right approach for a woman whose business depended upon people thinking soft furnishings were vital.

26

She resurfaced with a sudden memory. Of Peter saying to her after they separated, more in sorrowful conviction than in anger, that she was far too slipshod to run a business efficiently. She laughed at the arrogance. But she nearly proved him right. It still made her shiver. She met Douglas, he of the stockings and suspender school, a couple of years after she opened the shop. It was called Love and she fell for him. Fell was putting it mildly. An avalanche on K2 would have been nearer the mark. It was Jenny who held the business together during the Douglas years. While Pamela went foolish and haywire, Jenny held on.

Ever since Euston and the holed stocking, she found herself thinking about Douglas. Just wondering how he was. Recalling the odd moment. Passion remembered in tranquility. She was over him now, of course, of that she was sure. She shivered again. She *needed* to be over him, remembering those final months together. She won, and nearly lost, the biggest contract of the shop's life, the big break, out of the domestic into the public arena. Pamela, in love, failed it. Peter's voice of doom was nearly proved right. The most valuable job of her designer's life would never have been successful without Jenny's tireless scouring for the right stuffs, the right tones, the right decorators. Pamela swanning around the shell of the Regency, and therefore site-sensitive,

27

Boxwood Manor after its conversion into an hotel and restaurant, with stars in her eyes, saying airily, 'We'll have gold there, indigo there, and goose green in the foyers . . .' and then dashing off to spend a weekend away somewhere with Douglas—it could only have created mayhem and failure without Jenny's dedication.

And it had come to nought, the dashing hither and thither. She and Douglas finally parted company about the time Boxwood Manor was finished. Amid all the accolades and attention she was practically crawling up the wall with self-pity and self-loathing. Jenny and her new husband Howard spent a lot of time with her. A lot. At the end of it she made three decisions. That she would never expand the business beyond what the two of them, a couple of assistants and outworkers could handle. That she would make Jenny a full partner. And that she would never let her down again. Or Daniel. He suffered during the blackness, too.

Remembering all this, she got out of the bath and padded guiltily to the telephone. The bloody Wilkinson woman had changed her mind three times about the trimmings she wanted, which accounted for the delay, and the bloody woman knew that. Pamela had it in black and white that it was not the shop's responsibility. If they were not ready in time Pamela had agreed to provide some muslin

28

drapes. It was all under control. Dull old people wanting dull old perfections. Sometimes, just recently, it all felt very dull indeed.

Jenny was grateful and apologetic for disturbing her, which made Pam feel even guiltier as she returned to the bath.

She topped up the water. Danny, on the other hand, could wait. His message, left on the answerphone, was a demand for her to pack up some forgotten things and send them on. No little endearments, no gratitude, just Do It. It was therefore not so high on her list of priorities. Once, yes. But not now. He was a big boy and he could wait. She plunged back under the surface hurriedly, a little shaken. Such a change in her outlook was disturbing. She hardly recognized this woman. How easy it was. The world did not fall apart because she put herself first for a change.

But dwelling on the past disturbed her equilibrium. God knows it had taken her long enough after Douglas to build it up again. Crossly she got out of the bath, weighed herself, felt it had spoiled things even more, and promptly went on a diet. Downstairs she found the old aerobics video that Danny banned, and tried it again. She went at it with gusto. And no Daniel to come in and laugh. She did the whole thing and felt very faint.

Then she sat down at her table and worked on a plan for transforming his old bedroom into a study. The spare room had a double bed for their future visits and she could give it a new look in time for Christmas. She enjoyed the exercise. With a proper study of her own at last, she could do more work at home. She chewed her pencil. Best not think about the implications of that. It didn't *have* to be more work. She could do anything in there. Even study. But first she must design it exactly to her requirements. She chewed her pencil some more.

She sat there happily absorbed for hours, conscious that she no longer needed to think about Daniel and feeding time. She could make a sandwich whenever she liked. Or not. She could probably lose half a stone like this. Just ducking the odd meal. And that pleased her, too. It was only when she got up from the table that she felt a strange new painful stiffness in her joints. Oh, my God, she thought, I have contracted some terrible disease, now, here, on the brink of my new life.

She stood still, hoping it was temporary and would pass, but it did not. Bloody Fate, she thought. Gives you freedom for one month just so you can appreciate the pleasure, then whips it away and bangs you into a wheelchair for the rest of your life. She prodded and poked at the offending joints—the pain of it— even her elbows were going. If only she had gone to church. Too late now. She always knew that God, whoever he was, was an unforgiving Deity.

She hobbled out of the dining room into the hall and tottered down the passageway towards the kitchen. Tea or gin, it was all the same to her now. It was probably the worst kind of wasting disease. Didn't Fate always wait until it could make a real entrance? It was so bad she was clinging to the walls. Only when she passed the back room and saw the empty video box lying on the floor with the mid-star-jump Green Goddess staring up at her from the box cover did she remember. *Aerobics.* Oh, thank God, thank God. She was so grateful that she laughed aloud. It echoed around her and she was brought up short by the sad little thought that there was no one at home, now, to share the joke with.

When she returned to the shop the next day she could barely crawl. Jenny looked at her sympathetically. She obviously thought she was seeing a new phenomenon: menopausal knees.

CHAPTER FIVE

Douglas Brown switched on the answerphone and checked his watch against the digital clock. Mary had given him the watch—which would have been fine if she had not also had it inscribed TO MY DARLING DOUGLAS THANK YOU FOR EVERYTHING. And then wept when he laughed. Apparently this was wrong. It was

31

not amusing, it was serious. He had not laughed cruelly, as he explained. It just felt a little sugary, a little adolescent. Which is possibly what you got for having a girlfriend so much younger. Her thirty-two had stars in her eyes. His forty-four had not. He liked the age difference at the beginning. Something new. But it soon palled. Next stop children and domesticity. No thanks.

He went back into the bedroom and pulled up the blind; his flat was six floors up. Below him the sunny September morning washed over the grey, densely packed buildings around Chelsea Harbour, and there, just a couple of miles away and proud on the skyline, was his office. Nearer to, he could see his gym, his favourite restaurant, the best place to have a suit made and Mary's accessory shop, all reflected in the watery light. He liked living at the heart of things. He was certain to get bored if it were any other way.

Immediately below his window he watched clones of himself or Mary getting into spunky little cars and driving off to their hives. To be style-conscious was fine nowadays, but it was done without flamboyance. That went out with the eighties. You should be seen to glory in nothing, to just proceed in a quiet and orderly fashion along the path of the cult of the individual. He had written something like that in his last editorial. It sounded pompous, but that was the tone of things now, even government. No one minded. Part of him cared so little nowadays that he almost willed the finding of himself as an entry in Pseuds Corner.

He turned away from the window, smiling. Once he might have opted out of all this— gone to live in the country with hens and baggy cords and actually *needing* a Range Rover. It was a silly temptation—thank God he had not succumbed—but coming at the beginning of the nineties, when everything was in the melting pot, it was seductive for a while. Or she was. He looked at his watch again, with irritation. Not sentimental Mary. The other one.

He had not seen Pamela for years. For some reason he had started to think about her again just recently. As dissatisfaction with Mary grew, he supposed. Odd, because Mary was exactly the sort of woman you would expect him to want, on paper, and the other one was a complete aberration. Such an aberration that when they met he felt safe from her, entirely safe and in control. Intrigued by what he took to be just another suburban woman waiting for her friends in a bar. She wore chain-store jeans and her handbag looked like something from John Lewis. He spilt a drink on her. Apologized. Bought her a glass of champagne to amend. Her friend was late. And the rest was very crazy and uncharacteristic history.

He wooed her, she was reluctant. He

pretended to like what she liked, and ended up doing so. He hid his sense of superiority when he found she had her own business, and came to be both pleased and annoyed, in equal measure, about how successful it was. And then he took her to a charity ball at the Albert Hall and she astonished his table by discussing how the rotunda was built. The engineering facts. He just sat back and smiled as his guests floundered. Pamela never had to act style. From then on the balance between them changed. For the first time he began to think about a future that was based around a relationship. He dared to think the unthinkable. That this was someone with whom he might spend the rest of his life.

His sister Zoe, independent as he was, voraciously socially conscious and proud of her stylish brother, was horrified at the change in him. She advised him to get out while he could, but by then it was too late. He was in love. He looked at the watch again. After that, Mary sweetheart, no one stood a chance.

Zoe complained of Pamela's bourgeois ways and took him to Barbados for Christmas. All he did was lie around wanting to be back in London. He took an early flight and joined her for the last couple of days of the holiday, he and teenaged Daniel glaring at each other across the festivities. She was the first woman in his life to have a child and he felt a terrible jealousy.

The only time she was really his was when he took her away, and she began to need no encouraging. Daniel stayed with friends or occasionally with his reluctant father. At first she worried about appearing to dump her son, then she exalted in the freedom. All he cared about was having her to himself. And he worked at it.

With her yen for the Cambridgeshire Levels, which he thought were exams until she took him there, he could get her out of London whenever he chose. She stood on the edge of that broad space, gesturing at nothing, laughing up at endless sky and down at seemingly infinite flatness—and he was almost persuaded that he wanted them too (but not, it was true, her son). And that was the picture that lasted—her, the sky and barren, brown flatness. After a couple of years he made the mistake of suggesting that Daniel should be sent away to sixth-form college. She refused. She would follow him to the ends of the earth, she promised, teasing him with that smile of hers, keeping it light, but she would not give up her son.

Well, neither, in the end, made it. Not to the Levels, not to the ends of the earth. Not together. That was all over four years ago. He took the phone off the hook for a month and steeled himself. Zoe saw him through. Kept him firm. Removed the telephone from his hand when he wavered, organized engaging things to do.

He survived. Never again.

He knew exactly where she was, living in the same house, working from the same shop. He had caught a glimpse of her a couple of times during the years. He had no desire to know if she had met someone new and had never spoken to her since. When Zoe asked him recently if he was completely over her, he said, 'Yes, of course.' And to prove it some imp in him suggested she use Pamela's services for her new flat. Why not? She might get a discount. It was a bravado that he regretted now and he hoped his sister had forgotten the suggestion. Zoe was right. She cost him too much.

He pushed his mobile into the Jesse briefcase and rescued a fountain pen rolling around in its depths. Pamela bought him this, though thankfully she had the good sense not to carve anything into it. All she said as he unwrapped it was 'I've bought it so you will think of me several times a day . . .' No laughter from him that time. In this, as in many things, she had been wise. Most times he took it in his fingers he remembered her, even fleetingly. And the oddest, and maybe the saddest, thing was that the years he had feared would crawl along, had flashed by. The teenaged son would be in his twenties. Still at home, no doubt. Still filling up the space like an unbudgeable cuckoo.

Ah, well. Not his problem. He threw the pen back into the briefcase, a gift from one of the women in between her then, Mary now. Imaginative, these women, he thought wryly. Or was it just that he was no more than a watch, pen and briefcase man? Well, if he was, he was also a free one. Touch and go that month of phonelessness. But he got through it. He was lucky she went so quietly. She was four years older than him and she used to say, 'Do you realize that when you were born I was grown up enough to read and write?' After she went, it seemed to him, looking back, that they had never closed that gap.

He picked up his car keys and jangled them to dispel the past. The hall was lined with photographs by Helmut Newton. She hated Helmut Newton, which presumably, a shrink would say, was why he had chosen them. Naked women in moody black and white doing strange things in cluttered rooms. Chic and vaguely S&M—not that he was, really. It made him look more dangerous than he was. Which he liked. Next door he could hear the flat-sharers laughing, talking, preparing for the day. It was a fresh lot, just moved in on a new lease—and one of the girls wasn't bad.

He ran a brush through his greying hair. Grey was OK. And put on the dark green Armani—also a present from Mary, though not, thankfully, inscribed. He checked his teeth in the mirror, ruffled his hair to fall more rakishly over his forehead, and pulled his cuffs straight. He would be forty-five next month. Mary was an infant. Time he traded her in, really, given that inscription. The wedding bells and babies couldn't be far off. If he had learned anything about himself and women, it was to stay on the move, not risk boredom.

He legged it down the stairs and grabbed his mail. Out in the day he felt restored. He always did. London. Great place to be. He pressed the remote and the car coughed itself unlocked. He slid into his seat, threw the mail down on to the passenger side, and revved. He glanced in the mirror and saw the girl from the adjacent flat just emerging. Dark suit, good legs, bright smile, VW Polo. Standard issue. Maybe in a week or two? Ask her for a lift. It was a good line. Mary would be away at the Fashion Fair in Köln.

He sifted through his mail at the lights. He opened a letter with an Irish postmark. From an hotel in Dublin. He had stayed there with someone last year. All very brief. The new owners offered him a discount weekend during the Winter Arts Festival. Presumably the new management did not know who he was. He remembered it as a nice, shambolic hotel of ageing grandeur. Maybe he could do an Irish issue? He tossed the letter on to the back seat as he turned the corner of Marsham Street. And maybe not. Dublin in winter did not sound that good. Truth was, nothing sounded that good at the moment. He needed a change, a lift, something new. He smiled. Maybe what he needed was what Pam Pryor used to call Fun?

He turned the car into the underground car park. Above his space was a notice saying RESERVED. STYLE AND CITY. EDITOR.

When he reached his desk Mary had already rung, 'Just to say hallo . . .'

She'd be talking about moving in next.

CHAPTER SIX

Ani Patel looked out of the shop window and saw Miss Phoebe Glen weaving her way along the road. A little later than usual. And very flushed. A bad sign. She went back to the counter and put the *Daily Telegraph* out in readiness, and waited. These people, this country, they never looked after their own.

Miss Phoebe Glen's suspicions were correct. The letter announced an increase in rent, approved by the powers that be, in line with government guidelines. It meant that her own small income, from home coaching the dim children of the rich, would be further diminished. It was pretty diminished, anyway, after she rapped that Benson boy's knuckles. She might even fall, finally, into this Poverty Trap she kept reading about and always

39

imagined had sharp, steel teeth. She held the letter up against the bars of the fire and burnt it. Then she took another little tot of sherry, just to brace herself, before leaving the house.

She shivered a little as she walked, hesitantly, up the road towards the newsagent's. September mornings might be sunny, but there was still a distinct chill in the air. Life could, she mused sorrowfully, be very cruel. If she did fall into the Trap, they would investigate her, wouldn't they? They would unearth all that stuff about her little difficulties in the past, the schools, the embarrassments, her little problem. She must not allow that to happen.

She paused for breath, leaning on the shop window, reading Ani Patel's notice. She shook her head with vexation. The times were all out of joint nowadays, if you asked her. She pushed on into the shop and in front of the counter her back straightened. She might be down but she still had standards.

'Mrs Patel,' she said severely, pushing her ragged white fringe out of her eyes, 'Mrs Patel—she pointed dramatically to the front display—'this is *not* a widow . . .'

Mrs Patel, who had temporarily forgotten the product of Ari's waggishness, had long thought that the English were nuts. She sold newspapers to men who ogled bare thighs and breasts and then beat up their daughters for revealing the same. She sold tubs of ice-cream

40

to women who every day, *every* day, stood in the shop bemoaning their weight, squeezing themselves into ugly, too-tight clothes. She longed, sometimes, to say no. She longed sometimes to say that a sari, in both instances, could help. Instead she smiled, nodded, ignored the teenagers' bruises, sighed with sympathy for the rolling midriffs. A little plumpness in a lady, she would offer if asked, was a sign of wealth and a properly conducted life, at which the doughbags would titter. Hardly surprisingly.

Now Mrs Patel followed the direction of her customer's pointing finger, shrugged and gave a cautious smile. 'Yes?' she said.

Miss Phoebe Glen arched an eyebrow.

'No?' she tried.

It had to be one or the other.

Miss Phoebe Glen arched both eyebrows. She went on pointing and seemed, though her mouth worked at it, to be temporarily devoid of speech.

Perhaps, thought Ani Patel, peering through the window and seeing no one—and certainly not a woman in black—coming along the street, perhaps it was something to do with the weather? It often was. Maybe what she spoke of as a widow was some kind of reference to the season? It was a reasonable assumption with the English.

Mrs Patel would have a stab.

'It might hold off,' she said, pleased to have

found the right vernacular. She handed the customer her *Daily Telegraph* and added the jokey conversational makeweight, 'I hope so, or I shall have to take in the washing.'

Miss Phoebe Glen's eyebrows returned to normal. She clung to the counter. Memories of her mother saying the same thing when her father disappeared returned. And now it seemed the same fate loomed for her. Taking in washing. Oh, the ignominy.

She nodded sadly. 'Yes, yes—it might come to that. Taking in washing. Although there are, of course, launderettes.'

Both women stared at each other.

'I have a washing machine, actually,' said Mrs Patel. And she added, so as not to appear prideful, 'Only an old one.'

'Tragic,' said Miss Phoebe Glen, who had lost the thread.

Both women stared anew. Ani Patel did not think that having a twin tub could be considered *that* bad.

The British usually had a way forward in sticky conversational moments, but Ani Patel could find none in her extensive, useful stock. And Miss Phoebe Glen was puzzled at the turn. She had merely sought to correct an error, not to discuss personal hygiene and she knew nothing whatsoever about launderettes or washing machines, managing everything with Persil and a bucket at home.

While they continued confounded, a woman

came in, a woman with the air of one who is slightly deranged, and asked, in the guttural accents of *Mitteleuropa*, whether Mrs Patel had any current diaries available. It being September, this went down considerably better than launderettes.

I am stumped, thought Ani Patel privately.

Even Miss Phoebe Glen recognized the absurdity.

'*Current*?' said Mrs Patel eventually. Verily, if the English were nuts, the Poles were cracked shells with knobs on.

The Polish woman nodded.

Ani Patel remembered that she never threw anything away. 'I have one somewhere upstairs,' she said. 'A present which I did not use this year. You can have that. I will ask Ari to drop it through your letter-box when he comes home from school.'

Mrs Patel looked pleased. She liked to be on top of her customers in a serving capacity.

The Polish woman said, gutturally and with no outward show of fulfilment, 'How big is it?'

Mrs Patel kept smiling. She made a gesture. 'Handbag size,' she said.

The Polish woman pulled a face. 'Probably not big enough,' she said. 'But you can send it anyway.'

She went out again without looking up.

'No probs,' said Mrs Patel. 'No worries.'

Miss Phoebe Glen flew to the door and called after the woman's back, 'In my country we say *thank you . . .*'

Not very often, thought Mrs Patel, but she went on smiling all the same.

A fat man with slightly soiled frontage and stertorous breath came in. He stood behind Miss Phoebe Glen waiting, pointedly. Miss Phoebe Glen ignored him in an effort to make sense of the launderette and the widow with Mrs Patel. He sniffed the air of fruity sweetness about the flushed woman ahead of him, found the way she pulled at her startling white fringe fascinating, and decided to wait with patience. He picked up a lottery form and began to enter his crosses. He had plenty of time and nothing better to do.

Eventually Mrs Patel explained that she wanted people to advertise on cards in her window. She thanked Miss Phoebe Glen for pointing out the mistake and said that were Ari not her only son, and she devoid of husband, she would throw him down a well and leave him there.

'You don't get many of those to the pound in Chiswick,' said the fat man wheezily. He was flapping his lottery form and in need of some conversation and he thought humour was best.

'What?' said Mrs Patel.

'Wells,' said the man. He looked pleased at the incontestability of the statement. Mrs Patel continued to look blank so he made a bucket-dipping gesture. 'You know. Wells.' He made another dipping gesture. 'Ding, dong bell . . .'

44

'Ding, dong, bells. In wells,' said Mrs Patel humouringly.

'Nice cathedral and a wonderful peal,' said Miss Phoebe Glen mistily. She took against the man and decided to loiter. 'Hot springs,' she added chattily. 'Once.'

'You know so much,' said Mrs Patel, thinking Clear As Mud, which phrase, she was confident, covered a multitude.

'I do,' said Miss Phoebe Glen. 'More than you will ever know.'

The fat man hung his head respectfully. He liked to hear women talk. He used to listen to his mother and her friends for hours. Unknown to them.

Mrs Patel looked at Miss Phoebe Glen and her clutching hands and tried to say something pleasantly dismissive to get rid of her—the British had taught her many such phrases—'Take care now,' she said.

Miss Phoebe Glen stayed.

'Mind how you go.'

Still she stayed.

The fat man waited patiently but Mrs Patel did not really see why he should have to.

She had one final stab at valediction: 'Well, then.'

Which she was relieved to see worked.

Miss Phoebe Glen held her head high and left the shop, tutting over the sign as she went out and pointing and mouthing silently through the window.

'Our Lady Wordsmith,' said Ani Patel, in a mixture of pity and compunction.

The fat man became animated. He fumbled with his hands, made a little bowing motion in the direction of the closed door, and lowered his eyes floorwards.

He said to Ani Patel, 'I had no idea she was a ladyship.'

He paid for his lottery ticket and backed out of the shop, deeply impressed.

Mrs Patel reminded herself, as she did every day, that she was here to serve. To see Ari through school. To see Ari graduate. To see Ari married. And then to care for his children. If she did not remind herself of this, she, too, would go nuts. She smiled at the Polish woman who popped her head back around the door and pointed at the rows of sweet jars.

'And half a pound of strong mints,' she said in her cracked voice, 'if you're doing deliveries.'

Mrs Patel nodded obligingly. She could only take heart from reasoning that if they kept the Poles out, then the English would also have kept her out. She tried to look on the bright side if possible.

CHAPTER SEVEN

Of course Pamela Pryor, mother of Danny, gave in eventually. And went up to his bedroom—his ex-bedroom—her soon-to-be-study, to look for the things he requested her so baldly to send on.

After she returned from the post office she rang his number to say the parcel was on its way. She got the answerphone.

'Dan Pryor and Lilian Watt are not here right now . . .'

So The Girlfriend had a name. She waited for the beep and then said, 'I have finally sent you the parcel which you do not deserve. It took so long because I am very busy at the shop at the moment. Next time you leave a message, how about some preliminary chatter? Along the lines of asking me how I am, that sort of thing . . . Works wonders.'

A bit stinging, she thought afterwards, but mothers had rights, too.

She could imagine The Girlfriend rolling her eyes at the maternal neurosis of the message. She no longer cared.

Truth was, since hunting through Danny's room, she could imagine The Girlfriend rolling a darn sight more than just her eyes.. .

The Girlfriend who, apparently quite untouched by a passable degree in philosophy, thought Crete was a great place for holiday nightlife.

The Girlfriend whose geographical knowledge stretched only to Malibu being a drink.

The Girlfriend who, with all these outward attributes, had captured Danny's heart and who, it was now clear, had captured all his other maternally proscribed bits as well.

This information was gleaned from going to his room, as requested, and finding some hidden, and presumably forgotten, pornographic magazines. She was still feeling most strange from the experience.

I'll open one, she thought, just at random.

She went into his room at seven and did not come out again until a quarter past nine. With nothing whatsoever packed up but with a very strange light in her eye. And a serious need for gin.

At first she decided that the magazines all belonged to some far-off adolescent time when he and his friends used to congregate up here. But they were dated last December and January. She was both fascinated and repelled and, although they were not hard core, it took a while for her to look at the pages inside. There was something very unedifying about knowing they belonged to her son. She opened them furtively, flicking through, trying not to dwell on the photographs that looked more like alternative positions for healthy childbirth

48

than hot poses. She realized there was an entire dimension to him that she would never know, could never know. She smiled, wryly. She must abandon the images of chuckling bathtimes and schoolday sulks. Her son was now a *Bloke.*

One of the magazines asked on its cover, 'Tell us the truth. Are you and your partner really hot together?'

How silly, she said to herself out loud. But she quickly turned to the page and found the questionnaire. Danny had filled it in. No use pretending. It was definitely his writing.

'Does your wife/girlfriend refuse any of your sexual needs or fantasies? Would you consider using a prostitute for these?'

Danny had written, a little too convincingly in her opinion, 'No' and 'No need.'

That made her think, as she sat there goggling.

Nothing?

Refused him nothing?

Ah, well, she consoled herself, he probably never asks for things. Whatever *things* might be. She tried not to think of polythene and whips.

She read on, trying to clear her mind of The Girlfriend as some sort of obliging orifice with a brain as secondary function. And she also, even more embarrassingly, tried to clear her mind of Oedipus. Had she done anything that might give him strange tastes? It was a thought best rejected. At times like this she wished Peter were more of this world. He was the only one with whom she could share any of this without it being a betrayal. Hopeless. She could imagine ringing Peter up now and reading some of the questions and answers aloud. He'd go whiter than his walls.

'What would you do if your wife/girlfriend told you she wanted to have sex with another man?'

Danny had written, 'Watch.'

She closed the magazine, red-faced as if he were in the room with her.

She very nearly did ring Peter at that. Just to share the burden. But if she felt a bit weak and wobbly, Peter would simply point a pale and shaking finger at her and say it was all her fault for putting royal blue carpet over the Furtzbangers and letting him have his way with the red and black.

Watch, indeed. Would he? She read on, abandoning the sense of guilt for the more urgent need to know. She was strangely moved to find that under the question, 'Was your wife/girlfriend more experienced when you met? Did you mind this?' he had replied 'Yes' and 'Yes.'

Pamela felt she had failed. Maybe there was something in the old fashioned idea of sending a young man off to Paris to sow his wild oats? She had done her best. Told him about caring for the girl, not hurting her in either an emotional or a physical way, told him that it was possible, and very nice (deep breath here), to have sexual experiences without, er—it taking place (God knows where she was looking when she told him that one—neither of them had found the kitchen ceiling so interesting before or since). And lots of other liberal-parent stuff that had them both writhing in a state of pink embarrassment and which she could never be sure he had heard. Had it all been for nothing?

The last question cheered her up. Danny had ticked the box which stated that he felt himself now to be a 'fully tuned-in, turned-on sexual partner'.

Well, thank God for that.

She felt like cheering.

Then she felt like crying.

Then she remembered and felt like a large gin.

Which was when she went back downstairs.

If anything was designed, she thought, cutting savagely at a lemon (she could hear Danny saying, What Has That Lemon Ever Done to You?), to show her, finally, that her son was now a separate entity, it was a questionnaire on his sexual habits. She banged the glass down on the kitchen bench and threw in the lemon so that it splashed. And that was good, was it not? So why did she suddenly feel so cross?

Best be honest. She was cross because he

had a love life and she didn't. She was cross because she had abandoned her own. The thought slipped out and into the gin glass before she could haul it back. Even though it was well over a year ago, she could still hear Danny's voice on the stairs, still feel the panic, and still get goosebumps at the thought of being caught *in flagrante* with a lover young enough to be her son. It was the end of Dean Close. Dean—final testimony to her recovery from Douglas. Dean, who a moment before was the object of her desire, became quite suddenly an expendable threat to her role as mother. She froze in his embrace as Danny called again, 'Hi, I'm back . . .' She was almost physically sick as she jumped out of Dean's arms. And that, she told the gin glass, was it. I simply could not cope with the guilt.

Friends said she was silly to be so protective. Rick, who was Danny's guitar teacher for years and a friend in whom she often confided, said that he, personally, would have *loved* to know his mother was having a good time. Not surprising, she thought caustically, since his mother was dead. Rick had a nipple ring put in when he was fifty, and a tattoo as a present from his wife saying SAVE THE PLANET, SING. So she couldn't take his cool advice seriously. 'Just tell him,' said Rick, playing an irritating little riff as if they were taking part in some sentimental musical. 'He'll be fine about it . . .'

Tell him indeed. She had only to say to Danny, Let's talk, and he would be backed out of the door, half-way down the street, saying, Don't wait up . . . As for telling him she was heartily knocking off someone young enough to be his brother? It would have sent him hurtling into outer space. He was his father's son, after all—both still seemed to have a proprietorial view of her morals. A mother should be above such things—the Virgin Mary was in there somewhere—and that was that. Whatever Rick or anyone else said, Pamela knew that her son would not be able to countenance the idea of her being sexy, let alone countenance her being Hands On and Doing Sexy. Free-thinking stopped with your parents. She wouldn't be able to handle his knowing, either.

She felt that sick feeling in her stomach again, heard the voice on the stairs, re-lived the panic in the dimness of a bedroom with the curtains pulled against the afternoon light. Ended, over, buried, gone. Might as well admit it as not. She *did* feel resentful. All it needed right now, given those magazines, was for her son to ring up and say, Mum, get a life, and she might very well tell him about the one he had taken from her. Or all three, she thought resentfully, still wondering what the erotic demands her son made on his amenable girlfriend might be, and trying not to. Oh yes, all three . . .

On entering their marriage, baby Daniel had put a gap between her needs and aspirations and Peter's that they had never managed to bridge. He had then grown into a teenager and grunted like a pig, glaring lout-like at Douglas when he appeared on the scene, his sixth sense telling him that his mother was in danger of putting him second. And finally there was Dean—whom he had seen off without so much as even knowing he existed. Dean—her oasis for the parched, whose youth made her feel ashamed of herself and whose pleasures were truly sweet in their simplicity. Or apparent simplicity. Nothing was simple, nothing was safe. She had to give him up, didn't she? After those magazines she was not quite so sure.

She put her feet up on the settee and sipped her drink. Well, well—they were all in the past. Over and done with. Gone. No going back, no second chances, that was for sure. She pressed the remote for the television. There was no longer even the comfort of fur to stroke. Piggins had gone to that Celestial Cattery in the Sky. She really was finally and completely alone. She could simply walk out of the house now and not have to worry about a thing. Not the state of the fridge food stocks, not what she'd find on her return, not even asking the people next door if they would feed the cat.

Why, Dorothy, she mused, You could just put on these spangly red shoes, take that yellow brick road, and do anything. But she didn't want to do anything. At the same time she felt restless. It was a conundrum. And it was then, against a background of Trevor MacDonald giving the headlines, and the chink of ice in her glass, that she remembered Vita Sackville-West's *All Passion Spent.* Of all the things to remember. It made her feel cold. All passion spent? She wondered if it was.

She hummed a few bars of 'The best is yet to come'. Second chances, she thought, second chances? Well, maybe. But not with any of them. That was certain. Musingly, she sucked on her lemon and thought sourly about second chances, while the depressing image of a snowball in hell came to mind.

CHAPTER EIGHT

Dean Close was not afraid of opening his birthday post that morning. He was not afraid of getting old because he had a safety net. If all else failed, he would join Exit and bump himself off. He and his mates all agreed. When it stopped being good, you went. The Sanctity of Life brigade gave him the pip. Who wanted to end up in an old folk's home?

Anyway, that was years ahead. Today he was twenty-eight. He rolled over to see the time. Presumably Keith and Julian had already

55

left—he couldn't hear the usual noises of them getting up and out at speed and there was no Capital FM pounding its lullaby through the walls. He scratched, yawned, stretched, rolled and opened one eye. Nearly ten. He had probably been woken by them banging the front door. Sods might have bought him a cup of tea before going. After all, it was his birthday.

He stumbled out, wrapping the duvet around his naked shoulders—first chill of the end of summer—and wandered into the bathroom. Damp smells of toothpaste and shaving soap clung to the walls and the shower curtain hung its dripping tatters on the wrong side of the bath. His feet flinched at the cold puddles on the floor. He peed quickly and plodded, like some snowbound monk, into the kitchen. The place was not too bad today—Julian's girlfriend had stayed the night and made a few inroads. The table surface had been wiped and only bore the slightest traces of spilt tea, scattered sugar and toast. The beer cans had gone. He picked up a buttery knife, dipped it into the Marmite jar, and licked it, while waiting for the kettle to boil.

He put his feet up on the chair opposite, wrapped the duvet even more firmly around him, and thought that Julian's girl, Alice, had her uses. She was also intelligent and decorative. Twenty-five, worked in an art gallery, cropped black hair and a stud in her

56

nose. Cheerful, chatty, she was the perfect example of the kind of girlfriend he was supposed to want. But it did not work out like that. Girls like Alice were no challenge and he always got bored with them. Pamela was different. She lived for the moment, she knew about things—took him to films he would not normally see, to places like Petworth and Blenheim and Sissinghurst, which she knew everything about, cooked stuff for him that was strange and different—so that he felt he was always learning, was fascinated, excited. And she made no demands. He used to wish, sometimes, that she would.

It was funny. The less she asked for, the more he wanted to give. Wanted to spend more time with her, even move in with her, and she was the one who laughed it off and said it would spoil things. That was usually his line. He had to accept it. He was not used to being refused, but he had to accept that this was the way she wanted it to be. Even that felt good. No arguments, no debates, no 'Which pub? Which film? Which pizza?' until you were blue in the face and fed up with the whole thing. He loved that, her decisiveness. She always said she was old enough to be his mother, but she was nothing like her. His mother never put him second in her life. Pamela did. She teased, cajoled, played around sometimes, but, basically, she made the decisions. This far only, was her message, and he enjoyed pushing to see if he could go a little bit more.

He yawned and sat down to think. He liked to remember her. When she said that they must think of it as fun and not for ever, he felt a sudden determination to change her mind. He loved her, he told her that, and she just put her finger to his lips and shook her head. He had never told anyone before or since that he loved them. He tried with girls like Alice, and he failed. No one in the flat understood about Pam. At first they just whistled the Mrs Robinson song at him whenever he came back from seeing her, and then, later, when they realized it was more than that, they got serious and tried to get him to back off. When he told them Pamela had ended it, he saw relief on their faces. 'Fuck you all,' he said.

He was miserable and drunk, and miserable and drunker, for weeks, and he remained unattached. He tried to see Pam a few times but she refused. Only once, afterwards, did they meet, and that was for a furtive drink by the river at Kew, when she reminded him, sad but firm, that it was never for ever. He would have gone on ringing her, but he got fed up with Daniel always answering. He also knew that what she said, she meant.

Alice brought her girlfriends round occasionally so that they could all get pissed together. Over the last year or so one or two of them had ended up in his bed. And that was all. He did not want anyone else. He found them boring. If he said a name like Wim Wenders or Lutyens, they hadn't a clue, and if he fooled around in bed instead of getting on with it . . . He licked at the Marmite again. They had no idea. None. So—if he could not have her—he would have no one. His mother kept hinting: the last of her boys and would he settle down now? Well, no. He could not tell her why.

Alice was really nice. Alice was really concerned about him. Alice would love to fix him up with someone just like her. Julian would like it, too—gave the whole thing a comfortable symmetry. But after the wild nights and frenzied beddings, he always kept his cool, kept his distance. They might ring (he was polite), they might call (he would be Just Going Out), and they got the message. Alice was nice but too young. He had nothing to learn from them. At that pub in Kew, when he complained, Pam said that maybe he should try to teach them about the things that interested him. He could not be bothered to try—they'd laugh. Silly girls. Not for him.

Not for him, either, were Keith's preferences. Dean had tried it once. Got picked up by a guy a few years older than him—thought it might work. It didn't and he would be forever grateful to the pick-up for recognizing that it was a bad idea. 'You'll freak,' he said. Which was probably true. And he told him to go home and find a nice girl to settle down with. Patronizing bastard.

He never told Keith. Keith, who would not bring anyone back to the house and discreetly kept his affairs elsewhere. Less, he said, to protect his flat-mates from the mortal sin of being party to the consenting act than to protect himself from losing the occasional lover he found. Keith had carroty hair, freckles and wore glasses. It would have been no contest with Dean. Julian was to be trusted by the presence in his life of an Alice; Dean was up for grabs, no matter how he laughed and denied it. 'Never had the horn for another bloke in my life,' he told Keith firmly when he was still seeing Pam. 'Always a first time,' said Keith good-naturedly. After all, he pointed out, he had been a virgin once.

Dean winced, remembering the pick-up. It was stupid. What she would call immature. He threw the knife across the table and it fell to the floor with a clatter. He did not bother to pick it up. Her rebuff still hurt. He was not used to being denied things. Anyway, it was wrong to give something that good up when any moment you could go under a bus or get cancer or anything. She held him for the last time on the pub steps, a quick hug, and was gone.

Live while you have life to live, love while you have love to give. He found that on a postcard and sent it to her. Picasso. One old bloke who got it right. Well, the words anyway—he wasn't too sure about the pictures—she liked them and he just pretended and tried to. When she walked off down the path at Kew Bridge, he wanted to run after her, scream in her face: What has your careful, planning older generation achieved?

A dying world. And now you are killing love in it too. He could still hear her saying, 'I'm really sorry, Dean,' as she said goodbye, and he could still remember how little affected she seemed to be. Her son was home. Bring on the fatted calf. Bye-bye, Dean; no hard feelings. Youth and beauty, she said to him, you have them both and they are great gifts.

He reckoned he knew the worthlessness of youth and beauty by now. He had been their star and their victim. If he sold trainers in pubs, the girls just melted. If he did clipboard market research, they queued up for him. Even getting the third room in this flat was to do with his looks. Keith just said yes. And that was that. He had even been picked off the street to do modelling, and now it was acting. But they did not look at him, they looked at his looks. When the poster campaign to stop people seeing only the disability rather than the whole person began, he wanted to scrawl across them, 'It's the same for me—no one ever looks at me.'

It was his looks that had brought them

together. He was waitering at the time. She said, 'I think my son's got a poster of you up in his room.' just for a laugh he said it probably was him. The next time she came in he was just going off duty. She screwed up her eyes at him and said, 'I'm sure it is you . . .' And he demanded to see it. He thought she was just a lonely woman, like his mother, but she turned out to be funny and interesting; he was sorry when she said she had work to do and he left. The next day he called at her shop, a bit tongue-tied, and then he waited to walk home with her in the evening.

Easy. One minute it was seven-thirty, the next it was two in the morning—and no tubes or buses. She put him in Daniel's room, he came into hers pretending he had had a nightmare—they fell about laughing—and afterwards, when he had been too nervous to manage it—she just smiled and said, 'Let's sleep.' And in the morning it was all right. No trouble. Easy.

At that time, Daniel the Beloved Son was only an empty room. An absence who had introduced them. He never seriously believed in his existence. When he came home for weekends sometimes, Dean stayed away. Naturally enough, she wanted to be with her son. He understood. And in the long summer vacation Daniel travelled in America. Which made the shock all the more devastating when he suddenly realized what Finals meant, and

Daniel came home for good.

One day you will want children, was one of her get-out lines. How the fuck could anyone make up another person's mind on that? Just because *she* had one. Just because she was half-way across London being a mother to *her* bloody son, and had almost certainly forgotten about him completely, it didn't mean that he was going to be grateful for the freedom granted to get someone up the spout.

He put a tea-bag in an unusually clean mug, poured in water, and stirred angrily. Birthdays were supposed to be days for reflection, he decided, and having the flat to himself this morning was the best present he'd received so far. He slewed the tea-bag around, pressed it with a spoon once more, and flung it into Alice's sparkling sink. All right, it just so happened that she was a bit older than he was—well, all right, much older than he was—but it didn't stop him (on the way to her house, on the rare occasions she let him visit) singing at trees, buying chocolates and African violets, anything to show her that he really cared about her. A fact about which she seemed not at all convinced. He pointed out to her that her theory was badly flawed. The world, and that included his mother, would have to put up with it. You are not my mother, you are the woman I love, he said. My mother is sitting in Ireland baking and cleaning, he said. You are not like her. 'It's a question of degree,' she

63

said, stroking his face.

The letter-box rattled. He hopped out to the hall, still clutching the duvet, and picked up a pile of cards. His parents, his sisters, a few from friends—he went through the lot hurriedly, his heart sinking, and shuffled back into the kitchen. He opened the envelopes listlessly, sipping his tea between whiles. Nothing from *her*. Though why he should imagine that after fifteen months, and with no word so far, she would suddenly send a birthday card, he could not think. Yes, he could. It was called hope. It happened on birthdays.

He picked up his parents' card. Yet again there was the delicate, lacy handwriting that always filled him with dread and, yet again, amid the blessings for his birthday there was the offer of his air fare any time he felt like coming back to Dublin. His mother wanted to see her beautiful boy. He loathed the phrase now. Beautiful Boy. Pam called him that when he gave her a bunch of flowers, or made her laugh, or lay quiet in her arms. She had even used it on that last afternoon. Before 'Hi, Mum, I'm home . . .' broke their world apart.

He touched the carton on the table. She had turned as pale as this milk. He saw it, remembering the draining colour. Then she leapt from the bed, wagged a warning finger at him with an expression of anger and fear that he found frightening, shoved him—bollock

64

naked—under her bed—clothes, African violet, and all.

'Stay,' she had hissed, throwing on her Happy Jacket. '*Stay . . .*'

Just as if he were a disobedient dog.

'Danny,' she called down the stairs. 'Danny. You're a day early. I'm just coming down.'

If he learned one thing that day, it was that women are consummate actors. She sounded delighted that he was home. Delighted. Then, as she closed the bedroom door, she turned, looked at Dean as if he were her worst nightmare, and almost spat out that he should not move until she called him, on pain of death.

Lying under the bed, it felt as if he were the mature one rather than her. So her son had come home? So she was having a fuck. So what? He should be glad for her, shouldn't he? Anger and frustration made him say that to her later. After which she ended it. Very quietly, in a few sentences. Then she got up and left and, like the cliché, she never looked back. She was still wrong about one thing: whatever her age, it made no difference to how he felt.

He looked at his parents' card and re-read the message. Dublin, Donegal, Dubai. It was all the same to him. But maybe he would go home on a visit. Maybe later in the year, when the acting course was finished. He had wanted to take Pam to Dublin one day, despite her

65

telling him it was the place where she and her husband first fell in love. No chance now. Remembering the conversation about Exit, he brightened. There was always that. Then he opened a beer. Why not, it was his birthday.

CHAPTER NINE

Ani Patel hoped it would work. Then she could stop her Tuesday-night visits to Miss Phoebe Glen, which she undertook as a matter of kindness and which she knew the lady relied on. She took her Tropicana, Miss Phoebe sipped her sherry and they listened to the serial on the radio. *Bleak House.* 'Very appropriate,' Miss Phoebe Glen said. 'Seeing as how any day or night I could be out on the street . . .' Ani Patel scarcely heard the radio. She suspected that, as she left the shop on a Tuesday evening through the front door, Ari let in his girlfriend through the back. She had no proof. But she was afraid. Very afraid.

Thus, with hopeful breast, she placed Miss Phoebe Glen's card advertising for lodgers in the window and said, 'No charge.'

Miss Phoebe Glen, in a burst of generosity, decided to stay on and talk.

'No man is an island,' she said firmly, eyeing the fat man as he approached the shop.

Mrs Patel bowed her head politely and went

on measuring out acid drops.

'Some of them are not far short,' said a pale, shrivelled woman in a mackintosh, grimly.

Miss Phoebe Glen was keenly on the look-out for lodgers. 'And do you own your home?' she asked.

'Yes, I do,' said the woman positively. 'My Ernie left me very comfortable.'

Miss Phoebe Glen lost interest. There were those who had Ernies and those who had to fend for themselves.

Miss Phoebe started to sidle towards the fat man. It was, she decided, the only way. So far she had been unsuccessful, but she hoped a little coquetry would oil the wheels. With a little coquetry, she could get him to look at the spare room. She used to be quite good at coquetry, if she remembered rightly. She just needed a little practice. Yesterday when she tried it out, she was unable to get anywhere near him. Whenever she approached, he gave a strange little bow, went red, and scuttled away. She very nearly pinned him to the magazine stand but he somehow managed to grab a copy of *The Budgerigar* and slip round her crying, 'Ah, here it is,' as if he had just found El Dorado. After he ran from the shop, Mrs Patel said that to the best of her knowledge, on balance, and all things considered, he did not keep budgerigars. Which made it all the odder.

Today, however, she would persist.

She rolled her eyes and puckered her lips. The fat man stared resolutely at an advertisement for Clarnico toffees.

Miss Phoebe Glen moved, rather unsteadily, a little closer.

Ani Patel watched.

Something must be done. Her customer could be unpredictable. The fat man was of a nervous disposition.

Diversionary tactics.

'The dustmen were late yesterday . . .' she began.

'Dustmen?' They took up the irresistible chorus. *'Dustmen?'*

And they were off.

Just to be safe, when that subject was exhausted, Mrs Patel added, 'And then there are the buses . . .' Which never failed.

'Get one, you get six,' said the fat man.

'Get six, you get half a dozen,' said Miss Phoebe.

'At least,' said the fat man.

Miss Phoebe Glen smiled at him vaguely and nodded at the magazine he held as if to defend himself. 'I like a man with a hobby,' she said. And left him to it.

Mrs Patel sighed. The danger was over. Under cover of the shop door opening, he fled. The new customer bounced in saying she was late, she was late, and she had to take her mother some mint imperials.

Miss Phoebe turned to her, focused as best

she could and said, 'And do you . . .' But Ani Patel shook her head very slightly to dissuade her.

'She has just lost her son,' she said, after Pamela had gone. 'And she is a homeowner on her way to see her mother in an old folk's home.'

Miss Phoebe Glen shuddered as if someone had walked over her grave.

*　　　*　　　*

Mrs Hilda Hennessy, mother of Pamela, adjusted her skirt so that it was neat, leaned back in her fat blue armchair (brought from home on her daughter's insistence and the only lively colour in the place) and, gazing out of the big picture window at the September day, posed for a picture entitled 'Elderly woman still active waits graciously for her daughter's visit to the well-appointed Surrey rest-home'.

If there were those out there who feared such institutions, Mrs Hennessy was not one of them. She welcomed the blandness, welcomed the peace and, of course, had the money to pay for it. While you had your breath and your wits, a place like this was no different from a friendly hotel, she told both her daughters. Why struggle against the inevitable, she thought, when you could pay other people, at last, to do all the struggling for you?

She was a happy inmate. Even, perhaps, a little smug. She had new hips, both sides, her hearing was still sharp, she could get up unaided and leave the room when the Jesus Band arrived for Guitar 'n Clappin'. And did. And, what was more, she had chosen to be here. Grounds, indeed, for smugness. It also meant that she no longer had to struggle up to Scotland or into London for alternate daughterly Christmases. Once in an institution, you could invoke elderly fragility any time you liked. Invaluable.

She folded her hands in her lap and watched the squirrels performing on the smooth landscaped lawn. This was Surrey at its tamed and manicured best. She could be looking out on the gardens of Burlington Manor Residential Home—or at the Leith Hill Golf Course. Around here every homeowner's aim seemed to be to have a garden that looked as much as possible like links. Husbands felt at home and could drive their little tractors, while wives fondly looked on. She had chosen Surrey and the Burlington for precisely that reason—it was hybrid town and country and it made no demands. This was neither sea nor nature untamed. The banality suited her very well.

Both her daughters were very shocked. They accused her of giving up.

'Yes,' she said, 'that is exactly what I am doing. I have spent a lifetime on active service and now I wish to retire.'

'In the old days,' Pamela said glumly, 'you would have become a nun.'

'Well, now—that's a thought,' said Mrs Hennessy.

Kay rolled her eyes.

Pamela said, 'Oh, Mum!'

And Mrs Hennessy smiled to herself. What was the point of reaching this time of life and not keeping them all on their toes?

She sat in the Burlington, folded her arms on the girls' disapproval and said it was either this or suttee. 'You have both had a good education,' she told them, 'which is something I never had. So you mustn't begrudge me this.'

In the end they acceded.

Kay returned to her Highland farmer and her three bonny bairns. Pamela returned to her world of interiors. And Mrs Hennessy settled in nicely.

She knew that if Harry Hennessy had lived, they would have looked after each other. But Harry Hennessy did not. Eighteen months after retiring, just when they should have been enjoying the dues of their longevity, he crossed the road and never reached the other side. Long Vehicle, it said. Must have been, by the state of him. Which made future efforts seem a waste of time and Why bother? Not quite so bad now—but she still felt it. All those years and to end up alone.

'You don't have to,' said her sister Ida. 'You

could marry again.' That had shaken her. She was shocked into swearing. 'I'll be buggered if I will,' she said, poking her finger into her plump shoulder. '*Buggered!*' Poke, poke went the finger, 'What? Get a secondhand job that might conk out at any minute? And no past nor memories to back it up? No, thank you. Now, put the kettle on, my girl, and don't be so wet.'

'You're a good-looking woman,' said Ida mysteriously.

'So was Queen Victoria,' she snapped back.

But within the week, Nobby Porter from Gwendolen Avenue had started to call, bearing pansy plants and rhubarb and a screwdriver to fix the gate. She did not need his fixings—if she wanted a man with a screwdriver, she could pay for one.

She kept her distance, but he managed to kiss her a month or two later over the cake stall at the Twickenham Strawberry Fayre—and enough people saw to make the connection. She saw winks and nudges behind every raffle ticket, realized suddenly that she did not want to run a cake stall, did not want to be on a committee, and did not want to be kissed in public by a man whom she knew to have piles. In short she did not want to be In The Swim any more. She rang the admirable charity Help the Aged, who gave her the right advice, and, after many a secret trip out, she found the Burlington.

72

Mrs Hennessy then summonsed her sister Ida up from Bournemouth for a few weeks, introduced her to Nobby Porter, and left them to it. That didn't take long. She liked to see people settled. Ida always accused her of being too controlling, but Ida did not complain about Nobby. Anyway, what was controlling but another word for concern? Once installed in the home, she had time to consider the vexed question of Pamela. Now that Daniel had left home, she wanted to discuss the vexed question of Pamela, with Pamela, today. That settled, she was really ready for the quiet life.

Not entirely quiet, of course. For she had made one new friend, Eileen, and one was quite enough. Eileen was something quite different. Eileen was once a fairly high-class callgirl. 'Tart, dear,' was how she corrected the euphemism. 'I was a *real* tart—very fruity. But second eleven. They don't get the husbands. So here I am.'

Mrs Hennessy felt pleased to have broken new ground in this way. She had led a decent and unremarkable life as wife and mother and had done nothing to set the world alight. It was interesting to be friends with a lady of the night. The sort of woman who knew everything while she, Mrs Hennessy, did not.

Eileen was also there for the peace and beigeness.

'When you've had to wear as many red satin camiknicks as I have, ducks, a nice cream and biscuit wallpaper is very acceptable.'

She also came here for the food.

'All my working life I had be dressed to the nines—and be undressed to the nines as well. And my regulars soon knew if I'd put a pound on. Now it's the cream buns and the chocolate and anything I fancy. And the biggest treat of all—know what that is?'

Mrs Hennessy tried to guess. 'Bread pudding? Butterscotch tart?'

Eileen nodded slightly. 'Yes, dear, those, of course—but no, no, the real treat is wearing tights. All those years and years of belts and stockings and garters and whatnot—always at half-mast so they could see the tops—and now tights. Pinch me, dear, I'm in heaven.'

Mrs Hennessy, waiting for Pamela, thought it was like a little bit of heaven really. With just an edge of defiance in her and Eileen to make it interesting. She settled herself further into the blue armchair, glad again that Pamela persuaded her to bring it. You could not reject everything. It was as if a part of Harry was with her. On the day she moved in here she said this to Pamela, who burst into tears. Mrs Hennessy was amazed. 'But it makes me happy, dear,' she said. 'Brings us close.'

'That is real love,' said her daughter solemnly.

'Possibly,' said her mother. 'But it's also to do with time and shared experience.'

She thought about Harry. Had she loved

him? Hard to say, they had been so busy all those years. She certainly *missed* him. She missed him very much. Which was not quite the same.

Footsteps broke her reverie.

Pamela, hurrying down the corridor, suddenly envied the picture her mother made. Twenty-two years to go before such contentment would be hers. Her breathless greeting cut through the peace. 'Hi, Mum—sorry I'm late.'

'You'd be late for your own funeral, dear,' she said. And she patted the regulation oatmeal tweed chair beside her. 'How's Danny? He hasn't written to me once.'

'Join the club,' said Pamela ruefully.

'Missing him?'

Pamela considered. 'Not exactly,' she said. And handed her mother the mint imperials.

The tea arrived, neat on a tray, beige and white cups and a cosy shaped like a cottage. Ginger snaps, digestives and chocolate fingers. Mrs Hennessy smiled at the display. 'Every day's a celebration here,' she said, and offered her daughter the plate. Then, leaning back in her seat, she eyed Pamela up and down carefully and said, 'All work and no play? You look a bit jaded.'

Thank you, Mother, she thought. This being entirely correct, and therefore Pamela's rawest nerve, she opened her mouth to deny it. But before she could, Mrs Hennessy raised her

75

hand to attract one of the staff. The helper, a pale undersized girl with beige check overall and a listless eye, brought a jug of hot water. There was barely the flicker of a smile at Mrs Hennessy's thanks. It was less aggression than defeat. Somehow she always looked *damp.*

Pamela put down her cup. 'Seriously, though, apart from the chocolate biscuits, I don't know how you stand it here.' And, without thinking, she added, 'Why don't you come and live with me now?'

They both looked at each other with fear in their eyes.

'Don't be *daft,*' said her mother.

There was an audible sigh of relief from both of them. After which they sat in pleasant silence for a while, looking out upon the perfect lawns.

'Don't stay on your own too long, will you?' said her mother eventually.

Pamela laughed. 'I'm all right,' she said.

'And how's Peter coping?' asked her mother.

'*Peter?*' said Pam, thinking this was a bit thick. 'Peter—coping?'

'Yes, dear. Now Danny's gone.'

'He couldn't care less,' she said. 'He couldn't even get to the station to see them off.'

'Never did like goodbyes, I remember that,' said her mother, which was quite untrue. But she wanted to fly the flag.

Mrs Hennessy was fond of her ex-son-in-law. She did not really understand what he did, or like what she saw of it, but he had done well for himself, very well, and she could never understand Pamela leaving him just when things started to take off. When Pam said at the time, a little heatedly on questioning, that she just couldn't stand the way he seemed to be disappearing up his own bumhole with the need to succeed, and trying to take her with him, Mrs Hennessy had no idea what she meant. Men went out to work and women went out to work when they were free to do so. It was the way of the world. And if you stuck by your husband, then eventually he brought home the bacon.

Well, Pamela went ahead solo and did quite well for herself—though not as well as Peter. She could be having such a comfortable life now. And he was very thoughtful, despite what Pamela said. He remembered Mrs Hennessy's birthday and Christmas, and even visited her a couple of times, though Pamela did not know, about that. Mrs Hennessy guessed that he was a bit lonely, and she was quite certain her daughter was too. It was simple common sense for them to get back together again. It would be so *settled* all round. Mrs Hennessy liked the idea of things being settled.

She refocused on her daughter, having been miles away. One of the nice things about being elderly was you had excuses for all kinds of rudeness. Pamela was staring at her very hard. She stared very hard indeed.

Mrs Hennessy only yawned innocently. 'You are very tough on him, you know,' she said. 'He really wasn't at all bad. And I expect he's quite lonely now that Kirsty female has left him.'

'Mother,' said Pamela warningly. *'Mother?'*

Mrs Hennessy put up her hand.

'I'm only saying—that's all. In my opinion your generation gives up too easily. You could have a very comfortable life now. I'm sure of it. And you're fond of him, aren't you?'

'Peter was very odd, mother,' said Pam firmly. 'And hardly domesticated.'

'Everybody's odd, dear. Your father wasn't exactly what you could call easy. And he never changed a nappy in his life.'

'That's different. You were made for each other. You could see that.'

Mrs Hennessy snorted. 'We most certainly were not,' she said. 'And you girls only saw what you wanted to see. We had our silly moments like everyone else.'

She stared out at the lawns for a minute, as if composing herself. At her time of life, she decided, there was no point in platitudes. 'The truth is,' she said eventually, 'that we met on a trip to Brighton just after the war. I went with your Auntie Ida, Harry and a boy called Reginald. We all went up in a plane together. Paris or Bust. It was only once round the

78

airfield. A bit of a nonsense really. Reginald was the good-looking one and I wanted him to take notice of me very badly. But it was your father who gave me his hand as I got out. That's all. It could just as easily have been the other way round. You father could have been called Reginald.' Mrs Hennessy gave her daughter a little look.

Pamela nibbled at a biscuit to stop herself saying anything else.

'I can assure you it was not a marriage made in heaven,' said Mrs Hennessy positively. 'It was a marriage made in *Brighton* . . .'

'It's a nice story,' said Pam.

'Oh, it's always a nice story when it happens to somebody else. But we had to get on with it. And we did.'

'You were happy,' said Pam.

Give me strength, thought her mother. 'Off and on,' she said. 'Just like everybody else.' And she thought, Happiness can go under a lorry just like that.

'What happened to the other one?'

'Broke Ida's heart and vanished.'

'You had a lucky escape.'

'Not at all. I was never romantic like Ida.'

The trouble, thought Mrs Hennessy, with bright young women like Pam, all talent and education and independence, was that they just weren't prepared to put up with things any more. Peter was only being what men were brought up to be: ambitious, successful, number one. Even Kay, married to her quiet countryman, was happy in his shadow. At the end of the day there were no winners, of course, but you couldn't have it both ways. Here was Pamela all on her own, and there was Kay contented for life . . .

Pamela looked around. At the paleness, the sanctity, the perfection of the restraint. 'He'd love this place—Peter,' she said.

'He would,' said her mother. 'Perhaps I should invite him down here for tea again.'

'Mother!' said Pamela again. 'Stop it. Don't you dare.'

Too late. Mrs Hennessy looked down at her cup. She had made up her mind.

Pamela was looking at her questioningly.

But Mrs Hennessy was already rising from her chair. 'I think I'd like to go for a little walk in the grounds, dear,' she said.

It was the right thing to do and calmed things between them. Mrs Hennessy waved at Eileen, who was sitting in the small conservatory reading the *News of the World.* But she did not look up. Later she would read bits of the more scandalous stories out to Mrs Hennessy over cocoa. It was one of the delights of the week, of which there were many.

'Do you remember your father's bits of poetry?' she said as they walked arm in arm past serried ranks of chrysanthemums. 'He was a one for self-improvement. Very proud of you.'

'Well, I remember the bit he used at my wedding.'

'Say it for me,' said her mother.

Pamela knew what her mother was up to, but she obliged.

'Let him first work out the number
    Of the dust of Africa
    And the twinkling stars above
    Whoever wants to number your
    Many thousand love games
    Play as you please, and very soon
    Produce children . . .'

Mrs Hennessy nodded. 'Didn't half make your Auntie Ida blush.

'It didn't do too bad a job on Peter,' said Pam. 'I think I only saved him from fainting with embarrassment by pointing out it was Catullus.'

Mrs Hennessy stopped walking and touched some of the drooping flower heads with her fingertips. 'It isn't everything, you know. There's a lot to be said for company. And you've managed without it very well. Haven't you?'

'It?' said Pam, mischievously. 'What's It?'

But Mrs Hennessy walked on.

Her mother knew about Douglas, of course. There was no hiding the pain of that. But Pamela never told her about Dean. She wondered whether she should do so now, just to let her know that she had not been an entirely erotic-free zone. But much as Mrs Hennessy liked to present an easy-going face to the world, she would find the age gap difficult to accept.

They walked on. The turf felt like velvet and not a daisy nor a clover leaf spoiled the pile. Even the trees looked neat and tidy and moved very little in the breeze. How dull, Pam thought, how flat and dull and boring all this is. She suddenly came out in goosebumps. Was this to be the measure of her days also?

'I like Peter,' said Mrs Hennessy abruptly.

'Oddly enough,' said Pam, 'he and I have been getting on quite well recently.'

'Nothing odd about it. You go back a long way. And he can be very charming and considerate. And interesting. All those different jobs of his. You could do a lot worse than have him come courting you. A lot worse.'

Pamela thought it was remarkable how her mother kept abreast of such things, considering that she had not seen him for years, apart from at Daniel's graduation. It was Daniel who must have told her about Kirsty.

'There really is more to life than passion. Don't you think?' The word came very oddly from her mother's lips.

'Not on your nelly,' said Pam. And she steered her mother past the weeping willow which could not have been more tastefully or picturesquely placed if it had been set-designed.

'Do you really like it here?' she said.

Mrs Hennessy nodded.

They were now walking along by the fading rose beds, all of whose bushes bloomed at the same height, around the ornamental pond and back towards the house. They passed an ancient gardener. Mrs Hennessy gave him a regal wave with her handkerchief as if she were the Queen Mother. When, wondered Pam, did one stop feeling embarrassed by one's parents?

She commented that all the staff here seemed to be either very young, bored and boring, or very old and half-decayed. 'That's right, dear,' nodded her mother. 'It's very peaceful.'

'It wouldn't do for me,' said Pam firmly.

Her mother stopped. She gave her a penetrating look, her eyes just as alert as they ever were. 'Exactly,' she said. 'Exactly. So don't you let it. Think about Peter. You could do a lot worse.'

On the way home Pamela very nearly lost concentration and crashed the car. What might it be like to take up the baton with Peter again? One thing it might be was comfortable. No shortage of money now. And it was true they had their profession in common. And the invisible, permanent bond of a son. She tried to imagine what it would be like to have sex with Peter again, which was the point at which she nearly crashed the car.

CHAPTER TEN

One morning, about a week after visiting her mother, and still a little shaken by it, Pamela arrived in the shop to find Jenny standing transfixed in the back office, still holding the telephone.

She looked half-amused ~~and half~~ incredulous.

'Sit down,' she said to Pam.

Pamela sat. 'What?' she said. She looked at the receiver still cradled in Jenny's arms. 'No.' She held up her hand. 'Don't tell me.'

'Deep breath,' said Jenny.

Pamela breathed. 'Let me guess. The Clarkes' handpainted is peeling off again?'

'Nothing so sweet.'

Jenny replaced the receiver thoughtfully. 'That was Douglas Brown's sister. She wants to come and choose some stuff.'

'The sister from hell?'

'Battersea Waterside, actually.'

'Wants to come here? She must have an ulterior motive.'

'Maybe she just wants a discount?' said Jenny, who always took the straightforward route.

'Hmm,' said Pam, not at all convinced.

84

Jennifer went back out into the shop.

Still thoughtful, Pamela watched her heave a large gilded book of new French tapestry samples off the counter. 'Oh, let's send those back.' She pulled a face. 'Vulgar, over-priced things.'

Jenny opened the book and also pulled a face. 'Appalling,' she agreed. 'What are the French coming to . . .'

'Retro,' she said absently. 'Retro. It'll all be over soon.' She stood there tapping her teeth with a pen. 'I wonder what Zoe Brown really wants? Odd. Very odd.'

'She definitely wanted to deal only with you.'

'Well, if it is a discount she's after, she won't get one. Somehow I doubt it. More like a dog returning to its vomit. She's an emotional basket-case, especially where Douglas is concerned.'

'Maybe she won't come.'

'Well, all will be revealed in the fullness of time.'

She went to help with the heavy book of samples. 'Just look,' she said, eyeing the price list. 'Talk about crass. And you'd need a second mortgage for these. Who in their right mind would buy them?'

Their eyes met. They both nodded. And they both said in unison, 'An emotional basket-case . . .'

'If she rings again,' said Pam, 'make her an

appointment.'

'Here or there?' asked Jenny.

'Oh, here,' said Pam. 'I feel like playing the Grande Dame.' She ran her fingers lightly over the gilded lettering. 'I wonder how Douglas is,' she said.

'Pamela,' said Jenny sternly. 'No.'

'Oh, I wouldn't,' she replied, as lightly as she could manage. 'Not with Douglas. Not after all that pain. I'm quite cured. Dean saw to that.'

She spoke to Daniel that evening. He was distant and clipped, as if she had got in the way of something. She tried not to think what. At the end of the call she said lamely, 'Do you need anything up there?' To which he said, 'Mum, they do have shops.'

Afterwards she found herself wandering around the house doing the phrase in a number of silly voices—Mum, they *do* have shops—Mum, they do have *shops*—Mum, they do *have* shops . . . By the time she completed the circuit, it was all she could do not to call him back and yell something unpleasant down the phone. But what? I'll stop your pocket money? Father Christmas doesn't come for naughty boys?

*   *   *

On the following Sunday she got up very early, breathed deep of the fresh morning air, threw her walking boots in the back of the car, drove east and cursed both Rick and Margie all the way up the North Circular, along the M11 and well into the B1049, until the beauty of Ely Cathedral finally put her rancour to shame.

She had not meant to drive east at all. She had meant to drive west, pick up Margie, and have a day out with her, maybe hiring a boat on the Kennet and Avon. Now she was driving east because she could not stop herself. Because there was no one here to stop her. Damn the two of them, she said to herself, and drove faster. And, for that matter, damn Zoe Brown, too.

If the cursing of the latter was understandable, the cursing of the two former was severally odd. In the first instance it was odd because Margie and Rick had never actually met. In the second instance it was odd because they were both supposed to be friends of hers. Unlike Zoe Brown. In the third instance it was odd because, as Pamela pointed out to herself in between her extreme bouts of scurrility, they had not actually done anything wrong. Which, of course, made her curse them all the more.

Rick started it. Finding herself with time on her hands, Pamela asked if she could have some guitar lessons and he agreed. They were supposed to begin on Saturday afternoon but at the last minute Rick rang, sounding extremely subdued, and said that his wife, earth-mother Vanessa, did not think it was a very good idea.

'Well—another time then,' she said, not understanding. 'Maybe Monday evenings?'

'Er—no,' said Rick. 'I think she means It's Not A Good Idea—Ever.'

'What?' said Pam.

'You and me. Alone.'

As the penny dropped it was as well that Pamela was made speechless. Otherwise she might have committed the unforgivable, because truthful, sin of saying, 'Does your wife seriously think I've got designs on a pot-bellied old rocker with hoops in his ears and hairs growing out of his nose? Grey hairs growing out of his nose?'

'I see,' was all she allowed herself to say, with icy dignity, before ringing off.

Immediately she called Margie. And, taking the view of Sisterly Rights that meant she was allowed ten minutes of uninterrupted fuming while Margie made sympathetic noises, was much miffed to find herself getting very short shrift—about three minutes—before Margie interrupted and said briskly, 'Oh, it's inevitable. It'll go on happening everywhere. Why do you think I moved to the country? You'll even find yourself in Lenny's doing your usual flirty thing over the carrots and then Mrs Lenny will whip out from behind the cabbages and give you the evil eye. You're even more of a threat now you are not a mother.'

'Margery Jane Harcourt,' said Pam with vexation, 'Danny hasn't died and gone to heaven. He's just moved to Liverpool. I am still a mother.'

How could Margie understand when she had never had a child of her own?

'You would have to be as circumspect and well behaved as Ani Patel to be accepted. How is she by the way?'

'Fine,' said Pamela shortly. 'Ari's doing A levels.'

'She's really seeing him through. Good for her. Will you give her my love?'

'Yes, yes,' said Pam impatiently. 'But what about Vanessa and Rick?'

'Oh, just accept it. Get yourself a woman guitar teacher. Or a dishy bloke.'

'But Rick's a friend.'

'Oh, no, he's not. Not any more. It's probably crossed his mind.'

'Margie!'

'Yes, well. What I mean is, we are perceived as bad enough being single, and a threat. Probably, as you approach fifty, a desperately lonely threat . . . Friendships with other women's menfolk are difficult. And Vanessa might be right. Rick could get carried away. What with you being so free now.'

Had Pamela not been smarting from losing one friend that day, she might well have put down the phone.

'I have got a business to run,' said Pam

indignantly.

'You could give it up tomorrow. Or leave it and let Jenny and that new girl get on with it for a while.'

'But I don't want to. I like what I do.' She was certainly not going to admit to Margie that she also found herself a little bored by it. 'I'm only saying that I'd have to be desperate to even consider Rick . . . let alone Lenny—his teeth move in and out. It's from cracking all those walnuts.'

But Margie's cackle of laughter was shorter than usual. 'Listen—I've got to change the subject. I've met someone new.'

'What, what?' said Pam. 'New? You mean brand new? Never been unwrapped?'

'Not quite,' said Margie.

There was a pause.

'He's married, Marge?'

'I told you,' she said. 'Desperate and lonely. I got tarred with the brush often enough so I thought I'd wear it—the cap.'

'You're mixing your metaphors,' said Pamela quietly. 'And I wish you wouldn't.'

They both knew what she meant.

It was then that Pam had the bright idea. 'I know,' she said, 'let's have a day out together tomorrow. We could meet half-way and—'

'Oh, I can't,' said Margie. 'I'm seeing Tom.'

'I thought mistresses didn't see their married lovers at the weekend?'

'Oh, he's moved in,' said Marge.

'You didn't hang about.'

'Time marches on,' she said.

Pamela felt a shiver run up her spine.

'So,' she said breezily, 'can't tempt you out for the day tomorrow, then?'

'Sorry,' said Margie. 'Talk soon. Bye.'

Thus here she was, transporting her walking boots, feeling dejected and dumped, on her own, with the beauties of Swaffham Prior to her right and the charms of Ely Cathedral ahead, and on her way beyond those to the Levels of Cambridgeshire. Cursing her two fair-weather friends for making a hole in her life through which the memory of Douglas could come creeping, creeping and against which she was as weak as any soppy Victorian maid. If Rick's offensive suggestion had not caught her on the raw, and if Margie had not been quite so brutally involved with someone new, and if Zoe Brown had not been in touch, she would have been fine. As it was, she was not fine, and she came to these parts as a thirsty as a Walsingham pilgrim.

She had never been back here since they ended the affair. It remained in her heart and mind as a sacred place. Just the two of them alone. She without Danny, he without Zoe and the shallowness that surrounded him in London. She knew exactly which pathways to walk, exactly which fields to skirt, exactly which pub to stop in for lunch and from where to sit and watch the evening sun go down like a great pink billiard ball sinking below the net.

She experienced them all over again. And it was hard to do these things without him. To run across fields of brown ridged earth towards a horizon that never came, opening her arms to the huge sky and thinking, in suspended reality, that he might suddenly come walking across the field towards her, smiling, laughing, arms out, smelling of country dampness and his own particular scent. She wondered what she would do if she ever saw him again. Would the desire to kiss him still remain? In the past she had always wanted to kiss him as soon as she saw him. Supposing she still did? Woman Arrested for Attacking Ex-lover Lookalike came to mind. She shivered. No, she would never mistake him for a stranger. If she saw him, she would know him. But she would not see him. Ever again. That was the whole point.

She stood at the edge of the field in the gathering darkness and willed him to be there. And then she turned back to the car, not sure if she was glad or sorry that it was only fantasy. He would not be there, of course not. He was probably even now rolling around in the sheets with someone wonderful, childless, with small hips, while she stomped around these fields playing Dido. With which embarrassing thought she went back to the car. Shriven.

Driving home, caught up in the traffic cones and roadworks, she listened to Vaughan

Williams, whose very Englishness fitted the day so perfectly. And she was aware of hearing Daniel's voice saying, 'Oh, not that classical stuff again, Mum. *Please . . .*'

But, of course, the passenger seat was empty.

She turned it up all the louder, letting the rippling music fill the car.

She could do anything she pleased now. Anything she wanted. Well, almost. And even *that* was a possibility . . . Not that she ever, really, would. She had given Jenny her word.

CHAPTER ELEVEN

It was Saturday morning. As Pamela left the shop and made her slow way home, nose furtively buried in a nice tabloid headline and urging herself to savour the decadence, Miss Phoebe Glen passed her in the street without a glance, oblivious to all save her goal that morning: to win the fat man. He would come into the shop eventually, she knew, and when he did, she would be ready for him.

And she was . . .

'There is more to life than budgerigars,' she said jauntily, as he sidled in. She was very pink and her eyes glowed strangely. The fat man froze, no response coming readily to his lips.

Mrs Patel kept smiling while she sorted the

Maltesers and the Bounty bars.

He first shook and then nodded his head, made a curiously muddled motion that was half-bow and half-curtsey, and thought, How strange. Because after buying that copy of *The Budgerigar* he *had* been quite taken.

'But your landlady, Lavender, would not like them, would she?' She came even closer. He flinched. But stood his ground. He had to. Short of climbing into the upright refrigerator, there was nowhere else for him to go.

'Lavender?' he said cautiously.

Mrs Patel dropped one of the packets and tutted.

Miss Phoebe continued, still quite playfully, 'And you must get so lonely living on your own in that dreadful place in Pumping Lane. You deserve better. It must be hard for you to live with someone unintelligent.'

Coquetry, she thought, I'll give him coquetry. She hoped she had not gone too far. Ani Patel, who was absolutely certain she had gone too far, just went on sorting chocolate bars. It did not do to look at all censorious if you had darkish skin.

The fat man, who only knew his landlady as the Widow MacNamally, and as a woman who kept herself to herself except on the odd occasion when she brought a friend home from The Five Bells, was impressed.

She came closer. He quite liked the sweetish smell that hung around her. She said, 'I offer

94

you the opportunity to come and lodge in a cultivated household. Conversation, higher things. The gifts that lift us above animals, as Hazlitt would have it.'

In her desperation Miss Phoebe would have turned a somersault, or done a conjuring trick, or abracadabraed up the Turin Shroud, in order to impress him.

He said, 'I'm not very fond of haslet,' pressed pigmeat not being his favourite.

Miss Phoebe immediately said, 'Neither am I, oh neither am I . . .' as the desperate supplicant will.

And the fat man found the way her pointy fingers danced through the whiteness fascinating. A bit grubby, but definitely fascinating. And she was doing something ever so strange with her eyes. He looked across at Ani Patel, who gave him a little look of encouragement. If this worked, she would be safe home with Ari on those Tuesdays.

He almost said yes, and then, like a drowning man, he saw *Karaoke for Beginners*. And grabbed it like a life-raft. Shielding himself with the publication, he slid across to Mrs Patel, who felt sorry for him.

'It is last week's,' she said. 'Have it for half-price.'

He was not there yet. But Miss Phoebe felt in her fingertips that she had him in her thrall.

'A packet of strong mints,' she said to Mrs Patel. 'In case the social services call.'

Mrs Patel nodded and thought, yet again, how strange were this nation's habits. What was wrong with offering them a cup of tea?

She would have asked Mrs Pryor to explain the matter, as she sometimes did, but Mrs Pryor had already been in. Very early for her. And she did not seem quite herself nowadays. Ani Patel's heart bled for her. She could see that Mrs Pryor was affected by the loss of her son. She thought about Ari again and hoped, very much indeed, that Miss Phoebe was successful with her lodger.

*　　　*　　　*

Pamela was banned from going to her own shop this Saturday. Jenny, obviously worried about finding her slumped in an exhausted coma over the paint-finishes one Monday morning, warned her about spending too much time on the business. The fact was, there was little to come home for any more. She did not say this, of course. But presumably it was obvious.

'There is no need for you to be there at nine o'clock,' said Jenny one Friday right, when Pam had rung her absentmindedly to ask her something. 'Get in a cab and come over here and I'll feed you.'

'I am not a chimpanzee,' she said crossly. But the truth was, she did feel a bit like an animal in a cage.

Both her mother's silly suggestion about Peter and her visit to Cambridgeshire were very unsettling. In her isolation the past kept tiptoeing in and tickling her. Forgotten things in drawers, a postcard down behind the piano—all these things were imbued with new meaning.

When she rang Margie to apologize for being so short with her and to ask her more about Tom—she did not in the least want to know, but she felt as a true sister she was obliged to ask—she ended up telling her all about her trip to the Levels. Safe within her blossoming new affair, Margie could afford to be high-handed. 'To this day I do not know why you gave up Douglas,' she said. 'He was absolutely gorgeous, and right for you. Gave you loads of fun. Kept you young.'

'Oh, yes,' said Pam, 'so young I was like a demented teenager. He also damn nearly wrecked my career and my relationship with Danny.'

'Well—that's all in the past now,' said Margie, as easily as one might dismiss Passchendaele as a scrap. 'Why don't you ring him up? He might be free.'

Pamela paused, stunned. And then she said slowly, as if talking to a vegetable. 'Have you gone barking mad?'

'And have you,' Margie asked, 'forgotten how nice it is?'

Pamela did not ask what. She did not have

97

to. If Margery was a vegetable, she was an extremely well stuffed one. No—she knew, by the creeping tone of smugness. But she let her go on.

'You could just say you'd rung for a chat. Be brave. You're nearly fifty. You can do anything. What have you got to lose?'

Pamela thought about her mother. She could be forgiven because of age. Margie could not. She swallowed, made her voice bright, and changed the subject. 'Tell me about Tom,' she said.

It worked, of course. Margie launched in. And he sounded wonderful. But then, they always did. A superior thought that made absolutely no difference to her state of mind. Which was low.

This morning she was again feeling crabby on account of ringing up her son. This time he and The Girlfriend were still in bed—at half-past eleven. She had been up for hours. She had been cleaning for hours. Cleaning! *She* had no one to lie with. She suspected the two of them spent their whole time in Liverpool bonking. How could she have been protective of him? He was streets ahead of her. Those magazines proved it. But then, she comforted herself, if she had not been so protective of him, had not put him first, he would probably not be so happily indifferent to her, and so happily involved and bonking The Girlfriend now. Disturbing but true. Her sacrifice, she knew, without a tinge of pride, had made him whole. Oddly enough, this thought did nothing to alleviate the crabbiness. Nothing at all. So, she had produced a well-balanced member of the human race? Oh, good, she thought, going at the plughole savagely. Well, that's all right, then. That really makes the sexual frustration, the loneliness, and the sudden metamorphosis into flounder-woman much more acceptable.

Such thoughts were not helped by the sight of her primly active rubber glove. Crash, bang, she went, throwing cutlery for one back into a drawer.

And now the past was really coming back to haunt her with a vengeance, because—as if Peter and Douglas were not enough—she suddenly thought of Dean. Sweet Dean. Oh, the ignominy. Oh, the panic . . .

In the shine of the sink she saw poor Dean's face as it looked out from under the bed, naked and holding an African violet (why on earth had she shoved that under there with him?), and she saw her own face, beetroot red, as red as her Happy Jacket, glaring at him through the crack in the door, telling him to Stay, as if he were a little dog. And then going cheerfully down the stairs, two at a time, saying after the initial strangled cry of surprised greeting, 'Oh, Danny—would you just run and get us some milk from the corner shop?' And he, just having arrived back, Finals completed, and a little travel-weary, looking back at her as if she were completely daft. Since when did Danny run his mother's errands anyway? And certainly not on the day he returned from university . . . 'I'll take it black, Ma,' was all he said. 'That's cool.'

So poor Dean stayed up there, under the bed, while down below Danny and she bantered, had tea, made toast and it was half an hour before she could escape back upstairs to help him dress and slip out.

Poor, sweet Dean. She remembered, suddenly, that it was his birthday last month. She counted on her fingers. *Twenty-eight.* Did that sound better than twenty-six? Who could say? She was still and always would be twenty years older than him. Old enough to be his mother. Their Catullian games might have eased her heart, but such liaisons had always been thus, she thought mournfully. Such liaisons had always been ill-received and just as shameful.

Poor Jocasta. Finding Oedipus. Horror, of course, would certainly have made her mute. But also disappointment, perhaps? After all, there was nothing like youth. Poor Jocasta—to give that up and gain a son? From where she was sitting this morning, it didn't seem a very fair bargain.

Crash, bang, crash.

She now realized that she was making quite a lot of noise on purpose. Good job Piggins was sleeping in the Whiskery Beyond or he might have got kicked. She considered the possibility of getting a dog until Ani Patel, sighing a little, said that dogs were such a tie and meant you could not go off on your own for tramps. Realizing eventually that her newsagent did not mean smelly old men in broken boots, but was remembering how she used to go off walking in the past, Pamela agreed she had a point.

Hardly one that mattered, she thought despondently. For here she was, free to do anything. Stay out all night if she wanted to. Even stay out all night with an old tramp if she felt so inclined. And she was cleaning.

Crash, crash, bang.

Enough!

She ripped off her rubber gloves and threw them down on the draining board like gauntlets. She had cleared every single surface in the kitchen and tidied everything away. Not one of her usual pursuits. The cobbler's children go unshod. Her home might be colourful, but it was no design set. She straightened her back. And it was still only half-past twelve. On the wall was a plate that Jenny had brought her back from a trip somewhere. It said, 'A clean and tidy home means a dull woman.'

'Oh, fuck,' she thought miserably, looking out through the gleaming kitchen window. It probably does.

Of course she could have gone to lunch with

the boring Baldwins—a banker and his charitable wife, for whom Danny had removed the B, substituted a W, and sung, 'There was a wanker and his wife,' to the tune of 'Barbara Allen'. She even missed that schoolboy stuff around the house now. It used to irritate, now she missed it—like a whole lot of things. She could just stay in and continue with her study plans. She looked at the clock. There was still time to ring the Baldwins and say she was coming after all. Though her hand hesitated on the telephone, in the end she decided not. Maybe she would just go out. She pondered. But where?

Well, she certainly was not going back to Cambridgeshire. And she was certainly not going to attempt to play gooseberry with Margie in Berkshire. So she decided to have lunch out on her own. Why not? Get a paper. Choose somewhere appealing. It was yet another perfect Indian summer's day. She put on her soft pink jumper, tidied her hair, applied some make-up and struggled into an alarmingly tight pair of jeans (shrunk in the wash, of course) and got into the car.

Now, she said to herself, pretending the question was real, where shall we go today? But she already knew. She set off for north of Regent's Park. Be nice to have a little stroll around there again—not having been for well over a year . . . Might look at the Heath. She hummed under her breath. A sure sign she was up to something and kidding herself. Which, of course, she was.

'Well, I won't go in,' she said defiantly, as she turned off the Marylebone Road. 'I won't even let him know I've been.' And, she thought, even more defiantly, after the Levels and memories of Douglas, it seemed oddly appropriate to be doing this. And the car was a new one so it wouldn't be recognized.

She found herself in the familiar territory of Dean's road. She doubted he still lived in the same flat with the same lads—he would probably be living with a girl by now, like Danny. He could even be married. But she kept her head down low over the wheel as she crawled by. This time there was no sense of sadness to overwhelm her. Only memory and desire. That old geranium. She had forgotten how carefree the time with Dean was. She had managed, for the first time in her life, to do what all those therapies suggest: she really did live those few months of theirs one day at a time. Funny how you sometimes only see the value of things once they are over.

It looked the same—big front window—first floor—curtains at half-mast—decaying skeletons of long dead begonias in a terracotta pot on the sill. Ah, but how many twenty-somethings lived like that in this road, in these conversions? She was just about to pick up speed and move on when the door beneath the withered begonias opened and out tumbled

103

Dean and his flat-mates—all three, the same ones, and each with their kit bags—so they *even* went Saturday training as they had always done. Time might have been standing still and waiting.

She stared. It was an extraordinary moment, taking her completely by surprise, because the whole of her seemed to turn inside out while her brain exploded and her ears rang to deafness. It was simply that she had forgotten how wonderful he looked—and, worse, she had had no idea—how could she know?—what fifteen or sixteen months would do to him. Something had matured, changed, deepened. She almost called him, but a girl appeared behind them all. Dark-haired, slender, moving delicate as a flower down the steps, catching them up. Dean reached out and put his hand round her waist, she clutched him for a moment as she stumbled—smiled, righted herself, stayed within his hold.

Pamela's mouth went dry. The exploded brain began to pound, her eyes went watery and she felt sick. But it had to be. What she had come for, she did not quite know, but what she had seen, had to be. It was right. She needed to see precisely this. The understanding made her feel better. The pounding receded. The sickness died away. Her mouth moistened. She was right to let him go. That was where his future lay. Not with her. As she said to Rick, in defence of herself, if it had been Danny and some old bag she would have gone crazy.

The four of them were close now but on the other side of the road—paying her and the other parked cars no attention. Dean still had his arm round the girl, she still giggled, and suddenly the other lad—Julian, was it? She seemed to remember that was the name—Julian danced over to Dean, grabbed the girl from him, and said, laughingly, 'Hands off, you bastard . . .'

She watched Dean's arm fall back to his side, saw that he relinquished her easily, that he did not care for her in that way. She felt stupid with gladness.

They advanced. She slid further down in the seat. She tried very hard not to look at him as he strode and jumped and cavorted along the pavement opposite, right past her car. If she saw a sadness about his eyes, she refused to acknowledge it. She smiled out of the car at him, not thinking, and then shrank back down again. Just for a moment she wondered if their eyes had met and decided it was illusion. And she drove off quickly in the opposite direction, just in case she did something to make it reality.

She did not go to Regent's Park but drove home listening to *Tosca*. It was painful really. Within the confines of her little car, where no one else could possibly know or share the thought, she indulged in comforting self-pity and thought, as she listened, that sometimes you had to acknowledge you were a walking tragedy yourself.

*   *   *

Half-way along the path she stopped to pluck a few dead heads of roses and thought, yet again, how shamefully she had neglected the garden.

Plenty of time for that sort of thing now. It was a chilling thought. She suddenly saw herself pottering about in a shapeless old skirt and no longer colouring her hair. That was what having the role model of her mother sitting in the Burlington did. It tempted you to think that giving up was a good option. Go back to Peter, put your feet up, settle right down and let someone else take the strain. Tempting. Very tempting.

Especially in the matter of being able to afford a gardener, she thought idly. She inspected the desiccated tendrils of the Nellie Moser and had no idea what to do about them. She stared up at the wistaria, which looked very seedy, and she ran an inexpert toe along the edge of the campanula. Have to ask her mother. Soon, soon, she would turn into her anyway. Remembering that comfortable smugness settled in the blue armchair, she was bound to admit that the prospect could be worse. But not by very much.

She frowned at the bright blue front door. Did she have a creeping feeling that she would like to repaint it in something pale? She plucked at the sleeve of her very pink sweater. Was she not considering that the next one she bought might be taupe? Save me, save me, she implored herself, and began to sing very loudly, to the tune of 'Vissi d'arte': 'I am not my mother, I never was my mother, I never will be my mother, I swear, I swear, I swear—' and at each enunciation of swear she gave it all she had got. Which was a surprising amount.

Something would happen. She was a great believer in doors opening when others closed.

Symbolically she was just putting the key in her lock and giving it all she had got once more, when her small, pretty, punk-blonde, thirty-acting-as-twenty neighbour popped her elfin head over the front fence and blinked her baby-blues.

'Are you singing, Mrs Pryor?' she said brightly.

Pam longed to say the usual thing about riding a bicycle. But she held off. 'Call me Pam,' said Pam automatically.

'And what was that you were singing?' she said, in the kind way helpers up at Lupin Lodge spoke to their inmates. 'I've never heard you singing to yourself before.'

The implication was wild lunacy. Pam smiled.

'Ah,' she said. 'How are you getting on now

107

you're on your own?' Her eyes screwed up with sympathy.

Pamela longed to say something four-lettered and Anglo-Saxon. Any shred of respect she might have built up over the last few years would now be as shrivelled as the Nellie Moser. Wearing skirts that actually covered her fanny line had begun the rot—singing bowdlerized Tosca must just about have completed it. She clenched her teeth, turned, smiled, and waited. There would be more. Oh, verily, there would . . .

She, this neighbour, Peaches Carter—once, long ago, in far-off Leighton Buzzard christened June and now, in a surge of post-*Baywatch* syndrome and removal to West London, rechristened in fruiterer's mode by her beefy, media husband Bud, whom Pam was certain was originally introduced as Bob—wore a puzzled look. It became her. As a matter of fact, thought Pamela crossly, grimacing from piles would probably become her. She kept the smile on her face and gritted her teeth. 'Marvellously,' she said, 'Thank you—er—er . . .'

It was always so hard to speak that name. And for some reason, because it was always so hard, but unavoidable, she found herself wanting to go mad and say Strawberry or Mango instead. Indeed, finding herself with a little drop taken at one of their interminable barbecues this summer Pamela had called out across the smoking entrails, 'Lovely ribs, Apricot, lovely . . .'After which there was nothing to do but smile at the shocked and youthful gathering and hope they would put it down to senility. Since the Apricot incident, Pamela was pretty sure that Bud and Peaches and their friends now put everything down to senility. They had a tendency to speak to her in bright, loud voices and mouth at each other that she was In Design. Of course, they could have been mouthing at each other that she was In Decline. It mattered not. Danny had liked them. He and Bud would stand for hours looking at Bud's GTI without, apparently, saying a word.

Pamela was squinting into the sun anyway, which probably completed the illusion of mental instability.

'Not like you to go singing,' added Peaches carefully. She could just as well have said, 'Not like you to go naked in Sainsbury's.'

Pam said, 'Sorry.' Which was fair enough, given the voice she possessed.

Peaches took the apology as her right. 'Don't worry,' she said. 'But now you're back I can ask you . . .' She gave Pamela one of her melting looks. Whenever Peaches saw Pamela, she metamorphosed into one of those greeting cards that says 'In Loving Sympathy'.

Pamela kept her teeth clenched. If it is yet another invitation, she thought, I will not go— I will riot. She prepared for the worst. They eyeballed each other and Pamela continued to try to love Peaches as she loved herself, which was a fairly successful enterprise at this juncture, since her self-esteem was somewhere in the primal sludge. Being thought wanting is bad enough, being caught doing something that apparently confirms it is quite another.

Peaches smiled with a horrible knowingness. 'Doing anything tonight?' she said, in a tone that encouraged Pam's first considered response to be, 'Yes, rogering Arsenal,' which she quickly changed to a gay and careless 'No.'

Peaches smiled again and tapped her nose. 'Good,' she said. 'Because I've got someone coming over who wants to meet you.'

I will not go, I will not go . . .

Peaches dropped her voice in pleasurable conspiracy. 'A man.'

Pamela accepted immediately. Pamela even brightened. Peter, Douglas, Dean all floated away in the afternoon sun. And her mother, Margie—even Rick. Doors, she thought, always doors to open.

'I'd be delighted,' she added. And went in.

CHAPTER TWELVE

It was all very well thinking another door opens, but there was still the afternoon to get through.

110

Pamela rang her mother. At first she thought she would give the glad tidings. Guess what, I've got a date. Then she realized how adolescent it sounded. So she said nothing of Peaches and Bud, and when pushed to say what she was 'up to this weekend', she just replied airily, 'Oh, this and that,' and quickly changed the conversation to Daniel. Of course there was nothing much to talk about there either. 'He always seems to be in bed,' said Pam.

'I expect he's tired, dear,' said Mrs Hennessy. 'You were just the same.'

Typical. Her mother would say that even if Pam announced that Daniel was drug-running in the Congo . . . Ah, well—you were just the same . . .

'Have you rung Peter?' she asked.

'No,' said Pam crisply. 'And he hasn't rung me.'

That told her, she thought.

'Well, I expect he feels a bit awkward,' said Mrs Hennessy.

'Like when he stopped the maintenance awkward?' said Pam with spirit. 'Or like, Well done, Pam, you've done a great job on your own, awkward?'

'Bury the past,' said Mrs Hennessy.

'Sorry,' said Pam.

'That's all right,' said her mother cheerfully. 'Everything's in a state of flux.'

Sometimes, in attempting to hit one nail,

her mother managed to get another completely different one right on the head.

'Better go,' said Pam, as if the afternoon ahead was packed with action.

'Yes,' said Mrs Hennessy. 'Enjoy your this and that . . .'

Pamela walked down to the newsagent and bought another tabloid newspaper, thinking how strange it was, what murky moral sludges surface in the name of pleasuring when we are on our own. She bought chocolates for Peaches and eyed them lasciviously, too.

Mrs Patel was not her usual placid self, and to Pamela's enquiry about her son, said she was just a little bit worried about him.

'How clever you are,' said Mrs Patel feelingly, 'to have achieved it all so successfully.'

Pamela was about to stay and give her counsel, yes, and even, maybe, point out the truth—that she had only stumbled through motherhood and somehow managed to look like everything was planned that way. But the funny old woman with the white hair tottered in, the one who gave Daniel his piano lessons years ago. She gave Pamela an oddly sympathetic look, not unlike Peaches' but swimmier, and said with great feeling, 'I was so sorry to hear about your son.'

'Oh, well—' said Pam. 'Always darkest before the dawn.'

'How brave,' said the woman.

112

'When they go, they go,' she said, wondering how many platitudes you could get to the pound.

The woman looked at Mrs Patel, leaned heavily against the counter, and raised her eyebrows. 'Well, I must say,' she said, looking heavenwards, 'that does seem extraordinarily stout-hearted.'

Not for the English, thought Mrs Patel, and she went on reorganizing the KitKats.

*   *   *

In the Burlington, Mrs Hilda Hennessy sat with Eileen, gazing out at the irreproachable gardens. Thoughts of Pamela were getting in the way of their customary peace. Around them hovered the dwindling smells of lunch— salmon fishcakes and salad—and sleep lay heavy on the air. In the surrounding chairs, comatose figures had propped their walking sticks and lay drowsing. Magazines and newspapers fluttered and flumped to the floor. It was usually a particular moment of congratulation for them both. Nothing to do until tea. But Mrs Hennessy, despite her silence, was agitated. Eileen could see this because her friend's fingers were drumming, very lightly, on the blue leather arm of her chair.

She coughed very gently. 'Nice fishcakes,' she said. 'Tomatoes were firm.'

Mrs Hennessy gazed out at the garden and barely nodded.

'You're worrying about your daughter.'

'I do like everything to be settled,' said Mrs Hennessy. 'Otherwise I can't settle.'

Eileen said carefully, 'I'd have thought you could give up that responsibility now.'

'Oh, no,' said Mrs Hennessy. 'You never do.'

'You're a wonderful mother. If my mother had only taken half the trouble you do,' said Eileen thoughtfully, 'I'd have been a lot better off.'

'Is that why you became a . . .?' Mrs Hennessy coughed delicately.

'Oh, no, dear, it was because of her lack of care that I didn't become a very good one.'

The thing about Eileen, thought Mrs Hennessy, was her directness.

'I expect you taught your girls things?'

Mrs Hennessy said, slightly agitated, 'Well—not those things . . .'

'I mean like pastry and hospital corners? That sort of thing. How to iron a blouse?'

Mrs Hennessy agreed. 'It was different then. Girls were expected to know.' She laughed. 'But you wouldn't catch Pam doing hospital corners or making pastry nowadays.'

'But still,' said Eileen, 'you did teach them. And that's something. My mother was far too busy being Queen of the Night to spend time teaching me anything. I had to learn on the job.'

'It isn't easy,' said Mrs Hennessy, 'being a mother.'

'It isn't easy being anything,' said Eileen, flicking a crumb off her cardigan, 'but it's a darn sight easier if you've been given the instructions.' Eileen's mother, it seemed, never let anything get in the way of her profession. She died, so Eileen said, in a very nice house in Edgware, paid for by a duke.

Mrs Hennessy said, 'You can't prepare your children for everything.'

'No,' said Eileen firmly. 'But you can try. I had to learn on the hoof. No help at all. Oh dear, yes. Good job you can't be sued in my line of business. There was one gent, a man of influence, and he was very taken. So was I. I told all the girls that marriage was on the cards. I was quite sure of it. But I didn't know the ropes. Literally, really. So there he was yelling, Oh, my angel, oh, my angel, and I was saying, Yes, my darling, yes, yes, yes—and he yelled again, Oh, my angel, oh, my angel . . . Before passing out.'

Mrs Hennessy leaned forward, Pamela temporarily forgotten. 'Heart?' she said.

'Not really, said Eileen sadly. 'What he was really saying was Oh, my ankle, oh, my ankle— I'd tied it up too tight, you see, and it nearly dropped off.'

Mrs Hennessy patted her hand. 'Well, we've put all that behind us now,' she said.

Eileen nodded. 'If he'd only *said* something.

115

I said to him, Well, why didn't you say? But he said he couldn't.'

'Ah,' said Mrs Hennessy, knowingly. 'I'm afraid they don't. Harry was the same. I said to Pamela when she went on and on about Peter never talking to her—they just don't and that's that . . .'

'No, they don't,' said Eileen. 'Anyway, he never came back. Left me fifty pounds on the mantel and went. And that's how I know he cared. Because he'd shown a weakness and he couldn't face me again. Odd, when you think he'd shown me everything else, and I do mean everything. You see him on the telly occasionally—waving from aeroplanes and whatnot—still limps. Married a very plain woman. Not happy. Might have been different if my mother had taken the trouble to show me the ropes. Well, *knots*, really. Course, I got there eventually. After a few more little accidents. Never lost a life though. Never. I was interviewed a few years ago. The young woman said I was a living history resource.' She leaned back, smiling, shaking her head at such folly. 'Biscuit?'

They both sat silently for a while. Then Mrs Hennessy said, 'What did you think of my ex-son-in-law? He came here last week. Brought white delphiniums. Those droopy ones.'

'Not my type,' said Eileen firmly. 'Either for business or pleasure.'

'Exactly,' said Mrs Hennessy with

satisfaction. 'Exactly.'

'Looked a bit seedy, actually. Like he needed looking after. Got a few bob, though, if I'm a judge. He'll be snapped up soon enough. They always are. Single men with a bit of money never stay on the shelf for long.'

Mrs Hennessy suddenly sat bolt upright. 'Pass me that telephone,' she said. 'I'm resolved.' She tapped out Peter Pryor's number. 'And if he needs any help, you and I can give it to him.' She waited for the number to be answered. 'Many thousand love games, indeed,' she said. 'He'll never get there on his own.' And then, leaning towards Eileen, she whispered, 'It'll give us something to do.'

Eileen's eyes gleamed.

*   *   *

At about five Pamela rang Danny. If they were *still* in bed with each other, it was just hard luck. The prospect of the evening's dinner with Peaches and Bud and Someone Who Really Wanted To Meet Her set her thinking too much. Talking to Danny, even for a few minutes, would soon cut out all this simpering nonsense. Worrying about the late September sun showing up all her wrinkles. Foolish, unliberated stuff and beneath contempt.

She tapped out the number quickly, and felt even more jumbled up when her son picked up the telephone and answered her bright 'Hallo' with 'Why, *Mum*. What a surprise!'

Surprise? *Surprise*? She could understand it if the Pope had rung him up, or Mrs Idi Amin—but she was his mother. That's what mothers do, she thought, ring their children. They bring them up, help them spread their wings, watch them fly, feel both glad and sad when they finally go. And then they ring them up.

He went on in that absurd way, saying things like 'Oh, *really*?' when she mentioned visiting his grandmother, or 'That's great,' with all the false enthusiasm of an American game-show host on discovering the participant was jobless for a living. She realized that she had passed over into that parental land called Tolerated.

Eventually she could bear it no longer.

'Danny,' she said, wishing suddenly to shock. 'I am thinking of turning your room into my study now that you've gone. Would you mind?'

And Danny just said, '*Great*.'

'You and—er—um—Lilian can have the big spare room when you come for Christmas.'

'Great,' he said.

'Christmas, Danny.'

But she knew he was not listening. She knew, then, that he was watching TV. He had pressed mute (it mattered little to him, she remembered all too well, if there was talking or not, so long as there were pictures).

'Danny?' she said.

118

'Mum,' he replied.

'Sure you don't mind?'

'Sure. That's cool.'

She noticed, with distaste, that he applied a slight Liverpudlian twang. So he was getting a bit posey, too. Just like his father.

'What are you up to tonight?' she said.

'Oh—hanging out. This and that . . .'

She waited.

Eventually he got the message and said, 'And you?'

She told him, making light of it. She could almost feel those rolling eyes again as he said, 'Oh, Mum—that is so *embarrassing* . . .' It was exactly the same phrase he used when he mistakenly smeared her expensive eye gel on his hair and she had to confess its true use. One day, promised all the magazines, they would be friends. Apparently not yet. You couldn't make friends with an embarrassment.

She put the phone down feeling dismissed. His door was temporarily closed to her, which was probably healthy. One of the statements on her last school report was 'Looks for the positive and makes the best of things . . .' It was getting harder. Much harder. Comfort she wanted, but there was none to be had. An arm round her shoulders, a cup of tea and a 'You put your feet up, I'll do it . . .' She returned to the notion of a snowball in hell.

What to wear for this Oh So Embarrassing date was another little problem.

119

Big issues, small issues, making up the weft and warp of her turbulent life. Oddly enough, she thought, living alone is not necessarily a peaceful experience. Should she, for example, expose her cleavage? Her knees? God it was hell. At least Danny was not here to participate in the sartorial debate. He would have had her in a *chador*, given his views on the acceptability of the sex life of mothers.

The phone beeped. She picked it up and said, 'Pamela Pryor,' very crisply. It sounded heartwarmingly well-adjusted.

'It's Peter,' said the voice. 'I just wondered how you are. Dear.'

Dear?

She nearly cried. Never had she been so pleased to hear his voice. Well—a bit of an exaggeration. But not by very much.

'I've just spoken to Danny,' she said. As if that explained everything. She clamped her mouth shut in case she added *Darling.* She was in an untrustworthy state.

'I am glad you are in,' said Peter, in a complete *non sequitur* and as if he had rehearsed it. 'And how nice to hear your voice.'

'What?'

He corrected the tone a little and said, 'I'm glad you're there. It's nice to get a chance to talk.'

Many things had been odd in her life just recently, but that was one of the oddest. She tried to sound casual. Her son was surprised if she called, and now her ex-husband suddenly thought the sound of her voice was Nice. Perhaps she *was* the Pope?

'Is something the matter?' she said carefully.

'No. Why?'

'You sound a bit wound up.'

He looked around him at the scattered paperwork and the upturned cup of coffee. Fact was, he had been unable to find the phone when his ex-mother-in-law rang. He'd lunged a bit and failed. The less furniture in a room, the more a telephone beep will throw itself. The coffee dribbled on to the plain wooden floor and he could see it dripping through the gaps in the boards.

It was, he knew, time to give up minimalism. Minimalism did not help the arthritis. *Arthritis!* Hardly the thing to go discussing over a Saatchi canapé. Nothing to be done, said the best young doctor in town, none of us is getting any younger . . .

He imagined himself living alone and arthritic with only a Stannah stairlift as companion. Even if he redesigned it, which he could do, it was not something to which he could ever confess.

He hesitated. How nice it would be to tell Pamela everything. Knees, eyes, fear of loneliness, everything. He very nearly did. And then he remembered Mrs Hennessy's urgency. Pamela was in need. That was what this was about. He cleared his throat, rallied himself to be protective, and said, as if he had just had a wonderful new thought, 'Hey, Pam . . .?'

She nearly fell off the edge of the bed. *Hey, Pam?* It was as shocking as if the Queen had said, 'Cut the crap' to a passing ambassador. What on earth was going on?

She made a little noise in response. She had a terrible urge to say, 'Yo! Pete,' but contained it. Instead she gave a very restrained, 'Yes?'

'What are you doing this evening?' he said. 'Would you like to come over and talk?'

Odder and odder.

'What about?' she asked suspiciously.

There was a pause. And he continued in a voice that was strangely soft, cajoling even, 'I just thought you might be lonely.'

And, because it got her on the raw and approximated to the truth, she responded tartly, 'Of course I'm not lonely. I have got a life, you know.'

Peter, recognizing the signs, changed the subject. Not for nothing had he known this volatile woman for nearly thirty years. He was treading on eggshells. 'How is Daniel?'

'He's fine. I think.'

'He certainly was last week.'

'What?'

'I talked to him last week.'

'He rang you?'

'Only briefly.' Peter felt a chill wind around his arthritic joints.

'Why?'

'Oh, he wanted to chat.'

'What about?'

'The car.'

Pamela hooted with something between amusement and derision.

'And his new computer. He was very enthusiastic.'

Danny? Enthusiastic? Her heart plunged. 'You bought it for him?'

'I helped.' Peter squirmed.

Pamela suddenly felt defeated.

'You bought it for him,' she said faintly.

Peter waited and then said cautiously, 'You have done a marvellous job. And now he's grown up, flown the coop. And we are on our own again. I congratulate you. We made it.'

Pamela went rigid. We? She waited.

He gritted his teeth. Why was it always such a battle? He knew she would say, as she had in the past, that it was a battle because he had never put either of them first. Well, he thought with spirit, Daniel didn't seem to mind all that now. Daniel was extremely friendly. And thrilled with his car. As a father, it was nice to be able to step in with something like that when it was needed. He was about to say something fairly sharp when the Stannah and the knee loomed large and the drip, drip, drip of coffee echoed like torture, and his ex-mother-in-law's voice nudged his conscience. Time to bury the past. Headlong, he rushed in.

'I'd like to take you to dinner tonight.'

Pamela went even more rigid. But she listened. Just for once she had to, because she was speechless. Beyond asking, 'And pay?' which she knew was not wise.

He avoided suggesting his favourite Japanese Sushi bar nearby, was tempted but abandoned suggesting a restaurant he had recently designed near Pamela in which all the chairs were draped in white cloths and where, in his mind's eye, he could just picture her whipping one off as if it were a dust cover, closed his eyes tight and said, 'Do come. Or we could get a *take-away* there if you would like that . . .'

In order for her to go any more rigid would have required surgery. 'Take-away?' she said.

'That curry place,' he said in a very small voice, 'is still there.'

She sometimes wondered if it was the opening of the Authentic Balti Curry House on the corner that finally broke up their marriage. There was just something marvellous about skipping off to the end of the road and coming back with those tin-foil containers. On each occasion Peter had opened all the windows and very pointedly boiled an egg. About all he could do.

'Look,' she said, 'I can't. I've been invited next door.'

He forgot that he was showing a new and warmer side to himself, and he groaned, 'How frightful for you.'

This she found comfortingly normal, and, though true, she said spiritedly, 'Oh, not at all, they are very, *very* kind.'

He kept his irritation to himself. This was her favourite epithet for those who were beyond the pale in every other respect.

'Well—maybe next week, then?' he said cautiously. 'Or lunch?' He realized he would feel much happier if it were lunch.

'Make it a couple of weeks,' said Pam with spirit. 'I've got a lot on.'

'Fine.' He looked at the invitation to Dublin, ran his finger around its edge, took a deep breath and said, 'Do you remember when the college took us to Dublin?'

There was silence. Then she said, 'Vaguely,' which was quite untrue. She remembered it very well. They had fallen in love with the city and with each other, and she had thought he was the cleverest, most wonderful man on earth, full of ideas and visions for a Brave New World. In a way she admired the uncompromising path he had chosen since. It just made him a hopeless husband and father. Like Brunelleschi and Wren and his beloved Corbusier before him. Good family men seemed not to make visionaries.

'We rather liked the place,' he said. 'I remember.'

'Yes,' she said.

'I'm going again and . . .' And then his voice

trailed off. Now was not the time. He could just tell. There was something in Pamela's breathing. So he just added, because his ex-mother-in-law had been fairly blistering on the subject of feminine persuasion, 'It was *really* nice talking to you. I'll call in a week or two.' And rang off.

He was sweating. This was going to be harder than he thought. He rubbed his sore eyes, glad the first round was over.

A little dazed, Pamela sat on the bed and stared at the telephone. *You've been marvellous* . . . She felt tears pricking her eyes. And remembering Dublin? She almost smiled. *Really nice talking to you?* Well—yo, Pete . . .

*   *   *

Time dragged. It always did, she remembered, if you were waiting for a new date.

Jenny rang when she had closed the shop. She was training up their new graduate work-experience girl, Belinda, who terrified them both with her hauteur, knowledge, Royal College degree and height of six-foot-one. She was, they agreed, a find, an Amazon, and would probably see them both out of the business one day.

Pam was running a bath and endeavouring to shake off the sentimental aftermath of Peter's sweetness. The steamy air in the house smelled of rosemary and lavender and she was

126

lying flat on her back on the bed with a piece of cucumber over each eye, though the cucumber was a last-minute thought and not entirely fresh.

'We did well,' said Jenny. 'Belinda stole the show. Oh—and your friend was in.'

'My friend?'

'Are you sitting down?'

'Oh, not her again.'

'No. Douglas.'

She shot bolt upright, scattering the cucumber pieces. 'Douglas? When?'

'Late morning. He said he was just passing through.'

'Passing through Chiswick High Road?'

'Perhaps there was a jam on the A4?'

'My *foot* . . .' said Pamela, feeling queasy.

In the old days she took Saturday morning duty in the shop if Danny was at rugby or cricket. Douglas would not know she had altered the routine. Or maybe it was just coincidence?

'Did he say anything?' she asked.

'Well, he didn't just stand there struck dumb by my beauty.'

'I mean—'

'I know.' She laughed. 'No. He just looked ultra-cool, asked if you were here, said he'd heard his sister was using us, and went.'

'How odd,' said Pam, wishing she did not feel so strange.

'Ray-Bans,' said Jenny, 'Hide the windows

of the soul. I expect he was crying inside.'

They both laughed at the absurdity.

'Ah, well,' said Pam, feeling better. 'Better go and get some more cucumber.'

'Cucumber?' said Jenny.

'Yup. I'm using it to stop my eyes being so puffy.'

'Have you been crying?'

'No, Jenny, I've been ageing.'

Instead of telling her not to be so silly, Jenny was characteristically helpful. 'Say no more,' she said. 'Try putting a pair of spoons in the freezer for a second or two and using them. Or knives.'

'You're kidding.'

'I'm not. It's an old Liz Taylor trick I think. Try it.'

'As long as it's not an old Bette Davis trick, I will,' said Pamela, and she went to turn off the bath.

She put two spoons into the deep freeze and then sat staring out into her garden. The warm, golden September evening made her melancholy. In the past, with Danny around, there was never any room to be melancholy. Especially in the kitchen. He was always in there, eating, with the radio turned right up. If she'd sat around looking melancholy, he'd have asked her to make him a sandwich. Next door she could hear the familiar preparations growing apace. Peaches' high little laugh, Bud's monosyllables, the clang and scrape of their wrought rococo garden furniture being hauled into place. Suddenly she was filled with dread again. Peter had been so kind—well, kind for him. Bad-tempered bastard. She wished now that she had accepted his offer and cancelled next door.

She turned the bath water off. In the steamed-up mirror she looked like a young girl. Well, that was all right then. Provided she could walk around in a cloud of vapour, she'd be fine. She rubbed the reflection with her hand, brought herself into sharp focus, a great mistake, and took to plucking her eyebrows ferociously to continue the theme of pampering. How such an activity could be part of any Love-Yourself routine beggared belief. It hurt. She plucked on. Too ferociously. And ended up looking like a surprised version of Barbie's mother. If there was such a thing.

Am I ready for this? she asked herself. Am I ready to swim in one of Peaches and Bud's lurid cocktails, and meet the mystery man? The answer was—roughly—yes and no. She wondered what the mystery man was like. He was probably, she decided, called Clint.

Back in her wonderfully tidy kitchen, she removed the spoons from the deep freeze. They were wonderfully cold. She settled herself on the old wicker sofa, leaned back luxuriously, and placed them both gently on her eyes thinking how wonderfully clever women were, *wonderfully* . . .

A long, loud stream of abuse, quite as blue as her carpets, was followed by a wonderfully uninhibited howl of pain. For what had been so wonderfully cold to the hand was like ice-fire to the tender flesh of the eye sockets. She tried to pull the spoons away and found they were frozen like a tongue on an ice-lolly. She howled again, not least at the prospect of tottering next door in her strappy high heels, in her strappy white silk, with a pair of spoons balanced winningly over her eyeballs.

She got them off eventually. Clint would be impressed. She remembered she had a pair of Ray-Bans somewhere. Douglas gave them to her. She squinted into the mirror. And she certainly needed them now. She tried not to think of Douglas coming to the shop. Because if she did, she found herself wishing she had been there.

*   *   *

Meanwhile, Bud had a little accident with soft fruit and Peaches Carter, in search of succour, flew down the street towards Ani Patel's shop. Wherein, yet again, loitered Miss Phoebe . . .

It had been a very sideboard sort of a day and she was feeling a little warm, a little fuddled. But hopeful. 'Only connect,' she said gaily to Mrs Patel, who wished she would Only Connect herself somewhere else, but did not say so. She merely provided a chair for her

130

customer, who was swaying, to sit upon.

Miss Phoebe Glen gave a quiet little moan, remembering the harshness of her lot, and then, looking up like a martyred heroine, she added, 'But were I to be transported in a tumbril I could not be more resolute.'

Mrs Patel gave her a nice glass of water.

She drank and moaned anew.

Certain things had taken place last week, certain things that she did not fully understand, but which she knew presaged the rumbling of those tumbril wheels along the path of her life. Things such as another letter from the new landlord in which he set out a list of repairs necessary for the preservation of the house and which, when done, would mean another trip to the tribunal, and a higher weekly sum accordingly. Things such as another slip of a girl, with a very bright smile this time, calling and showing a small card and asking if she could just look around. She was from Housing.

'Why?' Miss Phoebe Glen had asked.

'To see if I can be of any help,' said the bright-faced young woman.

Help? Miss Phoebe Glen knew what that meant. She could see it in the peering around her and into the hallway that was going on. They wanted her home and they wanted her out of it.

'Not today, thank you,' she called back gaily. 'No canvassers.' And she shut the door with a bang.

'We will write to you,' said the young woman through the letter-box, in the tones of one addressing the village idiot.

Miss Phoebe Glen shuddered to recall it. 'I must get a lodger,' she said out loud.

Ani Patel nodded.

Miss Phoebe eyed the waiting Peaches Carter. Ani Patel gave a little shake of her head.

Peaches Carter made her request. 'Where would we be without the likes of you, Mrs P?' she said.

Mrs Patel downcast her lashes. She thought how true that was. Who else would have Bacofoil in stock, as well as offering to let the customer have her very own hand of bananas?

'Bud sat on ours,' said Peaches. 'And we're matchmaking tonight.' She touched the side of her nose.

Mrs Patel dared not think.

'Mrs Pryor from next door,' added Peaches. 'And the thing about barbecued bananas is they're *erotic.*'

Mrs Patel remained impassive, though deeply sceptical.

'It's true,' said the young woman confidingly. 'But I don't expect it's talked about where you come from.

Mrs Patel gave the tiniest shake of her head. Erotic? It would not, in fairness, surprise her if the British used them as a substitute. She

132

lowered her eyes and said, 'Bananas? Never,' in admiring tones. No wonder these pale men were growing less and less virile. If they were given cooked bananas as a substitute for caressing looks and dainty pinchings, it was not at all surprising.

The girl gave an uninhibited woo-woo, picked up the bananas, and left. For all her fuddlement, Miss Phoebe Glen watched her go and thought nothing was worth that as a lodger—*nothing*.

The fat man it must be. Back at number twenty-five Disraeli Road, the last thing Pamela wanted to think about was erotic anything. And if someone had offered her a banana, she would merely have ground it to pap and applied it to her eyes. Sometimes life was just like walking through treacle.

CHAPTER THIRTEEN

Erotic or not, Pamela, in the Ray-Bans, was ready to leave. Well, she thought nervously, ready as she would ever be. The front door swung open in her hand and she adjusted her sunglasses. The evening had continued warm, so there was no escaping the raking outdoor sun. English weather. You couldn't bloody rely on it for anything. And here she was with eyes like Mr Toad, about to embark on an evening that, yet again, was to be stage-managed like something out of a TV soap. It was how her neighbours lived their lives. They were both In Television in some capacity or other, so she supposed that was why they appeared to live it.

Tonight it might be a Bondi evening, or they could be going American. They did sometimes dump the Land of Oz in favour of California. Bud had been known to come whooping out of the house while carrying a surfboard and wearing a T-shirt and white peaked cap both yielding the legend BIG BOY. With Peaches following on behind in little gingham shorts, little bow hair-slides, not much else, and hauling a cold box. The surfboard would be tied to the roof of the car, the engine would roar, the wheels would screech, and the fantasy would begin.

Thankfully Pam did not have much of a Baywatch or Bondi-type wardrobe to worry over. Nothing in lime green, for instance, or sugar pink, and nothing very sketchy. She stuck to white silk, enlivened by a large pair of red cherry-bunch earrings that The Girlfriend had given her with a curl of her lip, saying, '*I'll* never wear them.' Well, *good*. They were resoundingly vulgar, which took the edge off the virginal whiteness. And matched the eyes.

You have to remember, she told herself, that a flaw always looks worse to you than to the rest of the world. It was what she used to counsel Danny about his spots. It is the egocentricity of the visual self, she reassured him. Danny had not been convinced then; and she was not convinced now. At least with Peter she had never worried about her looks. With Douglas it was different—she wanted to be beautiful for him all the time. And Dean? Dean was restful because he gazed at her as if she *were* beautiful all the time. Oh, for a touch of that. She was not wearing the stockings and suspenders on the grounds that it was too warm. But she wondered if that was the real reason. Oh, well, on with the show . . .

*   *   *

When they left the gym, Julian suggested they went to the pub. Alice was going to a hen night, so he was free for the evening. After several beers and a serious discussion about Arsenal and the England cricket team's sad performance, Dean said, 'That's exactly the sort of thing I mean. If I had a girlfriend, I'd never be free. I'd have to ask permission to do things all the time.'

'Try a boyfriend, then,' said Keith slyly. 'We're much more easy come, easy go.'

They all laughed with suitable coarseness.

'But seriously,' said Dean, 'I don't want to be pinned down by anybody.'

Julian nodded in the direction of the barmaid, whom they had christened Breasts 'n Beer. 'What—not even her?'

135

More laughter.

'You know what I mean. This. Just sitting here, without having to ring someone up for clearance.'

'Absolutely,' said Keith. 'Blokes are much less possessive.'

Julian felt got at.

'Wasn't always like that, now was it?' he said. 'With that woman?'

'She was never possessive,' said Dean defensively. 'And, anyway, I'm over all that now.' He hated them getting on to the subject of Pamela. 'Alice has got you right under her thumb, mate. I was free. You don't get that with little girls.'

He leaned back and took a long, smug draught of his drink.

Too long, and too smug. 'Oh, really?' said Julian.

'Really,' agreed Dean. 'Your shout.' He dissolved into laughter for no particular reason other than the feeling he had scored. They'd scored off him enough over the last year or so. He winked defiantly.

'Never checked up on you?'

'Nope.'

Julian collected the glasses and got up. 'Well, then, you will be surprised to know that she was outside our flat this afternoon, watching you.'

'Who was?' Dean said cheerfully.

'Her.'

'Who her?'

'Oo-er,' said Keith.

They fell about.

Julian brought his face very close to Dean's and said, savouring each syllable, 'That woman.'

Dean stared. 'You are kidding?' His heart began to pound. The humour left his face.

Julian cursed himself for not having kept silent. He and Alice agreed to. He'd get it in the neck for that, too, he supposed.

'No,' he said. 'She was there. Sitting hiding in her car as we walked by.'

'If this is a joke—' said Dean.

'Am I laughing?' said Julian.

He went off to get the drinks. At the bar the barmaid said, 'Whatever's come over your gorgeous mate?'

Julian looked round. Keith was half-standing at the table, while the only signs that Dean had once been there were an overturned stool and the swinging of the heavy glass door.

'Said he was going to make a phone call,' Keith told him.

'So much,' said Julian, 'for being free.'

*   *   *

Just as Pamela was about to close the door, two things happened. One, the telephone in the hallway beeped. Two, beyond her garden fence a car pulled up at the kerb. The calculating woman in her observed it to be large and shiny and dark blue—no little family runabout—and a man in a straw hat got out. He, too, was wearing sun-glasses, very dark ones. The mystery man. Average was the first thought—height, weight, mien—average. Not likely to be called Clint. She was the teeniest bit disappointed.

The telephone stopped before she answered it. She tapped out the code to identify the silent caller's number. The strange, mechanical female voice gave it, and then proceeded to suggest, in its chilling robotic way, that if she wished to contact the caller she should just press.. .

Pamela put the phone down, stunned. Perhaps he *had* seen her after all? For the number was Dean's.

*　　　*　　　*

Dean plucked up his courage and redialled. He was drunk enough to ask her to go to Dublin with him. Again there was no answer.

As she closed the door, she heard the telephone begin to beep again. No, she said to herself, no, no, no. New doors, she told herself. New doors.

And she walked down the garden path determinedly.

*　　　*　　　*

138

The man was Peaches' father. Recently divorced from her mother. Peaches was clearly very fond of him. 'Hitting the action now, aren't you, Dad?'

And it certainly seemed to be outwardly true. New straw hat, new dark glasses (Pam suspected that he was wearing them for approximately the same reason she was— bags), designer linen, and a new car. This last, he announced proudly, was a GTI Three Hundred Series, which apparently meant something. He was a doctor by profession, a golfer, had surprised himself by doing well on the stock exchange, and told a good story. He kept patting his stomach with satisfaction as if he had recently lost weight and, indeed, later, he said he could now fit into the same trousers as when he was twenty-five. Pamela hoped she would not be asked to comment. What did you say to a statement like that? Bring out your bell bottoms?

Peaches was not so circumspect. 'That's good, Dad, flares are back in.'

Ah, yes, thought Pam, you can certainly leave it to the young to embarrass.

She smiled daintily and squinted through her sun-glasses looking for her glass. Everything seemed very dim. Except the sun on her wrinkles, of course.

The cocktails were, unsurprisingly, lime green. Peaches wore a clinging Lycra dress in the same shade. Both looked suitably lethal. Pamela downed her drink very quickly—one for the hit, two to get rid of it, and she noticed that the mystery man, Lionel, did the same. It was like imbibing lime juice and scented soap.

'Lovely,' they said in unison. So they were both nervous, she thought. She said, 'Tell me about Leighton Buzzard.' A sentence, she realized with a giggle, that not many people got to say. Mercifully the cocktails were doing their stuff.

Bud strode around the brick barbecue in a sleeveless white top which showed his muscles up a treat. When not striding, he folded his arms like Marlon Brando in *On the Waterfront*, and stared moodily down the garden at the pink pampas grass. The Brando revival had made its mark. Pam prayed to God he wouldn't go out and buy a high-handled motorbike.

Lionel said, 'It's a place to get away from.'

'And Dad has,' said Peaches excitedly. 'He's come to London. To start all over again. Haven't you, Dad?'

Pamela felt exquisitely embarrassed. Thank God for the Ray-Bans, she thought.

Peaches' father removed his hat and showed thinning fair hair, soft-looking, like Peaches'. But there the similarity ended. He was diffident about the situation, where Peaches practically spoke in words of one syllable in order to spell it out.

'You saw Pam, Dad, didn't you? And you said, Now that's a good-looking woman . . .'

He opened his mouth.

Pamela said quickly, 'I remember when I was first divorced—you want to make new friends . . .'

He sighed gratefully.

Peaches, smiling indulgently at him, gave her head a little shake, as if to say, What a silly coward you are . . .

'Could we have another drink, June?' he said.

His daughter looked at him as if he had said something very rude.

'Now, Dad,' she said.

'Peaches,' he said shortly.

Pam gave him a look of sympathy.

Peaches filled their glasses. 'June. I ask you.' And she shrugged.

Bud stopped staring moodily at the pink pampas and called her. 'Hey, Peachbabe—is this chicken done or what?'

Peaches popped off with a squeak.

Pamela said, 'I remember when Danny went to senior school, I took him on the bus for the first few mornings, just to settle him in. He made me sit right at the front, while he sat right at the back.'

'My sons were much more difficult than J—*her*. Never left home. Well, they did—but only to come back. I sometimes wonder if that's why the wife and I—'

141

'Oh, Daniel's gone for good,' said Pam crisply. 'I know it.' She raised her glass, astonished to see that it was nearly empty again. 'I'm free. Quite free. It's lovely.'

'My daughter thought you were lonely.'

'Oh, not at all, not at all . . .' She got so carried away that she took off her glasses.

He leaned forward.

'Not at all,' she added, once more with feeling. The tender flesh around her eyes felt *very* tender. She touched it nervously.

He leaned further forward. He looked concerned.

She saw him, suddenly, as the doctor he was.

'It's very early days. Talk about it if you want to,' he said. 'Do you cry a lot?'

He was staring at her eyes. She put her hands up to their puffiness again. 'Oh, no,' she said brightly. 'This was just some frozen spoons.'

If he had laughed, it would have been all right. But he stared In Loving Sympathy. Now Pamela knew where Peaches got it from. Mistake to come, she thought. Mistake.

Peaches called from where she was investigating the drumsticks. 'You two get to know each other. And eat up those nachos . . .'

The two guests stared at a dish of something shockingly orange on the table. Pam felt rebellious. Or maybe a little pissed.

'Chili?' he asked, raising an eyebrow.

142

'Getting warmer,' she said pertly, immediately wishing she hadn't. It only drew attention to herself and in so doing drew attention to her bulging eyes. He kept trying to smile into them kindly.

She just wanted to go home. She fervently wished that she had gone out with Peter instead. And that was saying something. She gave a little laugh, chinked his glass self-consciously, and they drank.

He said, 'Barbecues!' and shook his head, continuing to be kind.

'Look,' she said, 'I'm not a bit lonely. I'm really not.' Her voice rose. 'Really.'

'Of course you're not,' he said, in the voice of one about to administer an injection to a frightened child.

This happy accord was broken by a Lee Strasberg grunt. Marlon Brando was having trouble with the barbecue. What he had taken to be foil-wrapped sausages and had placed in a particularly hot spot with a macho flick of his barbecue tongs were in fact the individually wrapped bananas. These fruity amulets, perhaps wishing for a moment to emulate their masculine morphology, had overdone themselves and burst from their sheaths in a spray of viscid matter. Bud—from the way he handled this verbally—had never seen anything like it. Certainly where once only smooth oiled bicep led the path towards cool USAF T-shirt, quite a lot of liquid banana now

143

got in the way.

'Never mind, hon,' said Peaches, but she was obviously disappointed. 'I got something else in the freezer. No worries . . .'

He growled and ripped off his T-shirt and Peaches ran after him, twittering like an anxious Disney bluebird.

Pam marvelled all over again at how little liberation seemed to have clung on from the bra burnings of the sixties. That was where she went wrong with Peter, she thought idly. Instead of screaming, 'You daft bugger,' at him when he flooded the washing machine or put disposable nappies down the loo, she should have said, 'Never mind, hon . . .' And massaged his feet. They would probably still be married. She'd be nuts, of course, but who wasn't nowadays?

'Something's amusing you,' said Peaches' father.

She pretended it was the exploding bananas.

'My daughter says they're erotic,' he said.

'They seem to be suffering from premature ejaculation,' said Pam, giggling. It took her completely by surprise and it certainly shocked him.

'I'm glad you've cheered up,' he said cautiously, and she could tell that he very nearly patted her hand.

Dates, as she knew from the few she had attempted over the single years, were difficult. And unless you were gasping with attraction,

144

truth to tell, they were a little wearing. It was all about learning history that was being told to you in the best possible light. And returning the compliment. If there was no gasping attraction, it became rather like two salesmen vying to talk about their product.

She found herself drying up in the middle of the tale of her conservatory. Christ, she thought, if *she* was bored stiff recounting the flooring arrangements, what must Peaches' father be feeling? She was hunting for a spark, she was desperate to find one. But the space between them was as damp as a rained-on squib. She was at that point where, if you can't be bothered to finish talking about something, you can be pretty sure that they can't be bothered to listen. With a spark between them, she could have been recounting the experience of watching paint dry and he would be hanging on her every word. Or she his. Instead she was fed up to the back teeth with his table-side manner and his sympathetic, doctorly nodding.

Later, the chicken cleared away and the strawberry gateau yet to come, Pamela relaxed in the cool darkness. She could have done with something round her shoulders but did not want to attempt getting up until it was absolutely necessary. Lionel had brought a very decent bottle of wine which both Peaches and Bud had ignored. Standing up could be tricky. Bud lit some huge flares—far too big for their little garden, but they gave a nice glow, a little warmth. Soon it would be over.

Peaches, returning with the extraordinary cake, Iceland Shopping Hall's best, proceeded to cut enormous slices. It was pink to the lime's green. Lionel said quickly, 'Just a little piece for me,' and slapped his stomach again.

He gave Pamela a look as if to say he was in fine fettle.

It's all disgusting, thought Pam. Like a cattle market for elderly beasts.

She, perversely, breathed out and gave a sigh.

'That's right,' said Peaches encouragingly, and looked across at her father.

He was asleep.

'I'll just go and check out the new car,' said Bud, taking advantage. He stood up, pointed broodily at the gateau, and said, 'Save it.'

Smoothing his blue jeans, he walked off as if he had two very large melons between his legs.

'Pam has an interior design shop, Dad,' said Peaches loudly.

He woke with a start.

Men, thought Pam, were truly amazing, for he immediately said, 'Really—and how do you operate?' All she would have managed in similar circumstances was, Where's the fire?

'Well—I get people to come into the shop first and we talk and they look at samples and ideas and catalogues, and then, once I've got a picture of the kind of things they like, I go to the site and we take it from there. It's simple.

146

Most people know what they want, they just need directing.'

'Dad's got a new apartment. Haven't you, Dad?'

He nodded, mouth full of ersatz cream.

'So he'll be along.'

Peaches, a veritable Cupid in lime green, beamed.

'Where is it?' asked Pam.

'Battersea Waterside,' he said proudly. 'Do you know it?'

'No,' she said, too past it to care, 'but you hum and I'll see if I can play along.'

Father and daughter blinked. It was time to leave. Verily.

She got up carefully, shook hands with Lionel, saw again the sympathy as he smiled in the flickering flare light. Peaches said, 'Aah,' as they locked hands, and Pam felt a spurt of irritation. She almost said, Round one and come out fighting, but thought she might slur. She would save the wit for another day. And with straight back she marched, veering a little, down the side entrance and out into the street.

Bud was just pulling up in his father-in-law's car as she turned out of their front garden into her own. She held on to a branch of her hedge and waved at him with the other hand. Quite a difficult manoeuvre. He leaned out of the window and called, 'Hey, there—talk about a love waggon,' flicked at his cap with a finger and thumb, winked and moved on, melons still

147

in place.

She scooted up the path and let herself in. Enough was really enough. In the kitchen she poured water into a glass and heard, very distinctly because the skylight window was open, Peaches' voice saying, 'There you are. Not difficult now, was it?' As if she had just given her father a rather nasty injection. Touché, Herr Doktor, she thought. She marvelled, yet again, how impossible it was to convince people you were all right, really, if they did not want to know.

On her way up the stairs she passed the hall telephone. It seemed to glow and wink at her and before she knew it—cocktails, wine and adrenalin withstanding—she felt a tremendous and powerful urge. She tapped out Douglas Brown's number. Just like that. She heard it beeping, heard it answered, and bravely held on, despite a further tremendous and powerful urge to throw down the receiver and run.

It was answered by a woman. A woman who sounded Scottish and quite elderly. 'I'm sorry,' said the voice anxiously, before Pam had time to speak, 'I'm only babysitting.'

Crash, down went the phone. Pamela was really shaking now. *Babysitter.* So the bastard had done it after all. Had a child. She went cold. She went hot. So that was why he had gone to the shop. He wanted to tell her. The proud father. No doubt Zoe, the most poisonous auntie in the world, would be

148

longing to tell her the news when she came in next week. She'd cancel her. Cancel everything. Get a train to Liverpool immediately and see her son. *Her son.*

And then she remembered—the cocktails were fuzzing her brain—and when she remembered, she laughed. Of course, of course—Douglas no longer lived in that rambling old Fulham flat of his. He had changed jobs and moved to Chelsea not long after they split up. Anyway, what was it to her if he had or had not become a father? It was all in the past. Every bit of it. She was glad that Douglas had not been at the end of the line. It would have been embarrassing and it would have been pointless. After all, disregarding the failure of tonight's date, had not a new dawn begun?

She went to brush her teeth. Her eyes really did look very peculiar. A new dawn? Not really. Not at all, in fact. Unsurprisingly, all she felt was a wee bit sick.

She fell asleep immediately and, even more unsurprisingly, dreamed vividly and rather upsettingly of Peter, Douglas and Dean. They were each growing in a garden, very similar to her own, all tangled with weeds, and she was standing there with a pair of secateurs, unable to move.

She awoke at five, drank several glasses of water, and then lay there until it was time to get up and fetch the Sunday papers. This cannot go on, she told herself severely. Firstly, from now on she must do more constructive things with her time. Secondly, from now on she must enjoy her time. It was not enough to find fulfilment in telling a solicitor and his new wife to paint their dining room scarlet and hang a beautiful Venetian chandelier from the central rose—though that sort of thing had once been entirely fulfilling—now she must find the equivalent of repainting her life scarlet and hanging a three-drop Murano from its centre as well. Get that study sorted, my girl, she admonished, and get it sorted soon.

CHAPTER FOURTEEN

Peter Pryor closed the door on the departing client, Mrs Evelina Rosen. The lock made only the slightest of clicks. Satisfying. Perfection in door furniture, almost non-existent. If you had to have the stuff, then this was the way it should be. Mrs Rosen did not quite see it that way. Mrs Rosen, despite knowing that his fame and skills rested on the Design of Absence, was a woman who liked to see something for her money. And Mrs Rosen certainly had a lot of that. She was also in the position of offering him a great deal of glory, too. Enough to be irresistible.

She wanted to endow a building for

Brigham College in her dead husband's name. Student accommodation, a library, a refectory, study areas—the Grand Plan. And, if Mrs Rosen had her way, a swimming pool as well. The Cambridge establishment would need to be convinced about the latter, but Peter thought they would be. He doubted very much if anyone ever stood in the way of Mrs Rosen. She chose Peter, she told him, because he had clout. Not because she liked what he had done. She declared herself a sensual woman—she gave him a very straight look at that point— and said she was prepared to pay for what she wanted. He shivered. Formidable widows who stood too close to him made him nervous. Formidable widows who knew what they liked, even more so.

Nevertheless, he accepted the commission. It was far too prestigious to turn down—and he did not want anyone else to take the laurels. He wanted the honour very badly: it would certainly clinch his knighthood. It was the kind of commission that might not come up in a century of opportunities, the first on the hallowed ground of Brigham for a hundred and fifty years, and a long time since he had worked to such a conventional brief. He must create something to sit perfectly between Wren and Gilbert Scott, and yet be of today.

He did not want anyone else to have it—he wanted to keep it for himself. His final glory— his own version of 'If you seek my monument look about you'. He had an urge to do something luscious and fun, and stand back to watch the shocked cognoscenti.

He had not felt this excited about a project for years. He leaned back, imagining, lost in the desire to begin. He considered Wren—saw the trussed roof of the Sheldonian, the austerity of the Doric barracks at Chelsea and the Baroque splendour of Greenwich. He considered Scott, with the high Anglo-French Gothic of St John's—not a genius like Wren, but very great. How to marry the two, how to link them? He shivered with pleasure. It was the living proof, the accolade, that he was right to persist. You could not succumb to the pram in the hall if you had a spark of genius within you. Brigham College would accept Mrs Rosen's offer *because* she offered his name with it, too. That made up for accusations of selfishness.

But it terrified him. Was he physically up to it? On some days, with his knee the way it was, he even found it impossible to drive. And then there was his eyesight. Not going blind or anything, but not getting any better. For the first time he felt unsure of himself. For the first time he realized that there was nobody but Pamela to whom he could turn for help. And for the first time he realized how much he needed her. The prospect was considerably more frightening than the Brigham commission.

It was no good his ex-mother-in-law urging him to be big and strong. He did not want to be big and strong and in control. As a matter of fact, at this precise moment, with a cortisone injection whizzing around in his system, he wanted to be very little and babyish indeed. Pam was strong. Pam was *always* strong. She had only ever had to deal with professional responsibilities at a very low level, and be a mother to Daniel, at which, he had to say, she was very good—but then women were supposed to be very good at it. Hence the courts awarding them custody.

But she was free now. So was he. And, given what his ex-mother-in-law had told him about her loneliness, it seemed foolish to waste their past together, their familiarities. He did not want to look for anyone else. He was not a seeker-out. He only found Kirsty because she came up and hit him, so to speak. One day she was his student, the next she was in his bed. And it was over just as quickly. One day she said, 'Old guys aren't cool any more,' and she packed her bags and went. He thought again of the departing client. She had left behind her a scent of something animal and unpleasant— peppery, musky, rich. He had been forced to switch the airconditioning on full. And she had given him a very meaningful smile as she said she was looking forward, really looking forward, to working closely with him. Quite suddenly he had felt in need of protection.

It would be calm with Pamela now. He could help her. They could both help each other. Despite his knee, he jumped up and began pacing the room excitedly, carried away at the prospect of all this potential goodwill. Between them, they would get the job done. Pamela would be flattered to help. After all, they were both once medallists in the college Young Designers competition. It was her choice to have Daniel, her choice to go into soft stuff, her choice to abandon him and his ideals for a bourgeois existence. He tried to help by suggesting they got a nanny; she said it wasn't a nanny she wanted, it was him, there, with her, sharing. He suggested they have at least a mother's help and someone to do the ironing, and she went to stay with her mother for a week. And what was he supposed to do? Abandon everything and take up babysitting? She chose to complicate things by doing it all herself. She made impossible demands. And, ultimately, she never gave him the respect he needed. The Peter Pryor Design Concept was not something to laugh at. Oh, bollocks, indeed. The business was worth enough to prove the point. And now Brigham.

Well, Daniel had gone now. They could be a real partnership. He would abandon this place, she could abandon the house and the shop, and they could unite. He would find something other than Furtzbangers to put on the floor. Compromise. That's what it came down to.

Compromise. Even the odd take-away would be acceptable. She had time on her hands—his ex-mother-in-law told him that. Lunch . . . in a few weeks' time. When the cortisone course had had some effect.

He returned to his chair and his drink. He had taken to using frosted glasses, otherwise a vodka and tonic could be lost for good in this space.

He focused on a notepad and something he had jotted down: Dublin and travel agent. Now why? He felt very tired; his memory was not what it was. His electronic diary helped, when he could locate it. Everything was going home; even his stomach, once flat to the pleasing point of emaciation, was now showing a definite little bump. If he ate any less, he would be anorexic. He was losing his grip and he needed looking after. He gazed around at the perfect white space he had created. Party's over, he thought. And then he remembered— about Dublin, the festival in the New Year, Bill Viola. And how he had made up his mind to ask Pam. He began to feel around cautiously for the telephone again.

*   *   *

The girl in the red suit was a disappointment. He knew, as soon as she arrived in the restaurant, that it was going to be like that. The wrong perfume—high, thin, sharp to the

155

nose, when he liked something soft and flowery. Balenciaga or Chanel.

And she ate sparingly, in a pecky, twittering way, like a bird picking over a nest of ants for an egg or two. She also drank her glass of champagne as if it were medicine—in little sips, to be suffered. When she was seated opposite him, and he could not see her legs, he wondered what her attraction had really been. He was glad it was only lunch—how useful the civilized etiquette in these matters could be: a cab to take her back to her office, on his account, and that would be that. No bones broken, face saved, nothing lost. She was no compensation for whatever it was he needed to have compensated.

He was being unfair and he knew it, which irritated him even more. She was pretty and she was making intelligent remarks about an Italian film they had both seen. At the same time, rather cleverly, he thought, she managed to let him know that she had gone to see it with a girlfriend rather than a boyfriend, and that the space was there if he chose to step into it. And she was looking at him with just the right amount of cool flirtatiousness. He had certainly thought about her a lot over the last few days. Since making the mistake of trying to see Pam at the shop, he felt an urgent need to begin something new, something to take his mind off the past—quickly, before he made another mistake like that. Now, here he was, had got what he wanted, and already he was planning to push her out of the door once the bill came.

He drifted for a moment, thinking about this absurdity, and then suddenly pricked up his ears as she said, 'So the rest of them are going down the Nile on a boat next week. I'm going to be the only one left in the flat . . .' Her eyes widened at him like the shutter opening on a lens.

He remembered that he had once planned a similar trip. Luxor, Karnak, Abu Simbel. Some of it on a paddle steamer. Exactly the sort of thing he would never do before meeting Pam—go down the Nile on a boat full of cardigans and M&S leisure wear? As Zoe said, it was the naffest thing she had heard. To him it was from the sublime to the ridiculous, to go from the Levels to Egypt. It made him laugh when they decided to go. 'We will go there,' Pamela said firmly, 'when we have discovered all we can discover about the Levels . . . I will take you off to Egypt and cruise down the Nile in a felucca feeding you dates from a dish.'

'She'll forget,' Zoe said, when he told her. 'She's crazy, brother dear, just crazy . . .

But she did not forget. Once she came running across that brown, barren waste up near Wisbech to say that a man with a measuring pole had told her the marsh was over three thousand years old. Which was nothing, she had added, to the ancient past of

Egypt. And she had kissed him excitedly and, like a teenager, said, 'You'll see—we *will* go there one day—next stop . . . Oh, yes, we will!'

'Not if she's got that son of hers trailing behind her,' said Zoe. 'You should really get her to do something about that . . .'

And that was the moment he suggested it: we could be so free, if you send Daniel away to sixth form. And she replied that you never were free. Egypt was put back into its mausoleum, she went from his life, replaced by Mary, who was not one for sailing or the countryside or anything that could not include her Manolo Blahniks. She was probably wearing them this very minute as she lunched with some fat cat Hamburger, and the fat cat Hamburger was probably eyeing her legs and wondering . . . But she was safely his. No amount of short skirts and mascara meant a thing—if he snapped his fingers, she'd be right there. Mary loved him and he felt dulled by it. Sometimes when they were in bed together, he imagined it was the other one and that made things better. But, really, it was just degenerating into boredom and habit. They both knew it—he resigned, she panicky. Couldn't be helped.

It was the reverse of a few weeks ago— when he had parked and walked round the corner to the High Street, his pulse was racing. So much for the gym. And in that state he was almost glad that when he finally dared venture into the shop, he saw only Jenny and some new young Amazon. Relief and disappointment. Jenny was cool but gave nothing away. In the end he had not asked. The shop smelled the same: fabric, leather, cinnamon; it looked the same: materials swagged and bunched, lights low, small tables carrying vast stacks of samples books. It was her empire. That and Daniel. He had not been able to penetrate either of them. She was strong, though she accused him of being the stronger. But he always knew he was weak. If he had been stronger, he might still have been with her now.

His pulse continued to play havoc for most of the journey home. If we each have one *grande passion* in us, she was his. He was right to get out; Zoe was right: you couldn't go through life feeling like this for someone. It made you too vulnerable. If his pulse was racing at just being in a place without her, what would he be like if she were there? Best not find out.

He kept up the pretence of being cured with Zoe. His eyes gave nothing away when she looked at him very pointedly and said she had rung Pam's shop. She asked him if he would help her choose what to put up at her long windows. Put nothing, he advised, and give the Chelsea Pensioners across the water a thrill. But he agreed. They were due to go there next week. Once he was curious; now he was no

159

longer curious. You could never go back. But he was only half-convinced.

Maybe he would just duck out of it. Tell Zoe he had a last-minute call. That was probably best. Why dig up the past? Pamela must be happy now, with somebody else. She had that capacity. It would be best to leave her alone, as she had asked, and as he had agreed. No good could come of anything else. Zoe was right: they were chalk and cheese. Zoe could be very over the top when she felt threatened, but in that particular she knew him well enough. Their own childhood was the opposite of Daniel's—rich houses, remote parents, boarding schools and bleak lives. It left neither he nor Zoe anxious to repeat it with children of their own. Pamela always said they should set down their pasts. But that was easy for her. She came from something approaching normal. Zoe still had the marks on the wrists.

The girl in red was leaning towards him now, smiling, saying something else about Egypt. He leaned back in his chair. He smiled and he put down his napkin. Then he signalled for the bill.

'Really?' he said. 'How nice. I've always wanted to go.' He reached into his inner pocket for his pen and felt the Dublin invitation. He had brought it with him just in case there might be an opportunity to float the idea past her. Now he pushed it back down

160

very firmly. And when the bill arrived, he signed it with deliberation.

The girl, hiding her surprise at his abruptness, said smoothly, 'Nice pen.'

He stared at it for a moment, in artificial wonder. Then he said, 'Isn't it?' and replaced it in his pocket. He stood up. 'You must come over while you are on your own,' he said, and, before she could answer, he added, 'and meet my girlfriend.'

*   *   *

Dean Close yawned while his mother went on and on about the good time they were all going to have once they got together again.

'We can go up to Wexford and stay with your Auntie Kath,' she said, 'and then over to Ballymena to stay with Billy. It's only Christmas. Not so far off at all.'

'Yes,' he said, 'Yes, yes, yes.'

And then there was a loud silence—while he was in mid-yawn—which meant either that he had to say something, or that his mother was building up to the fact that *she* had to.

'Deanie,' she said, and there was both an air of resignation and coaxing in her voice. 'You will come over, won't you?'

'I will as far as I know—but—'

'But me no buts,' she said anxiously. Then another pause. Deep breath. Then, 'Dean?'

'I'm here.'

161

One more big, big breath before she pushed off: 'Dean—ifitisbecauseyouhaveagirlwhoyou wantobringyoucan.'

For a moment it was as if she, he and the rest of the world had stopped all motion. It was extraordinary, he thought, to be loved that much. His mother, devout Catholic, would look the other way, sacrifice her faith, almost, to make sure of him?

'No,' he said. 'There is no one.'

He felt a very real twist in his stomach. He remembered Pam once saying to him, 'And what would your mother do if you introduced me to her as your girlfriend?'

If his mother knew . . . If his mother knew . . . She was always fielding that one.

'Deanie?' came the little voice.

'Maybe there is someone,' he said, 'Maybe I can come. But we're doing some filming next month. I'll just have to see.'

'Sweet boy,' she said.

He winced. His mother made him feel like the eternal baby. Pamela made him feel responsible for himself. Grown up. Kept him on his toes. Took her place with him as an equal, or even a superior. But never anything less than equal. He recognized this even in the simplest act. Like bacon sandwiches. His mother would never make one for herself but would stand, watching, while he sat and ate the one she made for him. Oh, she might wipe the pan round with a little piece of bread and nibble at it, but no more than that. His mother would never make them one each and then light a candle in the kitchen, sit down opposite him, and say, 'Race you.' With mothers there was no balance. With mothers it was all For You. With Pam he had to fight for every inch of ground, every moment of tenderness. The difference being that every moment of tenderness he won was his victory, had meaning.

He remembered running his hand over the tops of her naked arms and marvelling at how soft they were compared to those of his previous girlfriends. She laughed and said it was the way skin went—soft and floppy with age. He said it was like touching a marshmallow pillow. She just smiled and rolled her eyes as if he were being silly. 'Oh, you Irish,' she said, 'you'll say anything.' And the more he protested, the more she teased. 'The poetry's in your blood. You rut like rabbits and you sing like angels. It's all the same to you. But you can't catch me, because I'm not in love.'

Which, somehow, it was all right for her to say.

He wanted to see her again very badly.

That was the problem. He had promised everyone, from Julian to Holy Mary Mother of God, that he would not do it. But he really, really wanted to.

'Be good,' his mother said. 'I'll light a

candle for you.'

'Thanks,' he said, and rang off.

He knew the hope that such acts could carry. And the Mass. He, too, had lit candles. He, too, had stood at the base of the statue of the Queen of Heaven and prayed. The Queen of Heaven, being the right sort of mother, had not granted fulfilment. How could she when the request was so profane? He sweated now at the very thought of taking that request into a church when he remembered that most of their time together was about being in bed. If his mother ever found out, it would kill her. But he still wanted to see her again, very, very badly. Alas, he was on his own in this.

No more candles. If you wanted something, you wanted it. No more candles, action.

He might go and see her—that was all. Just see her. What harm could that possibly do? If Danny was there he would say he was just an old friend passing through. He would take her out for a drink—wine bar not pub—and he would say that he was a fully fledged grown up and how about that then? Would she not reconsider? Would she not come home to Dublin with him, just to see?

CHAPTER FIFTEEN

It could be the first day of winter, rather than the progression of quite a benign autumn. It was chill and it was dull and Zoe Brown was coming to the shop without Douglas after all. So much for the Ferelli crêpe dress in a colour called gingersnap on which Pamela had spent a fortune (I need one for important clients, went the litany), and so much for the hairdresser's bill which, alone, she told Jenny, had probably accounted for any profit they might make from the poisonous snake's visit.

'Oh, in forgiving mode, then, are we?' said Jenny. And went on with her diagrams.

Vanity, all is vanity, thought Pamela. The diagrams were for yet another solicitor and his wife. She was beginning to feel even more bored with shoring up the domestic lifestyle of professionals.

So, come the day, she wore a very ordinary shirt, waistcoat and black jeans. She wore the ensemble defiantly. Jenny could not quite hide a smile. 'I see you're pushing the boat out for her, then,' she said.

Pamela considered the conundrum. Was it better to dress up and acknowledge the reality of her feelings of insecurity, or was it better to dress down and *feel* insecure? Sometimes she felt her head would explode. And that was only in the matter of what she *looked* like.

It was thoughts like that which led to her private understanding with herself that she was borderline sane, only borderline.

She was serving a customer with several yards of blue tassel rope when she looked up to see Lionel staring in at the window. Her first thought was that perhaps she was no longer borderline but a fully fledged hallucinatory nutter; her second was, It's real and I'm off.

Just what she needed. What on earth was he doing here?

She turned back to the tasselling on the basis that if she did not look, he could not exist. Out of the corner of her mouth she whispered to Jenny, 'Don't look now but it's the Barbecue Date.' She indicated the peering Lionel with her eyes. And noticed that the blue tasselling was jiggling up and down, apparently of its own accord.

'Oh,' said Jenny, with a sickeningly indulgent smile. 'Well, then. Off You Go.' And she took over the blue tassel rope like reins. For a moment they both stood there holding on, with the puzzled customer attached at the other end. Then, resisting a sudden desire to say Gee-up, she conceded defeat, let the rope drop, said, 'Thank you, Jennifer,' in a knowing way, and looked up to smile through the window at him.

She beckoned. He came to the door, which

made its customary ping, and stood very close to the exit. Some men did find the place a bit daunting. Peter always said they had taken the notion of the feminine a little too far. Well, he would. If he'd had a shop, you wouldn't have been able to find it. As Pamela pointed out, usually it was the women who made these choices. The men had other preoccupations. Like whether the Springboks played fair.

The curious gaze of both Jenny and the customer met his. He remained waiting, just inside the door, fingering a lemon-coloured chintz and generally gazing about him as if he were in a museum.

This was my date, she mused. Oh, please let me feel *something*. Passion, lust, the solar-plexus punch, even the tiny frisson that says, Maybe. She waited, like St Ursula, for the touch. Nothing. Today of all days she could have done with a quickening heart.

'Well, hallo,' she said.

'Just thought I'd drop by.'

He was nervous, eager.

She had the poisonous snake Zoe arriving at any moment. She had planned to be so cool. The last time she saw Zoe she was not cool. She was quite out of control—had not slept for several nights, was in pain, still wore the same leggings and T-shirt she was wearing when she and Douglas said their final, simple goodbye at the front gate. When he said his quiet 'Sorry.' And she watched him, unbelieving because she had brought it upon herself, getting into his car. Her pink umbrella was still on the back seat. She hoped it would stay there for ever.

She asked—no, *sent*—Daniel to stay with his father for a few days. The T-shirt, in her madness, she thought held a trace of Douglas's scent. So she kept it on. And then Zoe came to the door, pristine as a *Vogue* shoot, asking for his few things. They were in the bedroom, scattered about, touched and cried over. And when she relinquished them, she cried again. Dribbling, lank-haired, wild-eyed. Zoe raised an eyebrow.

'Sorry,' she said. Quite coldly. As if showing emotion was a crime. She put the pink umbrella on the hall stand and went.

Well, not today. Today she, Pamela Pryor, would be in control.

And now Lionel.

He smiled shyly. 'You said,' he offered hesitantly, 'that I could come to the shop first.'

'Of course. I'm glad you did. Summer seems such a long way off. I had such a hangover after those lethal drinks.'

That was better. He smiled.

'And I fell asleep,' he said.

'Ah, well.' If she had learned anything from years of using Ani Patel's shop, it was her application of appropriate nothings.

'I thought we might have lunch afterwards,' he said shyly. 'If you can.'

She was supposed to have lunch with Zoe.

Not Douglas.

She only said yes to lunch with Zoe because of Douglas.

He wasn't coming.

Now it would be her and the viper alone.

She thought hard.

She did not want to have lunch with the viper.

And if she could not have lunch with Douglas?

'I'd love to, Lionel,' she said happily. She encouraged him to browse further into the shop.

'I like this yellow stuff,' he said, going back to the chintz.

And so they began the simple steering procedure that she applied to all new customers. Jenny, she could feel, relaxed. More customers came in. Any minute now, she thought, and venom fangs will appear. She felt quite detached, even a little bored. Lemon chintz had its limits of excitement.

She took Lionel over to the new Italian paper samples. He glanced at them, unimpressed. Perhaps they were a little bright. And then, in that way that Sod is supposed to arrange his Law, he noticed the book of tapestries.

Jenny had placed them artfully in the window, with rolls of disgustingly expensive fringing cascading in a welter of autumn colour all over the place.

'Oh, I do like these,' he said.

Not wanting to destroy the display, she picked up a sample of one of the richly coloured Italian papers to divert him, and moved with it firmly towards the window so that he could see better.

'This would be lovely on the walls if you're starting from scratch and the light is good,' she said. 'And if you like colour.' Since Peter, that was always something she noticed about men.

He made a face, as if blinded by the brightness. She laughed. He was all right really. They held the sample between them at the window. And then she looked up. The Italian paper fell from her hand and Peaches' father caught it. She was a sceptical human being, on the whole, but at that precise moment she wondered if she had not seen a *fata Morgana* flitting through the cars and buses.

She could have sworn she saw Douglas driving by. Righting herself, she looked again. It was gone.

She laughed up at Lionel flirtatiously to cover her racing heartbeat. Everything she felt for Zoe welled up. She'd show Miss High and Mighty.

'Lunch,' she repeated, 'would be lovely. I've got a client coming in but I can soon cancel her . . .' She added another flirtatious laugh. God knows how she would extricate herself if he suggested over the Beaume de Venise that they book themselves into an hotel for the afternoon. He would be more than justified on this performance. Revenge might be a dish that is best eaten cold, but you can't help it if the heat stays in. Zoe was expecting to be taken out to lunch, was she? Well, fuck that.

It was almost half-past twelve, the appointed hour. In very little time Pamela and Lionel had done well. She had steered him away from the tapestries and other possibilities had been chosen. If they were conservative, men were decisive. Easier by far to deal with, though perhaps not so interesting.

'It's a brand new development, isn't it? The Battersea Waterside? Do you know any of your neighbours?' she asked, making notes, trying to sound nonchalant.

'I've only been there a month,' he said.

'Of course,' she said. 'I forgot . . . I think another of my clients lives there too.'

'We might get together,' he said.

'You might,' said Pam, thinking, It is likelier than you think.

She would be lofty and superior with Zoe, and then pass her on to Jenny. Or even the Amazon if she got back from the leather suppliers in time. She would say, 'Here is our work experience graduate to help you . . .' That would really get up her dainty little powdered nose. Then she would tuck her arm into Lionel's and swan off.

'Where shall we go?' asked Lionel.

171

She was about to make a suggestion when she noticed that Jenny was staring hard at the door.

It went ping. And her partner, still transfixed, said, 'Crumbs.'

'What?'

Jenny looked aghast.

Pamela turned.

Illusion? Delusion? Was she the victim of her own madness and simply inventing everything? For here, looking a little like a stand-in for Oscar Wilde on *The Riviera*, was Peter.

Peter?

He bore a large bunch of white roses and looked horribly pleased with himself. It was a sight, Pamela thought, staring as if she had a sudden desire to rehearse the Banquo scene, that deserved something a great deal more linguistically positive than bloody 'Crumbs'.

Both women, with an instinct born from years together, avoided each other's eyes. To not do so was to court hysteria.

'Peter!' they cried in unison. He looked startled at the over-enthusiasm.

He closed the door as silently as he could but it still went ping, and he winced. It might be original, but he had always advocated removing it.

Then, very brightly, he said, 'Hi!'

Quite unable to resist, Pam said, 'Yo!' which stopped him in his tracks. And then she stared.

He was wearing a pink shirt and red-rimmed spectacles. Perhaps it was not Oscar? With the roses he looked a little like a character out of *The Boyfriend*.

As if rehearsed, he said, 'Pam, you look great.'

'For me?' she said.

'Who else?' he said in a voice that she was later to describe as spine-chilling.

Behind her Lionel gave a sort of exhalation.

She looked round at him. Was that the suspicion of an antler appearing in his forehead?

'This is Peter,' she said. 'Peter, this is Lionel.'

They moved towards each other. Lock horns and come out fighting, she wanted to say.

She noticed Peter's limp and felt a sudden stab of affection. All she could do was smile and smile and smile. If she opened her mouth, she knew she would say, Lord Lucan, I presume—or similar.

'Please excuse me,' he said to Lionel. And then, turning to Pam, said, 'I just wondered if you would like to have lunch?'

This time Lionel sucked in his breath.

Jenny made for the office, her back view freezing in the doorway as the door went ping again

Pamela jumped and prayed it was only the collecting nun.

Some nun.

Here she was at last, the thorn without a rose. Poison-chops.

If Zoe Brown had been treated cruelly by life, it refused to show. She was wearing black, of course, with long suede gloves and a hat. What did she think this was, Ascot? What was worse, both men stared at her with interest and admiration. Jenny returned from the back office. But there was nothing to say. The 'Crumbs' had done it all.

Zoe extended her gloved hand.

Pamela thrust the roses into Jenny's arms and touched those suede fingers as if they were contaminated. 'How nice,' she said. 'How well you look. Do you know my assistant, Jennifer?' She prayed her partner would forgive the downgrading.

Jenny did a kind of dance with the roses. Prick her, you fool, thought Pamela, but she did not.

'And Peter? Peter *Pryor*.'

Zoe moved her neck as if it were on castors. 'I have heard of you,' she said, as if she could eat him. Peter took a step back. He was not good with sirens.

Peaches' father advanced. 'And I think I've seen *you*,' he said firmly.

Zoe looked down her nose.

'Not surprising,' said Pamela curtly. 'You live in the same block.' She put the emphasis on *block* to give the impression it might be

174

Council.

Jenny disappeared with the roses.

'This has all got a little out of hand, I'm afraid,' said Pam, giving Zoe a very superior smile. 'I won't be able to see to you after all, because I'm having lunch with—'

And then the superior smile faded a trifle.

Who the fuck was she having lunch with?

Both men stared at her. She could hear her voice rising. 'Look, Zoe—I'm really sorry but I'll just have to leave you with my assistant.'

Jenny had completely vanished. It was all Pam could do not to clap her hands three times, as if summoning the houri.

Zoe gave both men a short, tantalizing, mocking (*infuriating* in Pamela's opinion) glance, and said, 'Well, I expected to have your attention. Especially since we haven't seen each other for so long. Douglas would have been here, but he had to do something with Mary.'

That worked. Pam felt an elephant kick her in the solar plexus. So he had a Mary, did he? Revolting name.

'That's all right,' said Peter, defrosting himself. 'You two go ahead. I'll try another day. When you're less busy.'

Lionel still looked quite put out. He was staring at Zoe and he suddenly said, 'Number nine,' just like on the Beatles' album.

Zoe stared at him as if he were an alien.

'What?' she said.

175

'I'm number twenty-two.'

Zoe stared again.

'Battersea Waterside. We are neighbours.'

This time her stare was tempered with considerably more warmth.

Pamela said, still high-octave, 'Lionel has asked me out to lunch, too. All these lunches suddenly, I don't know . . .' She trailed off before really putting her foot in it.

'Look,' he said, 'perhaps I could take you both to lunch?'

Zoe swivelled her neck again. Lionel was wearing his Paul Smith. She relaxed. 'Oh—' she said. 'Are you two—?' She pointed with a little black suede pinkie, from Lionel to Pamela.

Peter suddenly appeared interested, too.

And Pamela, curse it, began to blush.

'Lionel is my client,' she said. And, because she did not want to hurt him unduly, she added, 'And also a friend.'

Peter, in a burst of wholly inappropriate gregariousness, said, 'Well—why don't we all have lunch together?' After all, he had given up minimalism; he might as well apply it socially, too.

One day we'll all look back on this and laugh, thought Pam. If we don't die from it first.

'Yes, yes,' said Pam, quite beyond everything by now. This was another thing men were good at. Focusing on a sensible solution. She was still confused as to what her name was. 'Oh, *yes*, what a good idea. Can you hold the fort, Jen?'

Jenny did not look as if she could hold anything much. Having said she was going to take the roses into the office, she had reappeared, still clutching them. A burst from *The Bartered Bride* would not have come amiss.

Jenny nodded. 'Sure,' she said faintly.

And then something approaching horror appeared on her face. She was looking across the shop and out of the window. This time she did not say, 'Crumbs,' but, very softly, 'Oh, *shit* . . .'

Pamela followed her gaze and thought that if swooning had been an option, she would have embraced it.

Zoe said, 'Oh, look, there's my brother!'

Pamela said, 'Oh, really, where?' as if she had pointed out a particularly interesting bicycle.

Peter said, 'More the merrier,' so that Pam wished to kick him. And Lionel said, 'Ah, yes.' Which could have meant anything.

They all stared out of the window as Douglas's hunted, handsome (oh, still so handsome) face peered in, looked alarmed, and backed away on to the pavement.

Zoe leapt towards the door. Ping. And dragged him in by his sleeve.

'You said you were only going to drop me off,' she said, her arm hugging his tightly. She flashed a look of triumph at Pamela. 'Guess what, Douglas? We've got a lunch party.'

Pamela stood there, feeling dead in every particular save her heart, which beat and beat so that everyone must hear it. She raised her eyes. He was looking down at something on one of the tables—something made of glass, was it? Pam's focus had gone.

'Douglas,' she faltered. 'How are you?'

He touched the glass object. She knew those hands. She knew the ridges on the knuckles, the squareness of the nails.

'I'm well,' he said, suddenly bright, raising his head, defiant. 'And you?'

She nodded, dumb again.

'I can't stay,' he said stiffly.

Pamela was still trying to find a word. Any word at all.

'No,' she managed eventually. 'No, of course.'

And then Jenny, dear, sensible, land-based Jenny, said, 'Zoe, you really must look at these. I think they are just the thing. What do you think, Douglas?' And she ushered them both towards the book of tapestries and began to open it. The moment passed.

She thrust the roses back at Pamela, who very nearly chewed them.

Peter then said casually to Lionel, 'What block is that?'

Pamela, standing there, from somewhere on another planet, was impressed.

Here it was again, she thought, Immediate

178

Focus. Maybe they are better at running the world?

Lionel said, 'Battersea Waterside.'

And they were off. Masculine alacrity. If Pamela had not had to concentrate on breathing, in out, in out, she would have congratulated him.

Douglas, over by the book of tapestries with Zoe, looked as if he had a board up his backside.

'Will you give us five minutes?' Pamela said to Peter and Lionel.

But they were well away, talking noise levels, wind tunnels and the wonders of external piping.

She absent-mindedly gave Peter back his roses, who stared at them perplexed. She went over to join the others.

Jenny turned the heavy pages very slowly, which was soothing.

Pamela took a couple of swift looks at Douglas, but he did not look up. He made the perfect picture of a man deeply engrossed in French hunting scenes and medieval sprig. Pamela knew better. She longed to say to him that he did not need to go on with this. But Zoe was plainly delighted with the whole show. She must not be allowed to think that she had won any kind of victory. Pamela's pride would not allow it.

'What do you think, Douglas?' she said mischievously. 'Lovely, aren't they?'

Their eyes met. It was the old conspiracy. He suddenly smiled, sunlight in winter, and nodded. It was a small victory, and she squirrelled it away. It was hers.

She turned to Zoe. 'But, really, far too expensive . . .'

Zoe was piqued, as Pamela knew she would be. 'That's irrelevant if I like something,' she said. 'And I like these.'

Douglas looked down again. Pam knew the cast of his face, knew his thoughts. He began flicking through the designs with speed. 'Not fruit, not flowers—' he reeled away.

Zoe said, 'Not so fast.'

But he rattled on. 'Not stags, not fleurs-de-lis . . .'

Zoe nestled against him. 'What would I do without your eyes?' she said.

Walk over a cliff, hopefully, came to Pam's mind, but she held back.

Douglas had that little tiny smile at the edge of his mouth that said he was up to something. Then he stopped flicking.

'Perfect,' he said. 'Perfect.'

They all looked. It was a pale green background crowded with flashy peacocks.

'Peacocks,' said Pamela. 'Just the thing.' For a pico-second their eyes met and they knew.

Douglas nodded.

'Lovely,' said Zoe, and clapped her little gloved hands.

And then it was over.

180

Douglas said, 'I have to go.'

He went, and did not look back.

And then another miracle happened.

The telephone rang and Jenny went to answer it.

She came back looking very grave.

'Pam,' she said, 'I'm really sorry to do this, but there's been an emergency with the Barnetts' carpet. Wrong colour and they're about to cut it. They insist on you personally.'

'Oh, what a shame,' said Pam.

And so, thanks to quick-thinking Jenny, yet again, she did not have to endure the lunch.

Future appointments were made. Peter was appeased. 'Perhaps dinner would be better? I had no idea you were this busy.'

Pamela and Jenny took the compliment coyly.

Then, looking slightly confused, and still holding the roses, Peter followed Lionel and Zoe out into the street. She turned to give a little wave. Pamela stood to attention until they were right out of sight. Then, for want of anything else to say, she asked, 'Who was on the phone really?'

'A wrong number,' said Jennifer glibly. 'For Lupin Lodge.'

She began to tidy the books away.

'From where I'm standing it could have been right.'

Jenny pursed her mouth. 'OK?' she asked.

Pamela said, 'Yes.'

181

She would think about the veracity of that statement later.

The door went ping again. Peter came back into the shop, looking irritated.

He was still holding the roses. 'These were supposed to be for you,' he said, pushing them at her. Then he turned on his heel and pinged out. Pam watched him go and, out of the jumble of her feelings, wished, suddenly, that the two of them could have gone and sat quietly together somewhere. At least she knew where she was with him. Or she thought she did. But in that outfit she was not so sure.

Wearily she turned back from the window and smiled at Jenny.

'Excuse me,' she said. Tight-lipped, she went around the counter, through the back office, and into the small courtyard. She stared up at the grey, chill sky and, after taking what seemed like her first deep breath for hours, she filled her lungs and yelled, 'Fu-u-u-ck!' at it, thrice.

How many years?

Today of all days.

If Dean had popped in, they could have scored a hat trick.

Douglas, she thought, Douglas . . .

Taking another deep breath, 'F-u-u-u-ck,' she went again. And then, feeling a little better, she went back in.

In the companion courtyard of the charity shop next door, the Misses Avril and Elsie

182

Timothy, nearly a hundred and fifty years between them, but still sound of hearing, stood stock still, hardly daring to breathe. They were sorting plastic bags of cast-off clothing in the outside air (you never knew what was going to pop out) when the obscenity took place, and remained frozen in their positions for some time.

'Perhaps she's doing Amateur Theatricals again,' said Miss Avril eventually.

Miss Elsie nodded.

'Very *modern* ones . . .'

CHAPTER SIXTEEN

A few days after the strange experience in the shop, and feeling that fate dealt her hand unnecessarily harshly, Pamela decided to fight back. Instead of turning right on the way home, she turned left, and went to see Rick's wife, Vanessa. She rang the bell and realized she was palpitating. It had not occurred to her until that moment how very angry she was. To emphasize this, she knocked at the door as well. And when Vanessa opened it, staring in surprise, Pamela uncharacteristically pushed her way in and said, 'I want a word with you.'

Vanessa was a large, comfortable-looking woman, rubicund of face and with wayward grey hair. She baked. Even bread. Daniel always said she looked like everybody's mother, which made Pamela feel completely inadequate. The element of surprise in this sudden call gave Pamela the edge, which she knew needed and she felt she deserved.

'Can I come in?'she said. Once she was.

Vanessa just said, 'Oh,' and rattled her beads nervously. They went into the cluttered, plant-festooned living room and Vanessa offered her a cup of tea. Pamela declined. Vanessa offered her something stronger. Pamela said, 'Maybe, in a minute.' Vanessa pointed at one of the dark brown bean bags. Pamela also declined. Vanessa sat down—with such a rushing of air and grinding of seeds, that Pamela was glad not to have taken up the offer.

Dignity was all at this juncture. You could hardly push forward a point of cultural feminism whilst lying like a stricken doll somewhere near the floor and rustling.

'Vanessa,' she said. 'How long has Rick been coming to my house?'

Vanessa said, 'Oh,' again, rustled loudly and looked to the cascading plants as if seeking illumination.

'I'll tell you. He has been coming to my house since Daniel was sixteen years old. In fact, the guitar was Daniel's sixteenth birthday present.'

Vanessa moved around uncomfortably. The bean bag complained. She nodded, perplexed.

'And in all that time you never minded?'

Vanessa shook her head and said, 'Of course not,' as if she were genuinely surprised.

'But you do now?'

Vanessa did not move. Her puzzled, worried eyes gazed up at Pamela. 'Are you sure you wouldn't like a cup of tea? I've got fruit.'

'You've got cheek, is what you've got,' said Pam indignantly.

Vanessa sat up a little, not an easy feat. 'Oh?' she said, displaying a little more spirit. 'How's that?'

'Number one, in assuming that I cannot control myself. Number two, in assuming that—if I cannot control myself—then I'll go out of control over your husband.'

'These things do happen,' said Vanessa, still with spirit.

'Don't you lump me in with generalities,' said Pam.

Vanessa rustled some more and composed her features. 'Look at me compared with you,' she said, matter-of-factedly. 'I can't take the risk.'

'Risk? Vanessa, you are bloody lucky that I didn't decide to try to fulfil your horrible fantasy just to spite you. I've never heard such insecure rubbish. As far as I know, Rick loves you. I haven't seen or heard anything to disprove it.'

'Love,' said Vanessa, 'where men is concerned, if I may remind you, is not sex . . .'

It would have been interesting to go off at a tangent here and discuss whether, if Love was not Sex, there was any point in worrying if a husband did a bit of rogering on the side. If Love was not Sex, then, really, it was no more than, say, sharing a meal . . . Vanessa did not look as if she would be convinced. Pamela did not feel much convinced of it either. Still—she knew what Vanessa meant. But Pam was not going to back down and start wagging her tail. Vanessa's was an appalling calumny. It was probably representative of the view of at least half the married population—the assumption that she was husband-hungry was mortifying (and absurd, looking at most husbands), and she was not going to let it go.

'You do not have to remind me, thank you,' said Pam icily. 'And by the way—can you tell me when you first suspected I was having sexual relations with my son?'

The spirit in Vanessa died away completely. She went quite still, and the bean bag was silent. She put her hand to her mouth and looked truly aghast. *'Pardon?'* she whispered.

'Well, obviously,' said Pamela. 'You thought that while Daniel was at home I was no threat to your marriage. And now you think I am unable to keep my hands off any passing man, including your husband. And since all that has happened is that Daniel has gone away, I can only assume you think Daniel and I were an item.'

'Pam!' said Vanessa, quite horrified. 'That's a really disgusting thing to say . . .'

'Well, you make me feel disgusting,' said Pam, her voice rising. 'I've never been remotely interested in your husband except as a friend and musician. Do I make myself clear?'

Vanessa nodded. She looked quite frightened. Pamela probably did look deranged. Part of her wanted to stop the whole thing, do a re-run and go back to the bit where Vanessa told her she was desirable—she liked that bit—but she continued stern.

'And now this,' she said.

'This what?'

'You talking about the other kind of G-string. I was looking forward to those lessons.'

Light dawned on Vanessa's face. 'Ah,' she said.

'Yes, ah,' said Pamela, advancing. 'Well, you can just Ah-off out of it. I have never been so insulted in my life. If you think your—' She was about to go into an abusive description of Rick's lack of attributes when she stopped herself. Now that really would come back and slap her one. 'Anyway, I just wanted you to know it never entered my head.'

'No,' said Vanessa, with spirit. 'But it probably entered his. Oh, don't be so green.'

It was Pamela's turn to stare.

Vanessa struggled to her feet, leaving the groaning canvas mass behind her, and patted Pam's arm. 'If it's any consolation, he's still not speaking to me either.'

She lifted a small piece of paper from the table and handed it to Pam.

It read, 'I have gone to Greenford Estuary fishing for the day. Please don't worry. I will not be having it off with a haddock.'

'When he gets back, I'll tell him you've been round.' She fingered her beads. 'Oh,' she said, 'why not take it all as a compliment?' She shrugged. 'Or maybe as an indicator of just how insecure most of us married women are. What would I do if he left me? You're lucky—you went solo early and you've come through.'

Lucky? thought Pam. Doesn't anyone realize that luck has nothing to do with it? 'It cost me a lot, Vanessa,' she said.

Vanessa had the grace to look uncomfortable. 'I'll tell Rick you came,' she said, and offered Pam a drink.

'No, thanks,' she said, 'I've got to be getting back.' But for whom, she wondered, and for what?

It did not feel much of a victory when she left. She was reminded that if you loved someone, you assumed everyone else in the world would love them too. That was the fearful side of loving, that you might one day lose. At least she would always be Daniel's mother, wherever he was in the world, and that was about the only constant she knew.

*　　　*　　　*

When she reached home, she saw Peaches Carter coming down her path, in a bright orange puffa jacket that made her look like a walking Jaffa. She looked at Pamela coldly. Pam smiled and gazed all about her, indicating the dark chill of the night. 'It's a long way off from that lovely barbecue.'

Peaches sniffed.

'Your father seems very pleased,' she said cajolingly. And wondered why she was forever having to deal so delicately with the souls of the young. When did they ever stop to deal cajolingly with hers?

'I thought you'd look after him,' she said peevishly.

'We are,' said Pamela.

She had passed on both Battersea Waterside jobs to Jennifer. Since Zoe and Lionel lived in the same development, it seemed a waste of human resources to do otherwise. Well, that was her excuse.

'My partner and her assistant will take very good care of him.'

Peaches was disappointed. This was not the way soap romances should go. 'He's coming over tonight,' she said, looking hopeful.

Pamela did not take up the invitation. 'Say hallo for me.' Freedom, she thought, I will have it, and that includes freedom from guilt. I have done nothing wrong.

They both moved towards their front doors.

'Daniel will be back for Christmas,' she said. 'I hope you and Bud will come in then.' And she went inside quickly.

In the kitchen the table was covered in white rose petals. They had finally dropped. Unsurprising, given the traumas the poor things went through. Peter almost hurled them at her when he finally returned them. She picked up a petal and sniffed it. Of course, they smelled of nothing, being hothouse, out of season. If she remembered rightly, they were called Iceberg, anyway. Nevertheless, she was touched. It was not often Peter did anything so thoughtful. He was usually just mildly irritated with her, as if he had never quite forgiven her for letting him down. He really seemed to be trying nowadays. As if, with Daniel going, he, too, felt the need to bridge the gap.

She hung up her coat. No light was winking on the answerphone. Daniel never, ever called her. Twenty-two years, not including nine months in the womb, and he never rang. Margie said it was a matter for congratulation. That he was independent and free. A tribute to her fabulous mothering. Margie would say that. She was full of the joys of her newfound relationship (not affair, she insisted), and would probably have told Medea that she was doing a grand job.

She looked at the roses again. She and Peter knew each other inside out and back to front really. What a waste of experience and understanding. It might have been pleasant to have lunch with him. Ah, well, perhaps he would ask her again. Or dinner. Now the evenings were empty, dinner would be better. She thought about his limp and felt a little tug at her heart.

Amongst the petals sat a glass object, a prism, currently the stylish thing to have lying around on occasional tables in the politer kind of drawing room. She ran her fingers over its smoothness. It was the glass object that Douglas had touched in the shop. She remembered his hands as they toyed with its cut edges. Sentimental claptrap. She immediately swept the petals and the stalks into a rubbish sack and then, surprising herself, she dropped the prism in on top of them. She then replaced the sack in the cellar and went back to the dining room, where her plans for the study were still neatly laid out. She would work on that tonight. Something for herself. Whatever Herself wanted to do with it.

Later, admitting nothing, she went back down to the cellar and removed the prism from the sack and placed it near the drawings. She ran her hand over it, let its sharpness cut into her palm. Just as well Dean Close had not produced a hat trick. The way she was feeling right now, he would have been very welcome.

Later still the telephone beeped. Not Daniel but Rick. Fancy a lesson? he said chirpily.

CHAPTER SEVENTEEN

Dean Close tried to look nonchalant as he rose from the kitchen table. Four pairs of eyes gazed at him: Keith's, Julian's, Alice's and Alice's friend Deirdre's. He did not engage with any of them, particularly not Deirdre's, which were large, brown and moist, like a cow's.

'I'm going out,' he said, shortly.

'Bring us back a couple of Buds.'

'Get a pack,' said Julian.

'Not the off-licence,' he said.

'You mean really out?' Julian could not help giving Alice's friend Deirdre a glance.

'Yes,' he said, trying not to be self-conscious.

'Where?' said Alice baldly.

'Out.'

People on the tube stared at him. He pulled his Nike cap further over his eyes and ignored them. One shrivelled little woman in a raincoat kept darting nervous glances at him. She looked positively stricken when they got off at the same stop. Dean did not notice. He felt even more nervous now that he was here, and his feet dragged as he walked along the Terrace. He was keeping his distance behind the woman from the tube, who muttered to herself and kept clutching at her chest. He scarcely noticed. Then, at the top of the Terrace, they both turned right into the High Road. Dean kept his hands in his pockets and his head down. He speeded up and he slowed down, lost in anxiety. It was at the second corner that the woman in the raincoat stopped an idling police car and pointed to her stalker. A couple of seconds later, the two very bored policemen pulled him in.

'Good job you weren't black,' said Keith when he collected him. 'And a good job I'm a solicitor.'

'In training,' said Dean. 'Only in training.'

Keith laughed and set off for the flat. Dean sat up, touched his arm. 'No—' he said suddenly. 'Continue down here. I'll show you a route away from the traffic.'

Keith eyed the entirely empty road. 'Er—' he said, nodding at the emptiness.

Dean nodded impatiently. 'A brilliant solicitor—but occasionally a tad too fucking literal.'

Keith drove on. He did not, at first, realize why. And when he did, he shut up.

As they turned the corner into her road Dean's heart gave a surprising lurch. He peered through the windscreen. Halfway along the street, just about outside her house, he saw the lights of a car being parked. It must be her.

His heart lurched again.

'Inch forward a little,' he said to Keith, and he leaned across to switch off the lights.

Keith tutted and went to turn them on again. 'I'm a trainee solicitor, you nut—do you want me to get done?' But he steered forward slowly.

Dean's eyes never left the other car. 'Hey,' he said, 'she's got a GTI Three Hundred Series.' He smiled indulgently. 'But she can't park it.'

They both peered in the darkness. 'Pull in here,' he said suddenly. They were about a dozen houses away from hers. 'Maybe she'll need my help.'

The parking was finished. He watched the lights go out, heard the engine die, saw the driver's door open and the driver step out. He felt clammy with excitement and fear. Would he speak to her? Would he get out now and go up to her and say, 'Hi, I was just passing?'

He watched. Her house was lit up but everything else around it was dark. He watched the driver walk across the pavement, right up to her gate. Then Dean saw that it was not her. He watched the shadowy figure intently. He thought it behaved oddly, peering round her hedge, up at her bedroom. Particularly, he thought, up at her bedroom. He screwed his eyes against the darkness. It was a bloke.

'Fucking hell,' he said to Keith. His heart began to pound and, suddenly, he was out of the car, running along the street, driven by an emotion that was quite beyond control. She was being stalked. *Right . . .*

No knight on his steed could go faster. He gave a bloodcurdling yell, took a spectacular leap, missed the man completely, and landed right in the middle of the privet. He heard a yelp—then a voice, female, not hers, calling—a door opened, light flooded the scene and he heard the words 'Police' and 'Telephone' and 'Dad'.

Before he could rescramble his thoughts, and just about aware of a small blonde person yelling her way down the path, somebody heaved him from the hedge.

'Jesus, Dean,' groaned, Keith, 'do you want to get arrested again or what?'

Back in the car he kept the lights switched off until they reversed back round the corner, and then shot off in the direction of Kew Gardens.

'You're going the wrong way,' said Dean wearily.

'Why don't you just grow up?' Keith said furiously.

'I didn't hurt him,' Dean said righteously. 'I didn't even touch him. Wish I had—the dirty—'

'He was a neighbour.'

'He was a dirty peeper.'

'He was a neighbour,' said Keith. 'And what you did to that hedge was an act of criminal vandalism. You prat,' he said with feeling. And turned the car on to the High Road.

'She'd laugh if she knew it was me.'

'Dean, you are talking out of your arse. Forget it. Forget her. If you take the advice of your lawyer, you'll get stuck in with one of those friends of Alice's—'

'Get stuck in?' said Dean incredulously. The knight reared in shock. 'Get *stuck in?*' That was it. That was exactly it. Nobody of his own age really understood.

'Or whatever you straight blokes do,' said Keith serenely, as they drove back past Chiswick Police.

'Stop the car,' said Dean.

'What?' said Keith.

'Stop the car.'

He was fed up with being treated like an adolescent.

He got out.

He was going back.

* * *

He removed the hat and avoided any more oddballs in the street. He bought an African violet at the station flower stall, pink champagne at the offie, and chocolates from Patel's at the end of her road.

The son served him. Last time Dean saw him he was just a schoolboy. Now he had face hair and a giggling girl draped all over him. The giggling girl looked him up and down. She must have been all of fifteen. Suddenly he saw that she thought of him as old. He could have kissed her.

Just as he left the shop, the boy called, 'You're Danny's friend, aren't you?'

Their cover story.

'You taking his place now, then?' he added, indicating the gifts.

The girl giggled anew and clung on tighter.

Dean shrugged and opened the door to go. 'Sort of,' he said.

'I suppose she misses him. Is he lucky or what?'

Dean said, 'Misses?'

The boy nodded, fingering his moustache self-consciously. 'Now he's in Liverpool. Talk about freedom,' said the boy. 'Job, flat, girl. Brilliant.'

Dean stared.

The penny dropped.

He was enraptured.

Daniel had left home.

He strode up her path, noticing the hole in her hedge with amusement. She'd laugh. He pictured her face when she opened the door and found him standing there with all these gifts. He was about to ring the bell when he heard music—Danny's guitar, it sounded like. Puzzled, he waited. It definitely, definitely was his guitar. But who was playing? And then he heard the unmistakable sound of a male voice, not Daniel's, and her laughter.

He froze. In all the considerations that passed through his mind he never thought she

197

might have another man. Standing there on the step with the flowers and the chocolates and the bottle, he felt exactly what Keith said—a prat. He sat on the step, leaned against the wall of the porch, popped the cork on the bottle and drank the lot. All the time he could hear the voices, the guitar, the laughter from within. When he finished he put the bottle tidily with the milk empties, left the flowers and the chocolates where they would be tripped over, and posted the cork through the letter-box.

*　　*　　*

Putting on the hall light to let Rick out, she stumbled over a champagne cork. When she picked it up it felt fresh, slightly damp.

'Yours?' she said.

He shook his head. 'Gut rot.'

She opened the door and out he went into the night, guitar slung over his back, jauntiness in his step.

'Thanks for a great time,' he called loudly.

Oh, shit, she thought, and hoped Peaches was fast asleep.

Then she looked down. At her feet was a very pathetic little African violet lying on its side in a pot, its flower heads drooping with cold. Next to these was a box of chocolates. And in the milk bottle holder was an empty champagne bottle. She puzzled over it all for a moment. And then she knew. There was only one person in the world who thought that the Lady Really Did Love Milk Tray—apart from Danny—and that was Dean. They both seemed incapable of getting their heads around the fact that she preferred her chocolates plain.

Just as well he went before Rick found him, or he would have hauled him in, said, Bless you, my children, and left them to it with a cheery wink and a flash of his silly earring. When she told him about tracing Dean's call, he spent a lot of time trying to persuade her to call him back. 'You don't need the hang-ups of old guys like me,' he said, shrugging and smiling like a mystic. 'Seek him out. He just might be pining for you.' She stared at the champagne cork. Perhaps Rick was a mystic? She put the poor little violets where Peter's white roses had been. Only one left to go for the floral tribute, she thought. And her heart turned over. He would not, of course; Douglas was always capable of keeping his responses under control.

*   *   *

'Clubbing?' said Deirdre. 'At this time of night? As if . . .'

She got up from the settee, picked up her coat, rearranged her brassiere and did up her skirt. 'Anyway, you're pissed,' she said, and stalked out.

Nice Catholic girl, he giggled to himself, nice Catholic girl. How his mother would approve.

CHAPTER EIGHTEEN

The following morning, long after Pamela called in to buy her paper, Miss Phoebe Glen was leaning against the counter, wearing a pair of mittens from which her fingers wiggled and poked at the air.

The fat man watched, mesmerized.

'Everything is dangerous,' she said, having a little difficulty with the articulation. 'What's dangerous if not that sweet-tongued, red-mouthed girl from the Council? We are all in danger—every single last speckled one of us in the ocean . . . Our homes, our hearths, our freedoms . . .'

'Mrs Pryor's hedge was done last night,' said Ani Patel. 'Mrs Carter told me. And her father was knocked to the ground.'

'It's not safe to walk to the end of your street,' said Miss Phoebe.

And she gave the fat man a very penetrating, if slightly offskew, look.

'Every single last speckled one of us in the ocean,' repeated the fat man.

'You could have the top back,' said Miss

Phoebe Glen. 'It has a lovely view of the gardens. Together we would be safe.'

He watched her dainty mittens riffling through her fringe.

'How much?' he said.

This was beyond Miss Phoebe, who looked to Ani Patel for assistance in the matter. Since Ani Patel knew everybody's income from the post office, she named a suitable sum. *Tuesdays, she thought, I must have my Tuesdays back. Bleak House* had given way to *Lorna Doone*, which meant as much to Ani Patel as *The Story of Krishna* meant to Peaches Carter.

Miss Phoebe held her breath, the memory of that girl from the Council returning in terrible waves. Eventually the fat man nodded. 'I can suit myself,' he said. 'And I will.'

'All settled,' said Ani Patel, hoping they would go now so that she could be alone with her thoughts. She had a feeling things had been happening on the fireside rug upstairs. Something about the way it was placed. She must hope and pray. She bowed her head to the Goddess of Songs of Intercession, Ani-Vashtak, after whom she was named. Ani-Vashtak blew mournful notes through a golden shell and she lit the blessed way to loving unity with the fire from her eyes. At all times she wore seven silver snakes wound tight around her neck . . . 'With that lot strung round her,' she said thoughtfully, 'it's a wonder she could

201

sing or blow anything.'

'I'm sorry?' said Miss Phoebe.

Ani Patel apologized. 'I was miles away,' she said. 'Is there anything else?'

Surreptitiously Miss Phoebe Glen felt in her cardigan pocket for the scrunched up letter that had come from the Council that morning. It was the letter promised by that bright-faced young woman. Miss Phoebe Glen knew it word for word. It had three spelling mistakes and no commas. It said that she might find, if she thought about it, that she did not need all the room in her house. She *might* find, if she thought about it, that the bills incurred by having so much space were particularly wasteful. And she might find that she had some sympathy with the Benefit Department, who were having to rationalize all their commitments.

Yes, she could recite it with her eyes closed if required. And she knew where such arguments led. They led to one of those new so-called sheltered housing developments just by the M4. Cheap site. A ground-floor room with bath. That's all a retired person with no means of her own needed. And you were very likely deaf, so the traffic would hardly be a problem. If you didn't breathe too often, the fumes wouldn't make too much of a nuisance of themselves either. Your sight was almost certainly so bad that the lights of the traffic at night made no difference to the peacefulness of your bedroom. And, anyway—older people didn't sleep much, did they?

'Gather ye rosebuds,' she said, looking up at the Clarnico advertisement. 'For there is nothing sweet that does not end in bitterness.'

The fat unemployed man looked respectful. The Widow MacNamally seldom spoke to him and certainly not like that. He would go.

Miss Phoebe gave him a look of hope. He was very acceptable, particularly now that he had taken to wearing his beret like General Montgomery, with the perfect above-ear crease. She thought they could probably be very happy together. Had his jumper not been quite so dingy, he would have looked, thought Miss Phoebe Glen, very respectable. But she could put that in a bucket and wash it. No extra charge.

They left the shop. No more Tuesdays, hoped Mrs Patel again mournfully. Now she would be here to keep an eye. She put her ear to the door between the premises and living quarters, and thought she heard the faintest sound of tiptoeing on the stairs. Her blood ran cold. Ari was supposed to be in his room doing pure maths. Nothing pure about it, thought Ani Patel, and she added bitterly that it was a pound to a penny what he had been doing up there was extremely applied.

*   *   *

Pamela, with her thoughts bound up in the notion of a brave new world that morning, may have been the only one of her neighbours not to notice the hedge or pause to discuss the terrible goings on of the night before. She left for the shop with a song in her heart, a lightness of step and a sense that she was to be congratulated on finding the world a congenial place as a woman alone. Last night with Rick had been fun. It put Peter and Douglas and Dean in perspective. So who needed more than friendship?

She drove off enjoying the golden light and the hint of suburban woodsmoke in the air, congratulating herself on obtaining space in her life and the means to fill it pleasurably. And the benign sense of control and worth, and all those other matters that had long been an issue discussed with Margie and her other friends, lasted with her until late into the afternoon. You did not need to be a wife, mother or lover in order to survive extremely happily. Look at Jane Austen, she told herself, if a little vaguely.

It was the sports shop that did for this delightful equilibrium. Perhaps the goddess Nike felt a little meddlesome—understandable, given that one minute she was the great Greek Winged Victory and sister to the fierce river goddess of the Styx and of Zelos, and the next she was a brand name for sports equipment. If she was feeling a bit crabby about the ignominy, and Pamela happened to walk into one of her shops, who's to say? It was thus.

By about four o'clock in the afternoon, Pamela began to feel bored with work. It was happening more and more. She realized that she had been dealing with four walls and a roof for so many years that it was, in design terms, like a marriage in which the other partner no longer speaks. She decided to go home early and work on the plan for her study. Before she could take risks with her new freedom, she needed to have a place in which to think. She had an idea of producing the perfect small space, designed to hold everything she might need. A babushka of a room, space within space, items within items, depths within depths. It was as absorbing as designing a puzzle, and she set off completely absorbed, feeling happy and at peace. It would be the first space she had ever created for herself since she was a teenager, and she felt just as romantic about it.

And then it happened.

One minute she was heading home down the High Road, scarcely noticing the lighted shops, the hurrying pedestrians, the chill wind, and the next she found herself in a sports shop. I must want to buy something for Daniel, she thought, surprised. Yes. That must be the reason why I have come in here.

It was a very long time since she had been in a shop like this, the essence of which was masculine. She looked about her. Large posters portrayed athletes' shining biceps, glowing triceps, their gritted teeth above tensile neck and whipcord hands. She felt a little uncomfortable. Like a woman in a peep show. But, she told herself, she had a son, so she had every right to be here. And she eyed again the posters, the boxes of jockey shorts, the large pairs of socks and the massive trainers lining the wall. She could not take her eyes from it all, nor damp down the sense of being a deprived sweet-tooth let loose in a cake shop. She shook her head. She was not a deprived anything, she was here because she wanted to purchase an item of sports clothing. She practised saying it in just that high tone, in case she was asked to move on. Daniel, she thought, I have come in here to buy something for my son Daniel.

She was standing at a rack of shirts, *not* looking up at the posters any more, and wondering if it was *infra* dig for a mother to send her son something in Aertex while he was living with a female partner, when her idling eye noticed the changing rooms.

The doors were sketchy. She tried not to look but could not resist. In one, she could see over the top, was a man with his back to her and his neck bent downwards, as if doing up trousers or shorts. She could see the top of his shoulders, the curve of his neck, the utter concentration, the maleness. In another she saw under the equally revealing bottom half of the door a kneeling, hairy thigh. The combination of the two was so shockingly masculine, and the well of desire they plumbed was so deep that she nearly groaned out loud. She had to put her hand over her mouth and *keep* it there. And then she realized what was happening. She was now dispossessed of, and craving for, masculinity—a commodity of which, for the first time in her adult life, she was totally and utterly deprived at home. Unless you counted the yucca which had never flowered.

Coming into the sports shop was, she decided, subconscious—necessary, like getting a fix. It made her feel part of the whole world again, and not just half of it. You never thought twice about your right to visit a place like this until that right was removed from you. She closed her eyes as that hairy thigh came back to haunt her. This was no good, no good at all. If she carried on like this she would be arrested. Yearning was not too strong a word for what she felt now. A terrible, visceral yearning. Not for one man in particular, not even for a fantasy of one, just a yearning for masculinity. That was what the woman in her lacked—the opposing image to highlight what she was. Oh, she thought, oh, to feel that difference once more. She almost reached out. She had a sudden, dreadful picture of herself bending down and giving the masculine kneecap a grope, running her fingers over its bony, muscular hairiness, digging her fingertips into what could never be mistaken for feminine in a million years.

Instead, and very fortunately, she managed to remove herself from the shop as if nothing had happened beyond not finding the shirt she required. Once outside, she turned on her heel and fled. Putting away from her, as she hurried along, the picture of that neck, that leg, that knee. At least she had exercised control . . . She shivered. She could see the headline in the local paper now . . .

CHAPTER NINETEEN

Pamela, still much shaken, was caught on her front path by an excitable Peaches, and Peaches was incredulous.

'You mean you didn't hear? Nothing?'

Pam shook her head. 'I was having a guitar lesson last night,' she said.

Peaches looked at her with renewed interest. Not respect, just interest. Pam did not explain that it was elementary chords and that she was aiming to one day play Segovia.

'He was dressed like a real thug,' went on Peaches.

Pamela forbore to say that he sounded just up her street in her present deprived

208

condition. Her mind wandered free.

Peaches waited indignantly for Pamela's response, and, when none came, added, 'Anyway, this intruder nearly broke Dad's neck.'

Peaches paused again. Pamela, still in the sports shop with the triceps and only half-listening, had lost the thread but was aware she should reply. She smiled, non-committally. Was it something about Peaches' father's bravery?

'Pardon?' she hazarded.

'Dad,' said Peaches. 'Nearly broke his neck.'

Pamela felt on safe ground. Here was an opportunity for restitution. Paternal courageousness.

'What do you think of *that*?' said Peaches, even more irritated by the lack of response.

'Serve him bloody well right,' said Pamela firmly.

Peaches' mouth opened and a strange noise issued forth. 'Serve him—?' Her colour changed, and the redness sat very peculiarly above the orange of the puffa jacket. She appeared to be beyond speech. Pamela sought for something a little less tricky to say, something that would unite them again in their adversity . . .

'After all,' she said cheerfully, 'just look what he did to my privet.'

'My father had nothing to do with your privet,' said Peaches.

Had Pamela known it, she had just saved herself, for ever, from future lime green cocktails. Peaches, with a toss of her head, turned away.

Chocolate. Chocolate would have to do until she could work out what to do.

Having faded in the morning, Peter, Douglas and Dean all looked remarkably fresh and bright again tonight. Jesus, it was confusing. She marched off to Ani Patel's shop.

Ani Patel looked drawn.

'I am a little tired,' she said to Pamela's enquiry. 'My son.'

'Ah,' said Pamela with all the feeling, it seemed, of the world. 'Your son.'

The two women looked at each other gravely. Pamela had a sudden moment of understanding—both of herself and of Mrs Patel. She knew the meaning behind those words only too well. She knew that tone of voice. She knew that in the telling phrase 'My son' were hidden many griefs. And she knew that it would never be like that for her again. Not *quite* like that. Not so you lay awake listening for the key in the door. Not so you believed the Sixth Form Head of Year when he said your son would end up sweeping floors. Not so you felt his anger (at the world or at yourself, it mattered little) like a knife in your heart. And not so that every day, in every way, another little wrinkle of despair settled upon your brow. No—Danny was someone else's, and Danny was his own responsibility. He was her son, but he was now a fully paid up member of the adult human race. If she ever found herself saying this same 'My son' to half a stranger, it would be from the position of one who let wither the umbilical cord.

Where will it all end?' said Ani Patel.

Pamela touched her hand. 'All I can tell you,' she said, resolute in her new wisdom, 'is that, eventually, it does.'

And Ani Patel knew that she came from a different neck of the woods and that it never ended for the likes of her.

Pamela purchased her chocolate bar and went off to work on her plans for the study. If she could concentrate. If she didn't suddenly start doodling pictures of large masculine appurtenances in the margin.

In a way, she thought, chewing the end of her pencil thoughtfully, in a way it was a blessing that her mother was where she was. Safe. One less thing to worry about—and in a controlled environment where she could do no harm.

*　　*　　*

In the darkening gloom the view beyond the window was not inspiring. Apart from two elderly ladies standing staring at the leaden grey sky as if they had forgotten what they

211

were looking at, the outdoor area was full of soggy leaves—the last of them blown down in the first true wintry blasts the day before.

It all looked extremely gloomy.

'Christmas is coming,' said Mrs Hennessy, pleased. They linked arms and started walking again. 'I'm looking forward to spending it here with you.'

'You may be called away.'

'No, no,' said Mrs Hennessy with certainty. 'I shall be very happy here, thank you.'

Wind shook the bare branches. They both shivered but went on walking.

'How is that daughter of yours?' said Eileen.

'Well—I have to say I don't think Peter has shifted himself. Here we are, nearly December, and he hasn't done any courting of a substantial nature at all. One little attempt at a lunch is hardly Errol Flynn.'

They do seem a little cautious nowadays,' said Eileen, shaking her head.

'I shall have to swing into action again,' said Mrs Hennessy. 'Do you agree?'

'I do,' said Eileen. 'I really do. All this emancipation. Everybody's confused. Really, he should just pick her up, throw her over his shoulder, carry her off and say, Ugh!'

Mrs Hennessy was silent.

'I don't see Peter doing that,' she then said, looking back at the main house.

'Well, he'd better get on and do something quick,' said Eileen. 'A woman doesn't wait for

212

ever.'

Mrs Hennessy chuckled and pointed at the figure peering out at them. 'She thinks we're talking knitting patterns.'

Through the window peered a young helper, a nice girl, plump and consoling.

'She's got the brown pleats on again,' said Mrs Hennessy.

'And the orange cardigan,' said Eileen.

'Odd how they think we're not worth dressing up for.'

'They think part of your brain drops off over sixty-five.' Eileen paused, thought, chuckled. 'Useful, that.'

'Very,' said Mrs Hennessy.

The two women nodded in the direction of the girl, who tapped on the glass and smiled like a mime artist.

'Wave back and look uncomprehending,' said Mrs Hennessy.

And they both did.

The girl increased her facial contortions.

'Let's hope the wind doesn't change, dear,' said Eileen. And waved again.

Linking arms, they moved back towards the house, their sensible shoes squidging through the leaves very satisfactorily. As Eileen said, it had taken her nearly a lifetime to be allowed to mucky her shoes, and no slip of a girl in brown pleats was going to stop it.

'It all looks very dead,' said Mrs Hennessy approvingly.

'I don't see one green shoot,' agreed Eileen.

'She'd be best off with him,' said Mrs Hennessy thoughtfully. 'Grass always seems greener and then it's not.'

'Do you know,' said Eileen, 'I've had more of my gentlemen think they want to leave their wives for me than I've had hot facials, and lucky for them I've always declined. No idea what they're getting rid of. Oh, I'd say, you're a big, strong, powerful man, aren't you? Next thing you know they want to move in. I always sent them home.'

The girl waved at them from the window.

'Look at her,' said Eileen. 'Dreadful.'

They flapped their hands feebly and the girl gave them smiles of encouragement, as if talking them down for a dangerous landing.

Eileen stopped waving, resumed Mrs Hennessy's arm and said, 'Look at wars . . .'

They stood still for a moment, as if surveying a battlefield. Eileen gesticulated with her free arm.

'Heroes.' She sniffed. 'Stiff upper lip.' She sniffed again. 'All right until they're actually losing a leg or a life, then they suddenly realize how sweet it all is. Too late. It's the same with their feelings.'

They slowed down a little, giving the young girl another feeble wave each.

Eileen lowered her voice. 'I told them—I said, go home and tell your wives what it is you want. The fishnet stockings or the galoshes or the poached eggs on your chest.'

Mrs Hennessy made a strange noise.

'To be perfectly candid,' said Eileen, 'nine times out of ten, love is a great disappointment.'

'Quite,' said Mrs Hennessy. 'As I said to Pamela. But what's left after it can be rather pleasant. If you're still speaking.'

'Nice here,' said Eileen appreciatively.

'Very nice here,' said Mrs Hennessy with feeling.

'Some knitting pattern,' giggled Eileen. 'Shall we go in?'

They retraced their steps.

'I think I will tell that girl about those pleats,' said Mrs Hennessy. 'After all, one of the pleasures about being older is that you can say these things.'

'Well, I'd go further,' said Eileen. 'And say it's *expected.*'

'Quite,' said Mrs Hennessy. When they arrived indoors she made straight for the telephone with firm step and even firmer jaw.

Later, in the warm, dry, biscuity sitting room, as they sipped pale tea, Eileen suddenly smiled to herself and leaned towards Mrs Hennessy, dropping her voice. 'When I was in a brothel in Praed Street,' she said.

Mrs Hennessy raised her eyebrows with delight.

Behind them a swing door banged and someone advanced. They both looked smugly in the direction of the footsteps.

'Here she comes . . .' they both said.

And they returned the girl's bright, evangelistic smile with similar expressions of their own. Then they folded their hands in their laps and waited.

'Nice walk?' said the girl.

'Yes, dear,' said Mrs Hennessy, evenly.

'That's the spirit,' said the girl.

Both women stared at her. The girl gave them a pleased little smile. 'We are doing Third Age Therapy in the conservatory tonight,' she said.

'Lucky you,' said Eileen.

The girl smiled even more benignly.

'And Colour Me Beautiful.'

The two women looked at each other. Their eyes took on a little glaze of bliss. 'Impossible,' they said in unison. 'Impossible.'

It was, as they said afterwards, irresistible. And they filed the experience under the heading Cruel To Be Kind and spoke out clear and strong as a Greek chorus.

'Now,' said Mrs Hennessy comfortably. 'This place in Praed Street . . .'

CHAPTER TWENTY

Pamela woke early and lay in the dark. It was all right to admit it in the dark. So she did. She screwed her eyes up tight and admitted to

216

herself that not only was she alone, she was
lonely. Margie told her she would be, and
Margie was right. Damn her. She, mother of
Daniel, was turning into what Daniel would
call a Sad Old Git. A Sad Old Git who went
around groaning in sports shops. In the
darkness of her duvet she admitted to herself
that she was probably going weird.

At the end of the day what did it matter if
the two blokes in her life eyed each other
balefully over the morning toast? As Margie
had said, 'You're not proposing incest and
troilism. Put yourself first. One day Daniel will
be gone and then you'll wonder what all the
fuss was about.' Irritatingly accurate counsel
from a woman who had never had children
herself.

Oh, all right. She was lonely. Peter had not
rung. Douglas *certainly* had not rung. And that
left Dean. Who was too young. She stirred her
tea and smiled the standard rueful smile that
adorned her features whenever she thought of
her son. Given Danny's appalling disregard at
the moment, preventing Dean from having
children might be considered something of a
kindness.

Well, she thought, as the pale light of dawn
gave way to the stronger light of day, I have
seen my mother and I know her views. I will go
and see Margie and find out hers. In any case I
should go down and make this Tom's
acquaintance. And she hoped that she could

217

hide it if she found him appalling. She shivered at the memory of the sports shop. She would go down and see Margie that very night.

*   *   *

The first thing Pamela noticed when she walked into Margie's cottage was its neatness. And the lack of cigarette smoke. Then the man's jacket and cap hanging from a hook in the hall, along with Margie's outdoor clothes—a sight which made her burn with envy. And then, more transformed than all these, Margie herself. Gone was the cascading hair and the bright, generous mouth. In its place was a sober version. Hair held back in a velvet bow, make-up discreet, and several pounds thinner. It did not altogether suit her, though any weight loss between them was always a matter of green-eyed congratulation. But, Pam thought, it made her look a little gaunt. She was also, very uncharacteristically, wearing an apron.

They kissed. 'My God,' said Pam, 'you look great.'

'My God,' said Margie, 'you look fed up.'

'Thanks.'

They looked at each other again. 'I'm glad I came,' said Pam. Behind her an owl hooted and made her jump.

'Townie,' said Margie. 'Go and bring your bag in from the car.'

'I'm not staying, unfortunately.'

Margie looked really disappointed.

'Sorry,' she said, pulling a face. 'But I've got to open up tomorrow. Jenny and the Amazon are off on a job.'

This was not entirely true. They were going to see Zoe and Lionel, but not until midday. The real reason she was not staying was that she feared her strange state. How would she react to seeing her friend, whom she had never envied before, now in this enviable position? If her feelings on seeing the cap and coat were anything to go by, not very well. Before, she was always the one with the career, the son, the balanced life.

'Come on in, then, and close the door,' said Margie.

The place was cosy as ever. Margie always reminded her of a sleepy, cream-eating cat.

'Are you sure you can't stay?'

'Positive. Sorry.'

No, she was not ready for that. In the mornings she and Margie used to sit in bed together, with their eyes closed, sipping tea and communicating what little skipped in and out of their fuddled brains. Now Margie would be sitting up in bed with someone else. Pam would be alone in the spare room. And she was not ready for that. She begrudged her friend nothing, but she was sure she was not yet ready to see and celebrate this new-found intimacy of hers. Not until she had got something sorted out for herself. Something. Or *someone*.

'I really can't,' she said, bright and loud for the benefit of any third party who might be listening.

For he would be there, of course. She had steeled herself for that. She would meet Tom tonight and from there on in Margie would become part of a couple.

She looked beyond Margie towards the kitchen, expecting to see The Man.

Margie said, 'I've sent him back to his place for the night.' And then, a little sheepishly, she added, 'Well, he didn't need a lot of persuading. I said we hadn't seen each other for a few months and that we had a lot of talking to do, and he got a sudden, desperate desire to go over to his old place and lag the pipes.'

They walked through into the kitchen. Though neater than usual, it held the standard prerequisites of an opened bottle of red wine and two glasses.

'Isn't that dangerous?' asked Pam. 'If his wife's still in residence?'

'Oh, he's still bonking her,' said Margie, pouring wine, not looking up.

Pamela sat down and stared. 'Pardon?' she said.

Margie sat down. She pushed a glass across to Pam. 'We'll have something to eat in a minute.'

That was another change. The house smelled of cooking.

'I've got a casserole in the oven,' said Margie.

They looked at each other, compressing their lips.

'You've what?' asked Pam.

'You heard.' Margie was fiddling with her glass stem. 'Rabbit.'

'Is that a command or the contents of the stew?'

Their eyes met and they burst out laughing in relief.

'Casseroles? Oh, Marge,' said Pam, when they had recovered a little.

'And I've given up smoking,' she said proudly, immediately producing a packet of ten cigarettes from a pot high up on the dresser. She lit up thoughtfully. 'When Tom's around, anyway.'

'Are you happy?' asked Pam. Her envy at this new romance was diminishing moment by moment.

'What's happy? Sometimes yes, sometimes no. But at least something is happening at last.'

At what cost? thought Pam. But she kept it to herself. 'Does he really still sleep with his wife?'

She nodded. Her face bore the message, Don't criticize. Pamela knew that face. She first saw it when they were teenagers and

221

Margie told her she was going to leave school, just like that, and be an actress. Another bad decision.

'Will he leave her for good?'

Margie shrugged. 'He doesn't talk about it.' Back came the look. " "Oh, what it is to love . . . But—how *want* of love tormenteth . . ." *Venus and Adonis.* You can't say fairer than that.' She got up and put some plates to warm in the oven. She was an actor to her bootstraps and looked as if she had been wearing an apron and baking things for years.

'Come on,' she said. 'Let's talk about you.'

Later, leaning back and smiling, Margie said, 'Well, personally I don't think leopards change their spots, but if you think you have changed—it might work.'

Pam thought of the sports shop. She had changed. She was in need.

'Of the three of them, Douglas is the one, of course. You were mad to end it. He was the love of your life.'

'And the pain of it,' said Pam.

'No gain without pain,' said Margie.

Occasionally Pam felt like slapping her.

'Well, why not someone completely new? This Lionel?'

'Because his bedside manner was more doctorly than seductive.'

'Are you saying you want someone who is both nice *and* lustful? Not a hope.' She lit a cigarette, drew in smoke as if it were pure oxygen, and blew it around her thoughtfully. Then she sat forward. 'Oh, go for Douglas. You gave up the passion of your life when you gave him up.'

'My mother thinks I should get back with Peter.'

Margie pulled a face of extreme distaste.

'Rick thinks I should get back with Dean.'

'Too temporary,' said Margie. 'Douglas. Douglas. I always fancied him myself.'

Pam was shocked. But also rather amused. 'Did you now?'

'I did,' said Margie positively. 'And I certainly couldn't say the same about the other two.'

They both looked out of the window. It was inky dark and it calmed the atmosphere between them.

Eventually Pam said, 'I can't face trying someone new. Because it is all such an effort anyway. And I still might end up with something worse. Three seems possible. Three seems just about the number I can cope with. I could have dinner with them. Nothing more if I didn't want to . . .'

'It's like something out of a fairy story,' said Margie thoughtfully. 'You know—which casket will you choose?'

'I was identifying more with Ernest. I can just hear Lady Bracknell saying, "To have dinner with *one* ex is unfortunate, but to have dinner with *three* is . . ."'

'Three free dinners?'

Which they both found satisfactorily funny.

'Anyway—what's free in this life?' said Pamela.

Margie went serious. 'Ah. Exactly.'

'Freedom's just another word for nothing left to lose,' sang Pam.

They were both silent for a moment, contemplating this philosophical truth.

Then Margie got up and began serving the food, cutting up bits of hot bread as if it had done her serious wrong. It was a strange sight. Pam watched for a moment and then said, 'Neither of us wants to end up on our own, do we?'

'No,' said Margie, crashing down the pot lid. 'But you've got a better prospect than I have. You've got the future. I've been on my own so long that I had to grab a passing husband. Even if he was somebody else's. You've got a family. You really are someone.'

'I've got a mother who's put herself in an old folk's home *out of preference*—' they both let that one sink in for a moment—'a randy son in Liverpool whose randy girlfriend thinks I am senile, and an interior design business that has turned into a middle-class wank.'

'So? What do you expect from all your sacrifices? Happiness?'

Yes, thought Pam, yes, I do rather.

She began to eat. It was good.

'Tom likes his food,' said Margie, not

224

meeting her eyes. 'I went on a cookery course.'

'What?'

'None of us wants to be on our own,' she said. 'And we therefore have to do something about it.'

'You always said domestic skills were—'

'What I always said and what I now do are two different things. Much like you.'

'Oh?'

'If you ring those three up and ask them out. Whatever happened to, Never again, I swear it, never again?'

One thing about Margie—she was direct. Damn her.

Pamela said, 'I wish I was like Ani Patel. She copes with everything. Even those oddballs hovering around in her shop. They always make me feel privileged. I'm not so sure now.'

'We're all the same underneath,' said Margie. 'But you wouldn't want to be her. Not really. Ani Patel is a saint. And you know she never met her husband until the day she married him?' She was looking at Pamela as if this was a very significant statement.

'What does that prove?'

'They made up their minds it would work, whatever happened. Or *she* made up her mind. And it did. Like me with Tom. I just decided that whatever happened, it would be all right. And it is. You wouldn't be like that.'

Pamela said, 'Ani Patel's husband died after twelve years, and you've only known Tom for

225

e months . . .'

'And a half.'

'One man half-in, half-out, and you think you're the bloody goddess of wisdom.' She poured herself another drink, although she had not meant to.

Margie said quietly, 'But I was right about Douglas, wasn't I?'

'He's the one that worries me,' said Pam thoughtfully.

'The one that worries me is all of them,' said Margie, lighting up again, the food pushed to one side. 'Here you are, free if nothing else, and you're thinking of shacking up with Peter again? Or putting yourself back in the loony bin for Douglas? Or getting IVF at the age of ninety-two so Dean Close can have a son and heir . . .?'

'I am not.'

'What?'

'Ninety-two.'

They laughed.

'But why would you have dinner with Peter?'

'Company? Familiarity? Security.'

'And Douglas?'

'Love. Passion.'

'And Dean?'

'I liked his company. And it was easy.' She paused. 'And sex,' she said quietly. 'Unencumbered sex.'

'You disgust me,' said Margie. 'What's sex

226

to a woman nearing fifty?'

Before Pam could answer, the telephone rang.

Margie jumped up, crushing out her cigarette and practically standing to attention when she picked up the receiver. She spoke in softly hallowed tones. 'Of course,' she repeated. 'Of course,' and, 'You poor baby. It's fine. Absolutely fine. No. Really. I'll ask her if she minds. I'm sure she'll understand. Oh, no. Oh, no. You must.'

When she replaced the phone she lit another cigarette and laughed. 'He says he wants to come back here tonight after all. They've had a terrible row . . .' She clapped her hands, scattering ash everywhere, including all over the rabbit casserole. She peered into it, poking about at the bits. 'I said I'd save him some of this,' she said dubiously. 'Oh, well, what he doesn't know can't kill him.'

'What happened to Miss Sensitive and the Poor Baby?' asked Pam drily.

'Sod off,' she said. 'Anyway, he offered to wait another hour so that we could finish our *talking* before coming back. And I said I'd ask you if you minded going home after all. Because he's so upset.' She hooted with merriment, an owlish noise remarkably reminiscent of Pam's arrival.

'But I'm going home anyway.'

'I know that,' said Margie, rolling her eyes in similar manner to The Girlfriend. 'But *he*

227

doesn't know that. *He* will therefore now think that I've made a huge sacrifice just for him, and I'll have lots of Brownie points. Oh, Pam—don't you know anything?'

'I know that I'm a woman who's made a lot of sacrifices and someone else appears to have cleaned up on the Brownie points.'

Margie pulled a face and picked at the casserole again.

'Don't get bitter,' said Margie, winking. 'Get even. And while we're at it, if you do have dinner with them—make sure they pay.'

'Margie, you are a disgrace.'

'Pamela, I am pragmatic.'

'Anyway,' said Pam, rising with both dignity and envy and pointing at the telephone, 'that Brownie-point stuff. It is so dishonest.'

'Pamela?' said Margie sternly. 'Have you joined the Moonies?'

CHAPTER TWENTY-ONE

Wooing was all very well, thought Peter Pryor when he put down the telephone, if the one to be wooed was new in one's life. But wooing one whom one has wooed once is not so easy. His ex-mother-in-law had snorted and said that was called faint heart, to which he very nearly replied that Pam was hardly, as his ex-wife, a fair lady. But he stopped himself. He did not want a spat with Mrs Hennessy. 'She is lonely now that Danny has gone. Show her you understand. Twenty-odd years, after all. You could both do a lot worse.'

I am lonely, too, he wanted to say, but did not. And he wondered sadly where all that happiness they once shared had gone.

He was about to ring off when Mrs Hennessy said, 'Wait a minute, dear . . .' And he heard whispering. She came back on the line. 'Take her some underwear, Eileen advises. Take her something'—there was more whispering—'Not thermal, she says. Something a bit . . . interesting—satin, lace, bows—that sort of thing.' He flinched. There was more whispering. 'Red, she says.' He flinched again.

'What about flowers?' he said.

More whispering.

'Red, satin, lace and bows,' repeated his ex-mother-in-law.

'What about flowers?' he repeated.

'We think flowers would be gilding the lily,' said Mrs Hennessy.

He replaced the telephone carefully on its piece of black paper. The room had begun to take on the appearance of a human-sized chess board with all those squares of dark card placed around it. He sighed. His clients thought it was another departure in the Pryor Design Concept, a moving towards the millennium, perhaps, and it was catching on everywhere. What they would think when, chess boards in place, so to speak, he offered his proposal for the Brigham College Project, he dared not imagine. Soft, humane, decorative—he had even conceptualized Tufglass finials, *finials . . .*

His public would think he had gone mad. Or worse, they would all start sprouting TG finials and ribbed and coffered domes. It would be given a new style name—not retro, but something like it. Well, better that than they guessed the truth. The terrible truth about the human machine, he suddenly realized, was its built-in obsolescence. And built into that obsolescence was a need for each other. Like buildings. It was so obvious that he had never considered it before—you could only stay up if your wall or foundation was connected to something. Even the lone cottage in a field was sunk into earth that connected to the next field, the next cottage. Maybe he had been a little too precious. Maybe Pamela's fun-poking had some justification. They used to laugh at everything together once. When, he wondered, did it suddenly change into her laughing on her own and at him? He stood up carefully and winced. All is grass, he thought. Much is regrets. He patted the telephone as if to reassure himself. He would telephone Pamela later. First he needed to get more physio for his knee. Underwear, he went out saying. *Underwear . . .*

Zoe was furious with the bus. Full of horrible, grinning people staring down at the front of her car, at her own discomfiture. One particular baboon, a fat man in a beret and an extraordinary scarf resembling sea sludge, had actually pointed at her over and over again, as if she were an entertainment. She looked at her watch. Douglas planned to have The Talk with Mary tonight. By now he would have done it. She did not dare try to use her mobile phone again. Besides—the police had confiscated it.

*   *   *

Mary shed no tears at all. She knew there was no point. She said she was expecting it. That she had tried, that she had lost. Even to the last she was cool. He was glad she knew how to behave. It made the separation easy. He hated scenes, which reminded him of his parents, and he hated big displays of emotion. He had learned how to control his own. And he had learned what happens if you do not. Mary kept her head up and just walked down the stairs, rather than taking the lift, and told him not to follow. And that was that. Only once did she stop to stare back at him. With her white face upturned, she said, 'How many more times,

Douglas? You'll never make yourself or anyone else happy if you go on like this.' He turned away without speaking. She waited and he had nothing to say. It brought back memories. And while he listened to her footsteps, he remembered the other one saying something similar and how he had stayed silent and just turned and gone, as he did to Mary now. That was where not controlling your feelings left you, and he was still, he knew, not out of it.

Since seeing Pamela again, he had thought about her a lot more than he wanted to. Amidst all that foolery in the shop there were moments when it felt like they were just the same together. She looked older, of course, and not quite so slender. Zoe commented on this afterwards, Bet you're glad now . . . But he wasn't, and it didn't matter that her waist had thickened and her hair showed grey and her clothes were just thrown on. It did not matter one bit. If anything, he felt more tender about her. He wondered what she would feel like now if they were in bed together, he wondered what it would be like to walk and hold her hand and talk like they used to. And he wondered, but did not want to, if she had someone else. It was what happened inside when he thought about this last that finally convinced him it was not fair to hold on to Mary any more.

He went back into the flat, shut the door

firmly behind him, felt the familiar pain, the familiar relief, and felt alone. He needed to talk to someone. He telephoned his sister. He tutted with irritation when the answerphone clicked on. She had said she would be home. She had said that it was best to get it over with and that as soon as he telephoned, she would come. There was a big, black space here, now, in this room, which Zoe must quickly fill before he felt its emptiness. He tried her mobile but it was switched off. He felt a sudden sense of fear, a twinge of irritation. Her new flat was taking up her time, and her new neighbour with it. Lionel. She was probably with him again. Shopping for more stuff for their apartments. Zoe nesting was curious, and slightly disturbing. But Lionel? Anyone less like a lion was hard to imagine. He was more like Zoe's pet lamb.

Inevitably his thoughts went back to the peacocks and the shared smiles. Intimacy was painful. Maybe in a way he was paying his sister back for the way she behaved in the past. He had a feeling Pamela was. Or maybe he was paying her back for the way she was behaving now. Not there for him when he needed her. Since she took on that riverside place, she was more and more caught up with it. And Lionel. Useful Lionel. He tried Zoe's number again. Still the machine. He could wait. He was free, completely free. Maybe he would try again with the girl next door. Just to see him through this emptiness, until someone more permanent came along. As one eventually would. Maybe he would take a break—go to Dublin—do something. What he must not do was think any more about Pam. He waited by the telephone, glad the move had been made with Mary, sad for her, a little sad for himself. He tried Zoe's number again. And then some small part of the dam broke within him, and he surprised himself by telephoning a completely different number.

*   *   *

In the studio they were fiddling about with the lighting and a wind machine. Suddenly the photographer came over to him, took his chin between his finger and thumb and jerked it upwards, directly into the glare.

'You,' he said, scrutinizing him, 'are beginning to show your age.'

He laughed into the photographer's anxious eyes. 'Great,' he said. 'Great . . .'

Later, Dean sat on the edge of the settee in the front room of the flat while everyone else pissed themselves laughing about something in the kitchen. Sometimes, he thought, other people's laughter can feel like a knife. He had his eyes closed. He was nodding. Occasionally he was making little grunting noises. His mother was off again. It was his fault, of course it was. She had sent him the ticket. He had not responded. It arrived in the post the morning after the hedge, champagne and guitar incident, and he had not felt like saying yes to anyone, or anything, since. Tonight he'd been given three vodka Martinis in a row because Keith was just back from New York. He was not drunk, exactly, just in a different dimension from Dublin and his mother. She finally stopped talking. 'You will be coming?' she said, half-cross, half-anxious. 'They've a lovely lot of things happening here over the holiday with the festival.' She was wheedling, letting him know she would not tie him to her apron-strings. She would, of course.

'Sure,' he said. 'Why wouldn't I?'

'You're a good boy,' she said, and put down the phone.

Oh, for God's sake.

Good boy?

He'd once chased Pamela all round this flat when she teased him by saying that. It made him out to be a small dog. Absently he found his fingers tracing a number on the phone. Miraculously (it's a miracle, he wanted to say, and laugh) he heard a beeping at the other end. He began to giggle. And he could swear he had never touched the keys.

*   *   *

Pamela was sitting at the dining table writing postcards. Three postcards to be exact. One to

235

Peter, one to Douglas and one to Dean. Frankly, if Margie could find happiness with someone who kept a bum in both beds, and offered combined Brownie points and redemption through a rabbit casserole, then who was she, Pamela, to put her past behind her? What had once seemed so wrong with Peter, Douglas and Dean was, compared with Margie's lot, a mere flea-bite.

She was on her second glass of wine. To give her courage. And to celebrate the careful unpicking of the threads of her present, so that she could go back to the past and knit them anew. She liked that idea. What had her mother told her about her father and an aeroplane? By the time she was on her third glass of wine it suddenly seemed extremely profound. If she could only remember it properly. Well—*plus ça change.*

On the table next to the postcards was the finished plan for her study. She was really pleased with it. Of course, she still did not know what she was going to do in there, but she would do something. The builder was coming tomorrow, the decorator shortly after that, and she had all the final bits and pieces ready to install. It was her most interesting exercise in design since her student days. It was going to be lovely, just lovely. Quite a departure. It almost did not matter what it was for. It was simply hers to do with as she wished. It would be even better once she had

236

finished the postcards.

She was going to end each one with the words 'It would be lovely to see you some time' and sit back and wait. Well, she thought, now or never, and she picked up her pen. At which point the telephone beeped. The phrase 'her heart jumped into her mouth' took on tangible meaning. It was as if British Telecom had caught her out and read her thoughts.

She picked up the receiver. It was probably Daniel. She had left a message ages ago asking him to confirm Christmas dates. The spare room, now the proper place for Daniel when he came to stay, was freshly painted in neutral colours for neutral territory. Newly curtained in fabric that made no statement. Transient. For transient guests. She was fine about that now. Beginning to feel her way into the empty spaces. Thinking, somewhere at the back of it all, that she was capable of enjoying, or even revelling in, not knowing what the world held in store. All she prayed, in her hidden heart, was that her son would not end up marrying this one. Please, please, she prayed to whatever was listening, Not her—give me a daughter-in-law who thinks I am sane.

She said 'Hallo' warmly into the telephone, and waited for that breathless 'Mum?'

CHAPTER TWENTY-TWO

Pamela?

Peter?

Hi.

Yo.

I'm sorry?

Joke. Sorry. Long time no hear.

I'm sorry I haven't rung before.

That's all right.

Have I offended you?

Only when the maintenance stopped.

Pamela.

Sorry. Water under the bridge.

I wondered if . . .

Yes?

You'd like to have lunch.

No, thanks.

I have offended you.

No.

Why not?

I don't know. Perhaps you haven't been trying hard enough.

Oh, for—I mean, why not see me?

I haven't said I won't.

Pam?

I mean I'd prefer dinner.

Oh, I see.

More relaxing.

Busy at the shop?

Very.

Well, well . . .

No need to sound so surprised.

I wasn't. Don't be—

What?

Nothing. It looked like it was going well.

It is.

So? Dinner? You'd prefer it? Yes. Less rushed.

Of course.

More time to talk.

Talk?

Hallo? Peter?

Sorry, something going past in the street.

Evenings are better.

Lonely? Now you're on your own?

Well, I miss Daniel. And you?

Oddly enough, I don't miss him at all.

I don't mean that. You scarcely saw him anyway—

Pam!

I meant, are you lonely?

Oh, no. Not at all. I'm fine.

Kirsty?

No. Best thing.

When?

Oh, several months ago—

I mean, when shall we have dinner?

Ah.

I'm looking forward to it.

Ah.

Peter?

I'll get my diary.

*   *   *

Pam? It's . . .
I know.
I'd like to see you.
With or without Mary?
Just you.
Yes.

*   *   *

Mrs Pamela Pryor?
Yes.
This is the Acme Double Glazing Company.
At this time of night?
We never rest, madam.
Sorry, not interested.
Let me tell you about our special offer.
There's no point.
Don't say that.
It's very quiet around here.
There have been complaints.
What complaints?
Noise late at night.
Don't be ridiculous. I—Who is this?
Guitars, singing.
What?
Noisy hedges—and—hallo?
Really?
Hallo?

240

I'm still here. Noise?
Yes.
Ah. Noise.
Is what I said.
Not by any chance the sound of champagne
corks?
Ah. Could be.
And the rustling of chocolate wrappers?
You pigged them?
The lot.
Even the strawberry cream?
Even the strawberry cream. Dean?
Yes?
How are you?
I'm twenty-eight now.
I know.
You forgot.
I didn't.
No card. No call. That hurt.
Did you—
No.
No what?
I didn't.
What?
Enjoy it.
Oh.
Can I see you?
Ah.
You came to see me.
I was just passing.
Bollocks.
OK. It was fancy.

Let's meet. You're free.
What?
Danny. He's in Liverpool.
How did you know that?
Tell you when I see you.
Don't be cocky.
Never used to say that.
Dean.
Yes?
Isn't there anyone else?
Sure. I'm married with twins.
Dean!
Joke.
Oh, Dean.
Some joke.
I'm sorry.
Will you—?
How's your mother?
Do you want to see me?
Well, of course it would be very nice—
Fuck you.
Thanks.
Don't *be* like that. Do you?
Yes.
Better.
Dean?
Pam?
Are you working?
Told you. Acme Double Glazing.
We could have lunch.
Nope.
I just thought—

Dinner.

When?

Tonight?

Oh, *Dean!*

Why not? Seeing him?

Who?

The guitar man?

No.

Well, then?

Next week?

When?

Dean, it's not a very good idea.

It's a f—

Dean!

Excellent idea. Dinner.

I'll pay.

Will you fucking well stop that?

Will you stop swearing at me?

I asked you. I'm an adult, Pam.

And I'm still—

When?

CHAPTER TWENTY-THREE

Pamela stood waiting to be served. Ani Patel was in the middle of an argument with her son. 'He has mock A levels coming up in January,' she said, with eyes of fire, 'And he does nothing.'

She glared at her son, who stared pointedly

at a jar of sherbet lemons and fingered his infant moustache.

'I tell him that nothing is a mockery in this game and that everything is real. If his father were alive, he would not be like this.'

Ari rolled his eyes.

'Once a week,' said Ani Patel. 'Once a week I go. Now I shall not be able to do that. I must watch him all the time. And my old lady will suffer.'

Ari went very red beneath his smooth brown cheeks. He muttered what was possibly an obscenity.

'I,' said Ani Patel, 'have given up everything for him.'

Mistake, that, thought Pamela, shaking her head. She was glad to be free of it. She knew this scene inside out, back to front, and with knobs on. If you go out, he will not work. If you stay in, he will not work but he will sulk at home. Or he will go out slamming the door. Whatever he will do, he will not work. She remembered Douglas's perplexity and his conviction that if she stopped being so nice to Danny, he would soon learn to behave.

'Yes,' she had said. 'But learn what else? That I only love him when he is good? You are asking me to stop loving parts of my son.'

Douglas never understood. The divide between those who have begotten children and those who have not is vast and understandable. How can a sane person allow themselves to be treated thus? She saw that question in Douglas's eyes. She tried to explain. It is called unconditional love. It comes, if the child is blessed, as soon as it opens its little post-puerperal mouth to scream for attention. Time diminishes it, but it seldom goes completely. And, she thought, if it is the Kingdom of the Blind for those without children, for Douglas it was the Kingdom of the Certifiably Insane as well. What hurt him, and to a lesser extent Dean, and even, slightly, Peter, was that what they had to strive to win and keep from her, Danny got handed on a plate. Love, in all its complexities of loyalty and kindness and bestowal of happiness was his by birth. To the other men in her life it was theirs only by effort and good behaviour. 'Who takes the child by the hand,' she remembered from somewhere, 'takes the mother by the heart . . .'

Poor Douglas. Worse for him. She guessed, though he never really spoke about it, that the only unconditional experience he knew, growing up, was unconditional rejection. When she tried to talk about it, he gave the perfect imitation of a clam, even down to the thin rippling line of his mouth as it clamped shut.

Poor Ani Patel, now. Unconditional was written all over her. The terrible thing about this situation, Pam saw, was that Ari could not give a fig what Ani Patel had given up for him. Why should he? It was his due.

245

She looked at the boy. Only the amber of his skin and the colour of his eyes distinguished him from her son at that age. The pose, the mouth-line, the expression of impenetrable contempt, was the same. Suddenly the doubts lifted. Two brassieres and four pairs of knickers lying lonely in the bottom of a basket seemed heaven-sent. Where were those Dorothy shoes?

She, Pamela, had come through. She could choose. If she wanted, she could choose. Or try.

Mrs Patel said, 'And I want to take him to see my family for Christmas and he says he will not go. He wants to stay here on his own, he says'—and then Ani Patel remembered herself. 'Can I help you, Mrs Pryor?' she enquired.

Ari took the opportunity to slip away.

Pamela picked up her newspaper and touched Ani Patel's arm. 'It will end,' she said with feeling. 'Or at any rate, it changes. You will not always have to be so strong.'

'I do not think it will end for me, now,' said Ani Patel, which Pamela took to be rhetorical and uncharacteristically gloomy. She looked at her customer. 'For the likes of you, perhaps, but not for me.'

The sorrow and silence between them was broken by a sound like the rushing of wings. Miss Phoebe Glen entered the shop. Careless of any intrusion, she leaned against the counter, took several deep breaths, and began.

'I had a visitor today,' she said excitedly. Her hair was very much askew and her mittens were flying about all over the place, like birds fighting for the space.

And then, seeing Pamela, she stopped. 'You, of course,' she said, peering at her, 'have your own home? If I remember . . . Alas— your son . . .'

Pamela nodded.

Miss Phoebe flittered her hands about in a cheerfully impatient manner. 'Well,' she said, 'no matter, no matter. I am all sorted out now. Or very nearly. Soon they won't be able to touch me.' She looked at Pamela. 'Brave, brave woman,' she said.

Pamela shrugged as if it were nothing, which indeed it was, so far as she knew anything about it, and excused herself. She was expecting a call from Daniel and she was due to meet Peter at eight.

She walked along the empty road looking up at the black, starry sky. What was it Oscar Wilde said? Children begin by loving their parents, then they judge them, and rarely, if ever, do they forgive them. Maybe it was the same for parents? She pulled her coat about her and hurried up the path. One day, she thought, I might go somewhere exotic and warm for Christmas—but not yet. One day it would be time for Egypt at last. She sighed for it. Floating down the Nile on a felucca, past temples and pyramids and palm trees. Eating fresh-picked dates.

But no, not yet. Christmas was for families and that sense of being warm inside while outside the elements raged. Of course, it also had the highest stress yield, drove you quietly potty in the run-up, was always exhausting and inevitably a disappointment. But Christmas just would not be Christmas anywhere else. Daniel relied on it. Of that she was sure.

*   *   *

Ani Patel tried to look interested and concerned. Which was hard, for Miss Phoebe was full of her story. 'I shall have a little party,' she said, 'To celebrate. They came for me, you know. They came for me. But I have pre-empted them. Ha, ha! No little box of a place down by the M4 for me.'

Mrs Patel said she was very pleased to hear it. Humouring. She had spent all those Tuesday nights humouring. While Ari was humouring something quite different. She smiled as best she could and went to get a box of two-for-a-pennys. Better keep going while her customer unfolded her tale.

'Norman has finally decided to move in and Lavender MacNamally is behaving very badly about it. I washed his jumper. I think that is what did the trick. He was impressed with the colour it came up.'

'Norman?'

'The man with the corporation and no budgerigars.'

Mrs Patel nodded, her mind only half-engaged. 'Good, good,' she said, absently.

'And he is bringing his television,' said Phoebe Glen excitedly.

'So, no more radio serials,' said Ani Patel flatly. It was too late anyway.

'Probably not, dear Mrs Patel. I hope you don't mind.'

Ani Patel said that she thought she could just survive without it.

Miss Phoebe rattled on excitedly. 'But let me tell you the rest.'

Ani Patel went and fetched the chair. 'Do sit while you tell me,' she said.

Best to be safe.

Phoebe Glen sat. 'Well, it was most unfortunate that the girl should have called again and today. I had been celebrating, just a little. Now that I have the lodger question settled. So I had a little treat. Mules they were called, on a special promotion at the off-licence. PACK A HELL OF A KICK, said the poster. Anyway, they were half-price. I bought six and I have to say they were very acceptable. Slipped down nicely. Made a change. Being teetotal as a general rule.'

Mrs Patel did not blink.

'But I had a little difficulty getting up the stairs, so I thought I would lie down in the hall for a moment, just to get my bearings. And then she started knocking and calling and waking me up with rattling the letter-box because she thought I was lying there dead. She spoke to me through the flap as if I were a congenital idiot. I used to talk to children like that when they refused to come out of the lavatories. So I ignored her. I felt quite peaceful and relaxed. The hall floor is quite clean. I often have a little lie down in the afternoons. And *where* I have my little lie down is nobody's business but mine. Is it?'

Mrs Patel obviously agreed.

'I thought she would go away. And then I heard her say that the lock was a bit dicky and stand back. Well, I thought, if she can get the landlord to fix it, so be it. And went off to sleep again. One does get tired you know, Mrs Patel.'

Mrs Patel had been listening with her eyes closed, leaning against the ice-cream chest. 'You certainly do,' she said.

'And then she broke the lock. Just like that. Bang. Threw herself at the door and the lock came away. Well, of course, I could have told her there was a trick to it—you only have to lift and push. The landlord knows, too, but he doesn't care.'

She smiled and tapped Mrs Patel lightly on the arm. Mrs Patel opened her eyes.

'I expect he does now,' she said. And closed her eyes again.

'Yes, indeed,' said Miss Phoebe Glen. 'Anyway, bang she went against the door. Which, of course, flew open. And she came through it like a torpedo and landed head first right up against the banisters. She was out like a light. And there we both were, stretched out on the hall floor with the door wide open to the street and a whole crowd of gawpers peering in. It was like having no clothes on. Someone said it was the bailiffs, at which I stood up and pointed out that it was not. Certainly not. Well, we've had those once and they wear bowler hats. Then someone else said I had knocked her out cold. I kept quiet at that. I quite liked the idea. Though, of course, it was the banisters, not me, to be perfectly correct.'

'You always are most correct.' Mrs Patel smiled.

Miss Phoebe returned the smile graciously. 'Then I asked them all if they wanted an encore, to shame them, and slammed the door, but it just blew open again. And when the girl came to, she had thankfully lost all that infernal brightness and good cheer and said I should be locked up for such behaviour. So I said, Well, if you will go breaking people's doors down when they are having a nap, what can you expect?

'Not this, she said, very shrilly, indicating the lump on her forehead. It did rather resemble an egg. I pointed that out as rather

251

amusing. We need to keep a sense of humour at such times, do we not, Mrs Patel?'

'We do,' said Mrs Patel, sadly. 'Oh, yes, we certainly do.'

'She went off very shakily and said she would return. Rubbish, I said. *Rubbish*, I called out after her. I said, Who will pay for a new lock? To which she said something *extremely* appropriate to the gutter. So now I have to prop the door closed with a board from the fence in my back garden. I'm next to one of those big houses, you know. The Baldwins. Complainers. Not very satisfactory. One side is mine, the other side is theirs, and I am never sure which is which. They are quite unfriendly, so I would not like to give them the opportunity to accuse me of stealing. Would I?'

Mrs Patel shook her head. That was the other worry about Ari, which she did not like to dwell upon. The till. His girlfriend liked films and drinks.

'They don't like the idea of a rented house in the road. Dress it up as for my own good. An old woman living on her own. They've been to the Council before. So they will no doubt try again. True, I did once end up in their front garden by mistake. But it was a mistake anybody could make, and it was only for half an hour while I rested. As I said to the girl from the Council, I am not a statistic, a number is not a person, and I do not know

252

what my social security code is. What is wrong with a mule now and again? I said. She had absolutely no answer to that. Social security? I told her. I am not a number, I am real—I am old but I am real. I told her, You will be old and real one day. That's if that lump on your head clears up. I thought that was quite funny. Anyway, she stood on the doorstep and she said she would be back. You and whose army? I asked. Letting my language slip a little in the heat of the moment, I am afraid. Anyway, I shall have my lodger soon. Then we will be an army. A united front. All for one and one for all. Norman will mend the lock.'

She laughed.

Mrs Patel dutifully joined in.

'It certainly taught her, that bump on the head did.' She laughed again and tapped her mittened finger against her nose. 'Feeling mulish,' she said, and had to hold her sides.

Mrs Patel nodded. 'Will there be anything else?' she asked wearily.

'No, thank you, Mrs Patel. Except that I hope you will come to the little party.'

Ani Patel said, very graciously, that she would love to come.

Miss Phoebe Glen opened the door of the shop, thought, turned, and added discreetly, 'You may bring some wine with you, if you wish.'

And then, nodding, she went off into the cold, starry night.

CHAPTER TWENTY-FOUR

Peter Pryor took the telephone off the hook. Up to a point he was prepared to be led—he looked at the pale blue box and its silver bow. Up to a point. But beyond that point, he would not go. And one of the points beyond which he would not go was in the choosing of where to have dinner. Mrs Hennessy, he felt, had done enough. He touched the box nervously. *Quite* enough.

He therefore booked a table for them at his new conversion, a one-time gravy powder factory in Wandsworth Old Town. It would be perfect. Quite large, quite noisy, quite good food, and quite expensive. Mrs Rosen would not be there, which was another excellent reason for the choice. He did not want Mrs Rosen to meet Pamela. You had to keep the Mrs Rosens of this world sweet. They liked to think they were the only woman in your life, and Peter would keep it that way. Pamela did not exist. Not yet. If Mrs Rosen was dining out, she would be at his other restaurant, the one with the draped chairs. He was wearing a blue linen suit and a pink tie (bowing to *Style and City*'s sartorial suggestion of current chic), with which he was not at all comfortable, but which, he hoped, would impress his ex-wife. It was all getting quite urgent on the Pamela front. Mrs

254

Rosen had quite a penetrating look. As if she could see right through him. As if she knew he was fading fast.

So he was making an effort for Pamela. Indeed, during the past few days, making an effort for Pamela had become the only priority. He would talk to her about his plans to take her to Dublin after he gave her the blue box with the silver bow and . . . and . . .

Why did he have the sinking feeling, after imagining that proposed scene, that he would like to run for it? He was not at all sure what the etiquette surrounding the seduction of one's ex-wife might be. He could not tell her that he loved her, because that would sound silly. And he could not tell her that he was burning with lust for her, because he was not. What he wanted to tell her was that, if she would have him, he would like to come back to her with the minimum of fuss. All he knew was that he needed her. And he certainly could not tell her that, either. Perhaps she would read the signs. Women were supposed to have a sixth sense for these things.

He tapped the box. He relied on his ex-mother-in-law at this point. He had never got it right with Pam before, so his instincts must be faulty. Women were the same throughout history, underneath, was what Mrs Hennessy's friend said. And red satin and ivory lace, so the woman in the lingerie department assured him, was very acceptable. He was willing to be led.

As soon as Daniel said, 'Mum. How are you? Sorry I haven't rung. It's really nice to hear you,' she knew something was up.

Now, searching through her wardrobe for something to wear for Peter, she was in emotional turmoil. Up until the very moment when she rang Danny earlier that evening, she was fine. Ready to give him hell, but fine. She had finished the shop accounts, she had finished all her costings, she was on top of everything, and she had given some comfort to Mrs Patel. So she felt really very *good* and liberated. In her cosy tea-time nest of drawn curtains and teapot for one, with a pile of Christmas cards to write, she had even congratulated herself on how pleasantly surprising life could be when you opened yourself up to it. Exhilarating. As if all the playing cards had flown up over her head when she threw them, and were now falling down into place. That, she thought, yanking open the other wardrobe door and dismissing a nice little black number with a large dollop of something down its front (what? and when?), was what life did to you. She was now a snivelling wreck. For a moment she thought about cancelling the date with Peter. And then she flopped on the bed, put her head in her hands and repeated the mantra, Kids, Kids,

Kids.

She had got through three serious relationships, all of which had engaged her heart, and she had survived, regrouped, grown. Was even ready to take one back if it suited her. And that, surely, was growing some? And now this. If she tried to tell Daniel what he had done, he would be stumped. Or laugh. The part of her that felt ashamed tried to tell the other part to grow up. It was as if you had two hearts. One for the other lot, and one for motherhood.

And she could positively *brain* Daniel for doing it. Just as she was contemplating a flirtatious night out with his father. It must be nearly twenty-five years since she flirted with him. Before Daniel's conception. There was little time or inclination for flirtation after that. The prospect was interesting . . . And safe. Or maybe not . . .

And then Danny—with all his conciliatory, charming, am-I-talking-to-Mrs-Idi-Amin stuff —the upshot being that they were going to spend Christmas in Liverpool, on their own, which Pamela thought, quite irrationally, was a bit thick, and said so.

She was then treated to a lecture from her son—well, maybe not quite a lecture, more a tutorial—on how they couldn't go to one set of parents without offending the other. To which Pamela, reasonably, she told herself, pointed out that The Girlfriend's parents lived in

Tenerife, which was not at all the same as slipping down the motorway for a couple of nights. And then Danny said in a hurt, surprised voice, '*Mum* . . .?' And she was surprised at herself for the sudden sense of abandonment that welled up.

She managed to say she understood, ring off, and weep. Partly at the news, and partly at the effect of knowing that, for the first time since he was born, she would not see her son on Christmas morning. She heard, floating around in the back of her mind, I Gave Up Everything For You . . . Freedom was a double-edged sword. She might look in the laundry basket and gaze happily upon the paucity of two brassieres and four pairs of knickers—but to also have to gaze lonely and forlorn up a dead turkey's bum on Christmas morning filled her with a shocking gloom.

She could hear—already—Jenny's kind voice saying, Oh, you must come to us. And there would be the Clarksons' Boxing Day party. Traditional. And no Daniel to play his guitar and sing carols. It was the thought of all that pity that brought about the final turmoil. She was an object of pity over Douglas, and she did not wish to be so again. Pity was for the disadvantaged, or silly old bats like her mother, she thought savagely, suddenly remembering that she wouldn't even have her to fall back on because she was in a Home, and Happy To Be There, and because she had a new friend with whom she had already made it quite clear she intended to sip her port and play Scrabble and share the parson's nose on Christmas Day.

'Tea and Daniel will be very nice, dear,' she said. 'But I don't think I'd like to be out. It might snow. You and Daniel and Lilian (she even remembered The Bloody Girl's name) can come and see me when you like.'

Bums, she thought savagely, and ignoring the sensible solution of the little black frock, which could, after all, be sponged, she kicked it across the floor, out of the door, along the corridor and down the stairs. By the time she got to the kitchen and gave it one final shot, so that it skidded across the floor and sent two empty milk bottles into orbit, she was in even more turmoil.

This could be the first signs of madness, she thought, picking up the dress and smoothing it, as if it were a once-beaten child. She peered through the kitchen window into the darkness of next door. Unless they were out in their garden in camouflage kit and sporting binoculars (always possible if someone attractive in the Soaps had taken up birdwatching), Peaches and Bud had not spotted this particular aberration. She returned the milk bottles to upright. And then she felt another clutch at her stomach. If she was here and alone for Christmas, the In Loving Sympathy of those two would be intolerable.

She returned to the bedroom and put on a dreadful saffron silk affair that made her look like a brightly draped piece of furniture about to chant for Hari Krishna. And out into the night she went, ready, just *ready*, for Peter to wince as she walked through the restaurant door. Just let him, she thought. Just let him.

In Bayswater, Peter Pryor tucked the silver and blue box beneath his arm, tightened his jaw, and set out into the night.

CHAPTER TWENTY-FIVE

By the time she arrived she was ready for a fight rather than the gentle unlocking of a familiar casket and a flirtatious peep within.

He was sitting peering at the menu, right in the middle of a huge room of full tables. A downlight threw a halo over his head, and glowed upon the pastel shades he wore. God, she thought, he's even more The Boyfriend tonight. Well, she could hardly talk, now could she, given that she looked like a piece of tangerine peel on legs? She shrank from the expectation of the wince. Just say the word, she warned him, as she floated, head high, through the sea of quiet chic, and I'll scream. Comforting thought.

When she arrived at the table he did two

things. One was to stand up—a totally unexpected piece of gallantry—and the second was to say, 'You look very nice.' Without wincing once.

Surprised, defeated, confused and somewhat weary of it all, she burst into tears.

His face registered the thought that This Was A Tricky One. He knew he had said the right thing. Mrs Hennessy had reminded him about that. Compliments. Plenty of compliments. What she had not told him was what to do if the recipient of the compliment showed distress. He took refuge in safety and the only thing that came to mind and said. 'Bad journey?' As if getting stuck on the Marylebone Road were akin to a trip with the Ancient Mariner.

'No,' she said, 'it was a very good journey.'

No Hiding Place. This made it awkward. He did not think she looked like a woman who had just undergone a good journey. He put his head on one side and tried to look enlightened. Happily the wine waiter hovered and Pamela stood up.

'I'll just go—um—' she said, eyes still streaming, and she floated off with the silk rippling all around her, a noticeable and noticed deviant in a sea of good taste.

He ordered champagne. This was instinct. He had the blue box with the silver bow nestling in the cloakroom and a taxi booked for eleven. This was not instinct but Mrs

Hennessy. Between them, he thought, they ought to achieve the capture of one ex-wife.

In the Ladies, denoted on the door by a stencilled fifties woman in a pinny pouring gravy from a jug (Pam thought sourly that they may not have had liberation in those days but they looked a great deal happier baking their scones and welcoming home their pipe-smokers), she replenished her mascara. Why, she thought irritably, did he have to go and start being kind *now*? She took a few deep breaths, and marched out again.

'Better?' he said.

'Time of the month,' she said brightly, wondering where women would be without their hormones.

He kept the smile on his face. He had forgotten all that. Kirsty had been moody all the time, the prerogative of the young. Moody and passionate, it had to be said, but in the end it was an exhausting combination. At least Pam was cheerful most of the time. Well, now they were no longer married she had always seemed so.

'Champagne,' she said, pleased, if still a little dewy around the eyes, and she began to look around her. 'You've done this really well,' she said. 'It suits the restraint.'

She meant it. He had adapted the cool functionalism of the original building perfectly. And the only obvious tribute to its past was a series of enlarged, grainy photographs showing rows of seated women in white coats and mob caps, overseen by assorted standing men in horn rimmed spectacles, white coats, their breast pockets bearing pens. She stared, fascinated by the women's faces. The making of gravy powder was honourable industry in those days, it seemed, and if nothing else, it had prised the women out of their houses. But did they want to go? she mused. Did they really want to go? It could become very wearing, being a something outside of the home.

He tapped the side of his glass with hers playfully. 'A bit austere perhaps,' he said. 'You would have brought a little more verve into the proceedings. I was thinking—' he swallowed— 'how nice it would have been if we had done it together.'

She looked at him. He smiled. 'We'd have made a great team,' he said, forgetting the fierce battles of the past and believing it momentarily.

He was not going to mention Brigham yet. He thought he would soften her up first.

'I realize that much of what I have achieved has a coldness to it.' He raised his glass to her. 'You would have given it warmth.'

Behind his glasses his eyes looked quite dreamy and wet and just a little pink. What with thinking about her sisters in gravy, and the continuing kindness from Peter, she burst into tears again. His smile wavered. For a

263

moment he wondered whether to telescope the proceedings and bring out the underwear. But he restrained himself. The very thought of that startling lacy satin tumbling over the pristine white tablecloths made him go cold. He stared very fixedly at the salt-cellar in case it might offer a solution. 'Do you want to go home?' he asked, a little tetchily.

'Home? Home?' she said, on a rising note. *'Home?'*

'Pam, this is my client's restaurant,' he said crossly. 'For God's sake keep your voice down.'

'Bugger the client,' she said, sniffing.

That was better. And on this note, with Peter behaving more normally, she pulled herself together and settled down.

'Sorry,' she said, eventually. And she asked him to order for her, which she knew he would like to do. Then she leaned back in her chair and watched his familiar gestures—the pushing of the glasses up the nose, the playing with the earlobe, the stroking of the underside of his neck, all indicators that he was concentrating and taking the choosing of the food very seriously. Home? she thought again. Home? And had to swallow very hard. There was a limit—oh, didn't she know it—to Peter's patience.

He ordered jugged hare for her. That was odd, because it was exactly the kind of comfort food she wanted. Familiarity sometimes had its compensations. He chose lemon sole, but was not above leaning over and dipping a corner of his bread into her plate, which was a friendly thing to do. And then, in a strange kind of reversal of Judas, he sucked the bread end thoughtfully and said, in the voice of one who wished he did not have to, 'I feel I have not been much help.'

Baldly, that was it. Mrs Hennessy had put it in a more flowery way, but that, in essence, was the message. Partly he agreed, and partly he did not. But he went along with it anyway. He leaned forward. 'I want to try. So, tell me—how are you?'

And Pam, ready for a bit of sympathy, said, 'Well, I'm not completely sure—it's all been quite difficult in a way . . .'

Not as difficult as it's been for me, he wanted to say, feeling his knee twinge as he shifted in his chair. But no, no—he must not do that—even if what he really thought was that it would make much more sense at this juncture to cut the crap and get on with it, despite what his ex-mother-in-law and the other old bat said about wooing. Just to say, 'You're on your own, I'm on my own, neither of us is getting any younger and we like quite a few of the same things. How about it?' But the voice of Mrs Hennessy was so fierce that he did not dare. Instead he looked warmly non-committal and gave a grunt. Suddenly he felt all at sea. Kirsty used to throw things. Which was fine. All he had to do was duck. This, now—he shifted in his chair again and tried to think of something to say—*this* . . .

'The thing is—' she began. And then she looked up at him. He did not appear encouraging of intimacies. His eyes had gone a bit peculiar and he held up his hand as if to admonish her for speaking, pointing to the empty champagne bottle in the cooler. Nevertheless, she thought, he did ask. But before she could unburden herself further, he said, 'Shall we stick with that or how about a nice red burgundy for your game?'

Pam nodded impatiently and said, 'Burgundy,' flatly. To which he nodded, pleased, and said, 'Good, good.' She had a passing thought that he was ordering red wine—not part of the usual landscape of his considerations and some kind of breakthrough—but she let it go. And waited.

He grabbed the subject of burgundy wholeheartedly until the waiter arrived, and then, while he went away to produce the order, Peter waxed even more lyrical on the subject of the service here, which was, he pointed out, excellent. Listen to me, she thought. But she did not say it aloud as she would once have done. 'Lovely,' she said. Because she rather wanted to give this a chance to work. Somewhere, buried in Peter, was the man she once loved. It would be nice to find him again. She guessed he must be thinking approximately the same about her.

The waiter returned to show him the bottle. Feeling the air between them grow heavier by the minute, and himself grow heavier by the minute also, he pounced on the bottle and gazed at it fondly until the waiter became quite irritated and Peter was forced to conclude it should be opened.

He then began to talk shop. Pamela, realizing that to return to the personal was not likely to make the evening go with a swing, began to talk shop back. Peter then wrested his eyes away from the cow-moulded cornicing and relaxed again. Safe harbour.

Oddly enough, she decided that she did not mind. She knew him well enough. Once she would have been at the peel-me-off-the-ceiling stage by now, but—well, All Passion Spent was true, she supposed. She would enjoy the evening on his terms. At least he was paying. And at least with Peter she did not have to make an effort. They were what they were to each other, utterly familiar, despite his strange sortie into pastel shades and meat juice and talk about the feminizing of design. And, of course, between them they had a son. At which thought she very nearly made a dash for the smiling lady with the jug and pinny again, and would have done had she not thought the other diners might think her in the early stages of incontinence.

After half a bottle of champagne and a third

of a bottle of good red wine, she decided that she had quite enjoyed herself. Daniel and Christmas had not been raised. A few safe reminiscences—it was enough. She had attempted the odd little bit of flirtation. 'I like your glasses,' she said, lifting them off his nose. 'Very sexy.' She was about to try them on herself when he grabbed them, put them back, and went very pink.

'Nothing wrong with being sexy,' she said sweetly, 'even at our age.' And then added, daring to be roguish, 'You look cute when you screw up your eyes like that . . . Dangerous.' She raised an eyebrow and smiled.

It did not seem to get her very far. He immediately called for the bill.

They departed cheerfully. Peter was glad to be into stage two of the evening and hurried her along. Pamela felt good about it all. Easy. Relaxed. Nothing to hide.

In the taxi she leaned against him and said, 'Do you remember my father's speech at our wedding?'

He stared at her, panicking. 'Yes,' he said.

'Do you remember the piece of poetry he quoted?'

'Remind me,' he said, panicking even more. He had a vague notion of the quotation being highly unsuitable. And he was not altogether sure where his arm should be.

She was about to say that she knew perfectly well he could not remember it at all, when he held her arm by the elbow, which felt nice after the absence of any intimacy for so long. Even elbows have sensual possibilities in the right mood.

He then said, 'What I remember very clearly about our wedding is how lovely you looked.'

Her eyes pricked again. She forgot to pursue the Catullus.

Peter felt it had gone well. He knew what he was going to say when they got there; he had prepared the speech quite carefully, with his ex-mother-in-law's advice. Eileen, it seemed, had been in some kind of counselling business and knew a thing or two about these things. Her advice had been to pep himself up a bit, and he felt that he had. And now, here they were. He felt very confident.

As the taxi drew up outside the house, and Pamela was still protesting that he did not need to escort her all the way home, he hopped out, paid the fare, opened her gate and asked if he could come in for a cup of coffee. Even to him this sounded lame. But he could hardly split hairs and ask if she had anything herbal. He would just have to have those night-time pulse rates and accept them as part of the sacrifice.

'Of course,' she said, thinking nothing of it and getting out her keys while he lounged against the wall. She fumbled a bit, so he took her bag from her in what he thought was a debonair and proprietorial fashion and threw it over his shoulder. He was quite unselfconscious about using shoulder bags, calling them sensible things and even designing a couple for himself. He was so talented, thought Pamela. It was nice to be with a man who was so much his own person.

The door was opened. Pamela prepared to enter. Peter then went extremely peculiar.

From his casual leaning position he suddenly shot bolt upright, slapped his head and said, 'Oh, fuck,' twice. Loud enough, she thought, for Peaches to hear and conclude that she and her friends never said anything else. He then said, 'Fuck,' for the third time, jumped up and down, ran back up the path, leapt over the gate, showing a facility for hurdling she had never known he possessed, immediately got hooked on the post and bounced back against the gate by the dangling of her bag straps, yelled, dragged the bag off his shoulder and threw it at her, shouted 'Fuck' once more, with feeling, and ran off down the road calling, 'Hi, hi . . .'

Must be the drink, she thought, astonished, and tottered to the end of the path, retrieved her bag, and watched him run up the road and appear to rugby tackle the departing taxi with a Tarzan-like cry.

The taxi seemed unperturbed by this and accelerated, as, clinging to the door handle, did Peter. There was an exchange of unpleasantness before it finally stopped and she saw Peter give a little dignified shake and open the passenger door to take something out. He then came running back with it, arms outstretched, as if he were doing the relay. She opened the gate in case he hurdled and missed this time, and he thrust a box into her arms, saying, both puffed and irritated, 'For you.' He then went limp and gasped for breath. He bent his leg and rubbed at his knee. 'Fuck,' he said again.

'Do you mind?' said Pam. Even Daniel's friends had been circumspect about language on the front porch.

In the house she peered into the wrappings, puzzled. 'Is it an early Christmas present?' she asked. 'For me?'

He shook his head.

'For Danny?'

He gasped that it was not. 'Oh, go on,' he said, abandoning Mrs Hennessy's suggestion of seductive subtlety.

'Just as well it is *not* for Danny,' she said sharply, off on her emotional high horse at last, 'because Danny will not be coming home for Christmas.'

She delivered this very dramatically and paused for effect.

Peter stared at her, almost enraged.

'Open it,' he said, much more commandingly than he might have had he not just done the Olympic sprint.

She went into the kitchen and switched on

271

the kettle. Peter danced around her nervously. 'Open it,' he said.

'I only just found out today,' she said. 'Oh, yes—Daniel Pryor cannot come to London for Christmas with his mother because he wants to spend the whole time in bed in Liverpool with a tit of a girl having peculiar sex.' The wine was not helping restraint.

The tension was not helping Peter.

He indicated the discarded box with an impatient bash and creased the lid. 'For you,' he said.

'He's definitely staying in Liverpool. Christmas and no Danny. Can't quite believe it, really. I don't know what I'm going to do.' She looked up at him with welling eyes.

Not more tears, he thought. He picked up the battered box and shoved it at her. 'For God's sake open it,' he practically bellowed. And then something registered. He paused. Lowered his voice. 'Peculiar sex?' he said, with interest.

Better not go into that, she thought, so she opened the box instead.

While she untied the bow in a slow, methodical, smoothing process that nearly drove him berserk again, he began to think. And he had a sudden, wonderful inspiration. The speech he had prepared with the help of his ex-mother-in-law faded away. Here was an altogether better opportunity. While Pamela gazed in silent astonishment and attempted to

272

regain her eyeballs at the layers of tissue and the satin and lace, Peter lowered his voice and said, in the most persuasive tone he could manage, 'Then why don't you fly out and spend Christmas in Dublin with me?'

Pamela, holding up an extraordinary confection of satin and lace, the nature of whose application was unclear, looked up at him with wide, astonished eyes. 'What?' she found herself saying. 'Fly out on an aeroplane?'

Peter was not going to be diverted. And he was proud of himself for not saying, No—on a bloody donkey. Instead he just smiled, gave himself a great big red tick and ten Brownie points and said, 'We can go on a magic carpet if you like.' And his fingers, slightly squeamishly, it was true, touched the filmy satin very hesitantly, while behind him the electric kettle gave a long, low whistle, like a bawdy cherub, to indicate that steam was very definitely up.

CHAPTER TWENTY-SIX

Douglas was talking to himself. He could cancel. Even at this late stage, he could cancel. It would not be a very nice thing to do, but, then, this was deeper than nice, or polite, or any of those social things. He paced the floor of his office. He looked at the pad on his desk. There was the number. He had only to pick up the phone, cancel the table, and then it would be over. It was now a quarter to four. He was due to collect her at six-thirty—he heard her voice again, remembering the surprise at his suggesting such an early hour, and how he lied and said that he had to be back home early. She sounded—though it was well-disguised—disappointed. Which pleased him at the time. It made the whole plan more tantalizing. And now he was afraid of it.

He called Zoe, which was almost automatic, thinking she would produce the life-line he needed. It was the only thing he could think of as time drew on. He looked at his watch, felt vaguely uneasy about the inscription, but that was the way things went. Never look back. So what was he doing now?

Even if this proved a one-off—which is as far as he had thought it through—even as a one-off it was crazy. Already he felt weakened by longing.

When Zoe answered, she said she had the interior designer in, as well as Lionel. She gave a laugh that meant Lionel was nearby and said, 'Guess what—we're having the same curtaining. Isn't that sweet? The peacocks. What a hoot. And we are both being—' she turned aside from the telephone for a moment—'What would you call it, Lionel—hung? *Hung.*'

'Oh, good,' he said, as flatly as he could, hoping she would realize. But she did not.

'I must say,' said Zoe archly, 'that old girlfriend of yours did well in the end. Or her assistant did. She might not be much cop generally, but she knows her job.'

So how could Douglas then say, 'I'm seeing Pamela for dinner tonight,' and let her spin her dissuasive web?

'You could come over,' she said. 'See how they look.'

'Working late,' he said, feeling stupid, like an errant husband. He added, 'Your brother says beware Lionel.' He felt a stab of fear. Don't leave me now, he wanted to say.

She laughed again. 'I know what I'm doing.'

He sometimes wondered. Last week she told him, all excited, that she had persuaded Lionel to give her some highly suspect slimming pills. She also said, mystifying, that Lionel bothered to listen to her. 'Of course he's a bore, really,' she said this defensively. 'But what the hell? No one has ever listened to me like him before. I never thought of a doctor.'

'But Leighton Buzzard, Zoe?' he said, expecting her to capitulate.

'Oh, well,' she said, 'we don't talk about that.'

'And bald?' He felt angry. 'And boring?'

'Only slightly thinning,' she said. 'And someone who listens is never, ever boring.'

275

It wasn't love, obviously, but she was happy to use him for a while.

He supposed at just the wrong (or did he mean at just the right?) time he was off her hook.

He put the phone down, turned, looked out of the window at the London skyline, which he had once thought about giving up—and was resolved. He would go through with it. Why not? It was only an invitation to dinner. Not to breakfast. And not to the rest of her life. Zoe was right all those years ago. He was not cut out for the domestic life and he never would be. But having dinner was all right. He was offering nothing. Neither was she. It was dinner. Just dinner. With a little diversion on the way. If he cancelled, it would be the action of a shit. He did not want Pamela to think of him like that any more. He wanted to put some of it right. It was only dinner, only . . . And the truth was, he was looking forward to it.

*   *   *

Pamela gripped the telephone like a life-line. 'Margie,' she said, 'I can't hear you for the thundering of my heart. And I appear to be incapable of breathing.'

'Have a drink,' said Margie.

'I've already had a weak Martini.'

'Have a strong one, have a pile driver. Take

276

a Valium. No, second thoughts—don't take a Valium. You might end up slumped over the table and snoring with your mouth open.'

'Thanks.'

'You'll be fine.'

'It's the doorbell, Margie!

'Go and answer it, then. And remember—don't show your hand until he does . . . Or your fanny.'

'You are disgusting. And it is only dinner. An early one. He's even got his escape route lined up. Oh, Margie—what am I doing?'

'Go.

*   *   *

In the car it felt odd. So familiar, yet at such a distance. She knew exactly how he held the steering wheel, how he moved the gears, even knew his views on the value of gears over automatics. He liked to feel in charge. He was the same in bed. God, she thought, watching the grimy North Circular flash by, how much I would like that right now. And she thought about reaching out and running her fingers along his thigh.

She resisted. There was nothing in his manner to say she had permission to do more than give and receive the greeting kiss on the cheek. And she did not want the humiliation of rejection. They drove in silence for a while. Not an easy silence. But she did not know how to break it. She could hardly look out of the window and admire Leatherland and Ikea.

'I'm really sorry about this,' he said eventually. 'But I've got to see this contributor before the weekend. It won't take a moment and then we can go to a Greek place I know in Barnet.'

She felt humiliated. He was just fitting her in. The slight disappointment over his need to be back home early gave way to real depression. Why have I come? she wondered.

'Fine,' she said brightly. And she gave the pretence of a little relaxed yawn.

She expected him to take her somewhere of which the *Tatler* would approve. Quaglino's or maybe The Ivy. She was wearing the little black number, now sponged, and very silly high heels, along with black seamed stockings that cost practically as much as the dress. If not Tatler-friendly, she would have bet money on somewhere new, interesting and exotic, and that hardly sounded like a Greek place in Barnet. But she trusted him. And at least they wouldn't end up in one of Peter's creations.

'Where does this contributor live?' she asked.

'Oh—out of town a little way.'

She leaned back against the dark blue suede. Of course he would be driving a Saab, she thought sardonically. It said it all. Even she, who was what Daniel called car-illiterate, knew that. Before, when they were together, he drove a nippy little something that roared like a tiger, and laughed at the possibility of actually needing a Range Rover when they moved to the country.

She felt the barest possibility of a tear pricking at her eyes. 'Is this new?' she asked quickly, stroking the suede, which was so near to his thigh that she almost groaned.

'Got it yesterday,' he said.

'I like it.' She leaned back.

He was pleased. She saw his smile. So simple, men, she thought.

*   *   *

They talked of nothing for the next half an hour. Of shoes and ships and sealing wax, she found herself thinking, as she oozed into it all again. Of cabbages and kings . . . And she decided that this was a little bit of heaven—or something not far off, though she kept the thought to herself in case he laughed. She was even polite about Zoe, which cost her; they avoided the subject of peacocks. She congratulated him on his magazine and he, in turn, was pleased the shop was doing so well.

'And Daniel?' he said, perhaps a little too lightly.

'Got a two-one,' she said. 'He's happy.'

I am not going to discuss my miserably traitorous son, she thought. So she changed the subject to the number of contractors' traffic cones lining their route.

'Seem to have been building this bit of road for ever,' he said.

And then it began to dawn on her, very slowly, that they were driving down a very familiar route. But that would be nonsense. And, anyway, he probably wouldn't remember. Look at Peter and the Catullus. She had better say nothing in case he thought her sentimental.

She closed her eyes as they sped along. Truth was, even a Greek place in Barnet would be good. Or anywhere. Because whatever it was that caused her to be the opposite of what her mother called 'a bit jaded' was still there between them. She kept her eyes closed, savouring it all. Romance and passion, she mused, is the sparkle of life.

And then, God help her, she fell asleep.

This was hardly surprising, since she had scarcely slept a wink the night before and was rushed off her feet all day because Jenny and the Amazon were out and about. But to fall asleep? She was so ashamed when she awoke that she did not open her eyes at once. She tried, as surreptitiously as possible, to close her mouth. Which was very open. Not just delicately parted lips, but sagging, right open, probably with dribble. The car was still going fast and she had no idea for how long she was out for the count. For all she knew, they could have reached Wells-next-the-Sea by now. She decided to give the impression of one who has merely closed her eyes for thought.

She gave what she thought was a suitably positive 'Ah' and very casually looked about her. They were passing through countryside and, though it was dark, the moon and the stars were bright enough to show that it was very flat countryside. Not Barnet, not Enfield, and certainly not cone country. She must have been dribbling for nearly an hour. And then she saw the sign that said they were crossing the Little Ouse. She turned to him, as casually as she could. He stared straight ahead, negotiating.

'You snore,' he said, 'like a navvy.'

She prodded his knee with her index finger. It was as much as she dared.

She felt warm and lazy as a cat and had to remind herself that she was forty-eight and not exactly sinewy.

'How many navvies have you slept with?' she said, and then, not liking to think of what he might or might not have been doing during their years apart, added, 'So we are going to The Swan?'

'The Swan?' he said, negotiating an old humped bridge a little too bravely. 'What's that?'

She smiled. 'Sorry,' she said, leaning back, stretching, yawning properly this time, for now she knew. No more best behaviour, no more nerves. 'For a moment there,' she said, 'I thought you'd gone all romantic.'

281

'Did you now?'

She pushed her legs out in front of her to enjoy the warm blast of air. Sleeping, mouth dribbling or not, had done nothing to dampen her ardour.

She sighed and looked at him. And he ran his fingers lightly along her thigh. When he reached the fixing of her suspender and stocking-top, she saw him smile. She wondered, at that precise moment, if it was not the sexiest particle of time she had ever encountered in her life. She peered out at the darkness. The moon was very bright, the stars were clear as diamonds. And then, quite suddenly, he stopped the car. In the middle of nowhere. And got out.

She sat bolt upright. They were only about ten minutes drive from The Swan. Why stop? Maybe he needed a pee? Should she get out? She fixed her gaze on the headlit darkness, and waited. Sensuality had given way to panic. She was wearing high heels and not much else. And it was sub-zero out there. So much for the cat-like curling. Were all men mad?

He was round at the back of the car, opening the boot. Then he was back, opening the passenger side door, kneeling down, putting his hand in and gently taking her foot to slip off her shoe. Despite the suddenly bitter coldness of the air, she sat there thinking along the lines of just giving up and orgasming on the spot, and might have done, had she not suddenly felt him slip something else over her stockinged toes. Looking down she saw it was her old walking boot. He did not look up, but took the other foot, and did the same. Then he kissed her on the insides of her knees so that she went very faint, and needed the hand he offered to help her out.

Standing was quite difficult. She understood the meaning of the phrase 'weak with emotion'. I am Weak with Emotion, she thought with satisfaction. And took the opportunity to lean against him. A groan was not far off.

She looked down at the boots like a child, and then up at him. He was holding out a quilted jacket that was not exactly in the pink—she peered as he began to help her into it, and she recognized it as her own.

'You kept them?' she said, amazed. In the pocket she felt a half-eaten packet of Polo mints. Six years old. Six years . . .

He was already bending down, removing his shoes, replacing them with his boots. 'You left them in the boot of the car,' he said. She remembered the pink umbrella and felt she had triumphed over Zoe after all.

'I gave you everything back,' she said. 'Everything.'

She touched the back of his neck and felt him freeze for a second. Still she did not know. After all, they were such laws unto themselves, these wondrous lumps of masculinity, that he might simply have brought her out here for a midnight stroll and a packet of sandwiches.

When he stood up she could not read his eyes—but neither, she counselled herself, could he read hers. 'Dinner's in one hour,' he said, and he touched her face with his cold finger. And the other phrase I now understand, she thought, is 'his touch burned'. She thought she would enjoy telling Margie that, she being so disapproving of cold celibacy. Hah!

He took her hand and put it into his pocket with his own just like he used to do, and led her off. 'I thought we could work up an appetite.'

She went quietly, if you chose not to hear the hammering of her heart. Sparkle? *Sparkle*? This was full-blown Krakatoa.

She walked behind him, hand still in his pocket, like grandmother's footsteps, until the track opened out. It was impossible to know with Douglas exactly what method he had selected for the working up of an appetite, but she had her own preference. Nike was crowing in the trees, along with the complaining rooks. Douglas asked over his shoulder if she was all right and she just about managed to say that she was.

They walked, or—she remembered Mrs Patel—they tramped, along the footpath. It was dark, full of trees and rustlings, but she did not feel afraid. His holding her hand felt as natural as putting one foot in front of the other. This was where she felt at home, both in the landscape and with the person. Only once more did he speak, and that was to ask if she was warm enough. 'Oh, yes,' she said, thinking that the heart of a volcano feels no frost. It was so cold that their boots scrunched as if crushing old glass. A good sound, close to nature, all that.

Then silence. No more rooks, no more rustlings. They were at the edge of a field. Ridged and bare and bathed in moonlight. Far off, across the flatness, the lights from some house or cottage sparkled for them. The rest was cold stillness and absolute calm. They stood there, breathing. She let go of his hand. He turned to take it again. She shook her head. 'You go on,' she whispered.

He stared questioningly.

He said, with so much control in his voice that she realized he had not spoken before for fear of losing it, 'I haven't been here since. Have you?'

'No,' she lied, afraid suddenly of being so vulnerable. She wanted to stand here, alone, and watch him. That was all she could think of at that moment.

He went to take her hand again and she resisted, so he left her and walked away across the flat expanse, the moonlight making him a figure from a dream, all silvery and shining. Unreal. When he reached the top of the field she could still just see him. And then, before she knew what she was doing, she was flying. Not quite stumbling in the ridges and furrows of the ice-hard earth as she flew. She watched him open his arms and she ran, and ran, and ran for all her worth right up to them and into them, pushing her leg between his for warmth and wriggling and wriggling and wriggling herself as if she would burrow right into and through him.

He held her, almost squeezing out her breath, so tightly that he made her spine crack. And then she was reaching into the depths of the old quilting, pulling at her skirt, no longer aware of the cold, pulling at it feverishly right up over her hips, her belly, her breasts. Behind them an owl hooted, a fox screamed, but they were oblivious to it. She was aware of herself sinking into more than his flesh. Sinking and sinking. Stuck fast and like a holed ship, which metaphor seemed grandly appropriate at that moment, sinking and sinking even further, faster. Everything came out of her, every forgotten feeling, every fear, every hope. She knew—so clearly in the middle of the vortex—that he felt the same. Edge of the field, edge of the universe, edge of edge in every sense. And in another moment of clarity, when she was so happy it seemed the perfect moment to die, she thought, This is not safe harbour, this is disaster at sea.

Then she allowed the groan. A whole six years of it, carrying on the still night, scraped

286

from the insides of her, leaving her empty.

Afterwards she resisted saying, 'Love.' It was the first time she had ever held anything back from him.

*   *   *

In the car they were silent. Touching each other on hand, neck, hair, but not speaking, as if what had taken place was too recent for words. She just smelled herself into the quilting and thought the scent of it must be the smell of where he now lived. A new smell. She liked it.

'I'm hungry,' she said.

He drove recklessly until she put a hand on his arm and he slowed down again. 'Not that hungry,' she said.

In the restaurant he was surprised at how unchanged it all was. Pam feigned a similar surprise. 'Gracious,' she said.

It was only romantic because of what they brought to it. Otherwise it was regulation dark polished wood tables, spindle-backed chairs, Staffordshire copies and old brassware dotted around the walls. The log fire was still real, still generous. She felt a little afraid at the perfection of preservation—as if it were a stage set or a mausoleum to their memory. So much love turned into that saccharine thing called Our Place.

They smiled at each other and Pam let the

joy in. He leaned across the table and ran his finger over the backs of her fingers. Neither of them knew what to say so they laughed. They were self-conscious, shy of each other, desperate to touch again. No words seemed necessary. If it was a shipwreck, thought Pam, it was a bloody good one.

The waitress told them the soup of the day, parsnip and potato garnished with rocket, and they had to look away from each other or laugh. Or they could have morning-gathered, dew-drenched battered mushrooms . . . Douglas managed to hold on to his laughter. Pam dared not open her mouth. The waitress, politely waiting, looked down at Pam's boots. He had insisted. Boots and no knickers. 'It's a deal,' she had said. She rather regretted it now. Not for acceding, but for the sadnesses that lay behind the fun.

Douglas looked down at the boots and up at her pointedly. 'Can't take her anywhere,' he said to the waitress, who clearly sympathized. Her heart caught for a moment. She missed his jokes. Those things that made lovers private for ever, no matter where they were in the world.

Laughter and love, she thought, the relish of life. And on that note she picked up the menu.

Later he picked up her hand and kissed it.

'Are you OK?'

She shook her head.

'Me neither,' he said.

She said, 'I loved it. Out there.'

He put her hand back carefully on the table, picked up his glass, and drank. 'To you,' he said.

'And you?'

He hesitated. 'To me, then.'

'I didn't mean that.'

He was silent.

'Tell me, Douglas. And you?'

He seemed to hesitate. And then he put his hand in his pocket and took out an envelope. Before he handed it to her, he said, 'Why did we let it go?'

And a small spurt flicked out of the volcano. She thought, *We?*

Then he gave her the envelope.

'Have a look at that,' he said. 'I wondered if you would like to come.'

She drew it out slowly and read. Had the world gone mad or had she gone mad? Or had Dublin just become the epicentre of the universe?

'Maybe over Christmas?' He shrugged, a little embarrassed, waiting for her to be pleased.

And then the question came. Once more she could sense it, and she could hear the tightening in his throat. 'How's Daniel?' he said.

'Very well. Just the same.'

'He'll be—very grown up now?'

She was alert for double meanings. She

guessed he meant, Will Daniel want to come with us? It was understandable, she reasoned. And she held the contents of the envelope out, trying to make sense of it. The words moved hither and thither. She was remembering with both pain and anger how he had not stood by her during the difficult times. He had just fucked off, hadn't he? She controlled the thought. She could still feel where he had been inside her. Maybe that was enough?

'Still at home?'

'Yes,' she said, very deliberately, she who usually could never lie to anyone, and she watched his face.

'You could still come?'

She looked down at the letter in her hand and read it carefully this time.

It was impossible, wasn't it? Dublin again?

'For Christmas?' she said flatly.

'Why not? If you like,' he said. 'Daniel could go to Peter.'

Burned, she thought. *Burned.*

CHAPTER TWENTY-SEVEN

For a while—two days, to be precise—Pamela wondered if she was really up to any of it. Apart from two invitations to Dublin for Christmas, a state of affairs difficult enough to absorb, the open blue box sat like a simpering toad on her window-seat and a torn stocking hung raggedly over the bedroom chair. Talisman—or warning? She was not sure. She had asked for space from both of them. They gave it with quiet confidence. Women were ever neurotic. The Princess of Choices has breathing space, she thought. The Dowager has breathing space, you mean, replied the mirror helpfully.

She must see Dean. But unless he had obligingly done a fast-acceleration Dorian Gray and gone to wrinkled seed in approximately twelve weeks, the contrast between them would be as sharp as ever.

'And where would your mother like to sit?' She could hear the potential waiter's kindly voice even now. Which is why she suggested she cooked for them at home. Except Dean put his foot down. In the end they compromised and agreed that she would dine there. Dean would cook. She tried very hard to remove the feeling of being a visiting parent when he said he'd have to clean up a bit first.

Rick was irritatingly on the job. Almost coaching her. Ringing up, coming round, telling her it was what the Continentals did all the time: older woman, younger man. *They* understood all right.

'*They* might,' she told him. 'But we happen to be living in Chiswick, which is—despite the European Union—not a place given over to *la dolce vita*.'

As for crow's feet. In this light it looked more like she'd met with an ostrich farm. And has Elizabeth Taylor got any tips on how to rejuvenate? she wondered. Scrubbing down with bleach, perhaps, or a good rub-down with sandpaper? The embarrassment of the spoons haunted her. If she ever saw Lionel next door, she ducked. And she once spent several minutes draped over the passenger seat while he parked and got out of his car. She had not forgiven him for taking so long about it; she practically gave up, revealed herself and offered to help.

According to Jenny and the Amazon, things were hotting up between Lionel and Zoe. She felt responsible. The condemned man might eat a hearty breakfast, but Zoe would just have him for hers. Not my problem, she said stoutly, and tried to look on the bright side. A doctor ought to have more sense.

Some things were going smoothly. The builder had nearly finished the study. And Daniel, beloved, insensitive, lout of a son, was showing signs of conscience. He sent her a bouquet of flowers a few days after the Christmas announcement—red and white (like blood on the snow, she thought sourly) and a postcard of the Liverpool Tate. As if to tell her that he was being a beloved, sensitive, cultivated son, but with a life of his own. She supposed that was right. It just seemed so sudden. Anyway, she was female, and the flowers were a start.

Now for Dean. Lighten up, oh, please, she wanted to say to him when he rang to confirm. He sounded so excited. How can I possibly live up to that? she wondered. She nearly postponed the whole thing—to protect him, she told herself, but maybe to protect herself. Being with Douglas for just one night had dented her enough. If not holed her for good.

Dean might want to be treated like an equal, but she had news for him. You were not a big, grown-up equal person even when you reached her grand old age. Something always came along to make you little and thin and weak again. In her case Dublin's apparent transformation into a Mecca for rejuvenating dead relationships. The fact that Dean came from Dublin in the first place did not escape her. She refused to think about it. She was feeling rather battered—as much by her own hand as anybody else's—and she wanted comfort.

The study was a comfort as it took shape. Daniel was now erased as son of the house. It was like one of those photographs from Lenin's cabinet office. One minute Trotsky was standing there with a cheery grin, the next he was not and never had been. Sometimes she wondered if she should have done something so drastic so soon. But, remembering Queen Victoria's domestic shrines to Albert, she decided it was necessary and for the best.

Daniel was living and breathing out there in the world. Shrines were not necessary.

Rick called in, yet again, on the pretext of picking up some of his music, and stayed for two pots of tea. Vanessa only gave him herbal or fruit and so Pamela was his fixer for caffeine. But in the end she threw him out because he kept looking at his watch and saying things like, Well, better go so you can tart yourself up, or, Well, better go so you can make yourself seductive. And playing little riffs of 'It's Now Or Never'. People loved to live their braveries vicariously. Left alone, he would probably broaden out into a medley including 'Love is Lovelier the Second Time Around' and 'September Song'. He was high as a kite on Brooke Bond.

'Get back to your wife,' she said.

As he left he put his two fingers up in a solidarity V sign and said, 'Peace and Love. And remember why we went to Woodstock. Love, not prejudice. You are not old.'

But she never was at Woodstock. When everyone was at Woodstock, she was fresh out of college ready to burn into the world and change its shape and its colour for ever. The following year she married Peter.

Stop growling to yourself, she warned, as she went upstairs. And tart yourself up a bit . . . It was the jeans and the pink sweater again. So easy. She began to feel better. No standing on any kind of ceremony for Dean. He wouldn't care if she turned up in Crimplene.

*   *   *

Dean Close stood in the kitchen, holding a bag of mutton chops, waiting for the sound of the door to bang closed. When it did, he breathed a sigh of relief. That was the last of them. Keith had gone off to his mother's for the night. Julian was staying over at Alice's. At last he was alone. Well, him and two pounds of mutton chops. He was going to make an Irish stew, which was now on the menu of the trendy pub down the road. He asked his mother for the way to do it and she told him over the phone. It was more simple than he imagined. And it could be left to cook for hours if necessary. Or eaten for breakfast instead. He tried not to think about that. He had to concentrate. He turned the radio up loud and began the preparations. When she arrived he would put on the Segovia. He knew what she liked. If she wanted maturity, he could give her maturity.

He had never cooked a thing in his life beyond toast or eggs or stuff and he found himself enjoying it. As he chopped and trimmed and sealed, he thought he could do this for a living. He threw up an onion, twirled round, caught it as it came down. He just felt so happy. The others could take the piss all they liked, but happiness was happiness,

295

however odd it seemed to the rest of the world. As he said, if they were going to get all lathered up about an age difference, why not about colour of skin? Or being gay? That shut Keith up. But Alice just shook her head. She was still furious with him for the way he treated Deirdre.

He whistled. He pulled out the big pot from the back of the cupboard and washed out the cobwebs. He had three hours and then she would be here. The bed needed changing. The bathroom needed cleaning. Then he would hoover. Nothing would spoil the evening, nothing. And she was on her own now—no reason for her to go back home. Nothing, nothing, nothing. Great. And this time the chocolates he had bought were plain. He was learning. In fact, he was probably there.

Chop, chop he went at the parsley, as neat and small as he could manage, lining it up on the board next to the perfectly sliced onions. It was true, cooking was relaxing. As a career, it was a thought. Suddenly it really felt as if he had a future. That was the way she made him feel.

*　　　*　　　*

'The last time I was here,' she said, 'someone had thrown scrambled egg at the wall.'

'Alice,' he said. 'Hell of a temper. But she also does most of the cleaning so—' He shrugged. Small talk, small talk.

'It all looks pristine.'

'I did quite a lot.'

Her eyes took in the clear surfaces, the table washed down, neatly laid, with candlesticks and long white candles and the voluminous paper serviettes, best quality, which he had folded just so. And a flower, silk, she thought, but did not check. Would Daniel ever be capable of this?

'I'm impressed,' she said, trying to sound like a visiting aunt.

'Just don't pat me on the head.'

He said it mockingly. Age had brought confidence to him. She felt a little disconcerted to find him so completely unabashed. She laughed. Now she was here she was glad. There is something magical, she thought, about making any man's eyes light up when they see you. And also the openness of youth. Peter and Douglas disguised and suppressed. Dean, when he opened the door to her, wore his heart on his sleeve.

'You really are cooking,' she said.

And behind her she heard him say, 'And you really are here.' And her heart gave a little flip.

'Are we alone?' she said, mocking herself.

He nodded and came up and stood close. She kissed his cheek and moved away.

'It smells wonderful,' she said.

Now they were standing opposite each other, with the table in between, and he was pulling the cork from a bottle. He smiled. He looked pleased that she could remember such a small detail as scrambled eggs on the wall. 'Do you remember Alice? Julian's girlfriend?' he said. 'You met once at the Camden.'

Pam nodded. Touching the back of the chair lightly, she said, 'Does she still introduce you to her friends?'

He poured the wine.

'I've gone through the lot, I think.'

'In what way?' she asked. Dangerous territory, but she wanted dangerous territory.

'Every way.'

'Have you been a promiscuous boy?'

'Promiscuous, yes. Boy, no,' he said, and raised his glass. 'Cheers.'

She raised hers and responded. He reached over and touched her hand.

'You should always make eye contact with the person you are raising your glass to,' he said. 'That's the whole point of it.'

They chinked glasses again. His eyes spoke very clearly. For the first time her resolve left her and she wondered if they would end up in bed after all. It was an odd experience to be ambivalent. And relaxing. After everything that had happened since Danny left home, it was really relaxing to be here. She felt warm and indulgent and full of affection. And inclined to let what might happen, happen.

'It should be Guinness,' he said, indicating the bottle of wine.

'Why?'

'Because I've cooked an Irish stew. You always have the black Liffey water with an Irish stew.'

She lifted the lid off the pot and sniffed. 'It smells—' she could not resist saying it—'as good as you.' He came up close behind her but she moved away. 'Guinness? Well,' she said, 'let's go and get some.'

She picked up her coat and out they went. For tranquility's sake she kept her hands in her pocket as they rushed along the cold pavements. And she moved too fast for him to hold on to her. Never again did she want to be seen holding his hand. Dean was unaware what happened when they accidentally bumped into Alice at Camden Market that day. Of course she remembered meeting Alice. How could she forget? One minute they were standing there, hand in hand, the next Dean spotted her coming towards them and automatically, without thinking, tugged his hand away from hers so that Alice should not see. She understood, but at the same time it made her feel like a lecherous old quean.

She reached the shop before he did and pushed open the door. This was the familiar, scruffy little off-licence. The local. The one she used in the old days on the few occasions she went to his flat. Owned by the woman with the nice smile and the wall eye, the woman who had said to her one evening, 'Nice boy, that boy of yours. Polite.' And Pamela knew she did not mean *boyfriend*. She knew because people spoke to her in the same way about Danny.

In they went. Still the same woman, still with the elderly Alsatian dog stretched out in front of the counter. 'Do we want it cold or warm?' asked Pam, seeing cans of the stuff in the fridge.

'It's cold enough already tonight,' he said. And gave the woman a nod. She responded, her good eye flicking up and down over Pam. She was saying to herself that she knew the face, knew the face . . .

Pam turned away.

Dean took two large bottles of Guinness off the shelves. 'A pint each should do,' he said, 'or it'll lie heavy on us, what with the stew.'

Everything was subtext somehow tonight, she thought.

The woman said helpfully, 'You can always come and get another if you need it. Come round the back. I don't go to bed much before twelve.'

Dean said, 'Oh, we might as well take it with us.'

At the same time, without thinking about it, Pam said, 'One pint is more than enough for me. Don't forget I'm driving.'

And then it happened.

Dean walked over, put his hand on her neck, and pulled her to him.

He stared at her as if she were the only thing in the world. He said, 'Stay.' And stroked the curve of her neck with his thumb. 'Please?'

It was an unmistakeable gesture. The tone of voice was unmistakeable. She heard the hissing intake of the woman's breath. Pamela pulled her head away from his hand.

'Will you pay?' she said, and stood there with her back to the woman, gazing unseeing at wine labels while the transaction took place.

'Goodbye,' she mumbled, as they left.

The woman said, 'Goodbye,' in neutral tones.

Dean put his arm round her as they walked back. 'I'll let your tyres down,' he said, 'if you try to escape.'

The arm felt good. She gave in. Now she was blooded. The wall-eyed woman had seen to that. What did anything matter any more? She made up her mind.

'No need,' she said, and kissed him. 'I'll stay.'

They ate first. No rush, as they said. No rush about anything. Dean told her about his sudden inspiration to be a chef. And she thought, What a suitable career for him. She could see him as one of those television cooks, with bags of charisma and style. 'Well, if this is anything to go by . . .' she said, taking another drink of the Guinness. 'I've never made an Irish stew in my life.'

And he went very red and exploded with

301

laughter. 'You made me stew often enough,' he said. Which suddenly changed the whole atmosphere. 'Will you come to bed?'

She nodded. 'I'd be delighted,' she said, mimicking his accent. She meant it. It would be pudding.

'That's terrible,' he said. 'A cross between Welsh and Ian Paisley. You need to go over there to listen and learn it.'

They stood up. She picked up the candle. For a moment they stood facing each other and then he asked, 'Will you?'

'What?'

'Come home with me?'

'Home?'

'To Dublin?'

I do not believe this, she thought. I really do not believe this. What god mocks me?

Part of her wanted to ask if he had been colluding with Peter and Douglas. Part of her wanted to confess the coincident absurdity. Part of her, very sensibly, did not. 'When?' she asked, hoping he would say February or June. Anything but December.

He moved closer. Put his hand around her neck again. She shivered at the warmth of it. 'I'm going back at Christmas,' he said. 'Come with me. Meet the family.'

'*Dean!*' she cried, half-angry, half-astonished. And she almost did ask him if this was a conspiracy of some sort. Had he and Peter and Douglas decided to form a coven and show her the error of her ways?

'Dean,' she said again, but more quietly. 'Where did you get that idea?'

'Why not? My mother said I could bring you.'

'She did?'

He shrugged.

'You told her about me?'

He nodded.

'All about me? My age, for instance?'

'It doesn't matter. Not if we love each other.'

Ideals. He ran on ideals. Even though she did not love him, she longed to believe him. He gave her a hopeful look. The candle-light flickered on his face. It was ageing, wasn't it? Maturing? Taking on new depths? He could carry her with him on his marvelling innocence. If she could do anything, then why not this?

She was about to speak when the telephone cut through the silence. She jumped.

'Leave it,' he said, taking the candle, putting his arms around her.

The answerphone picked up the call.

They both listened as Dean's mother asked if the stew had turned out all right, had his girlfriend been impressed with it, how Niamh had laughed to think that boys cooked for girls nowadays. And that if the girlfriend did come and spend Christmas with them—and she hoped she would—then she would show her a few more of his favourite things to cook, as she used to show her daughters.

'Oh, Jesus,' he said, listening.

'Mutton dressed as lamb, is it?' she said, more harshly than she meant in order to hide the pain.

'You could still come,' he whispered. 'We could spend real time together. You'd love it there. We wouldn't have to stay with the family. Not the whole time. You not at all, perhaps . . . There's hotels.'

'I know there are,' she said. 'You are not the first person to point that out to me.'

I will wake up soon, she thought. I will.

CHAPTER TWENTY-EIGHT

Mrs Hennessy said, 'Did you give it to her?'

A quick and crude riposte sprang to Peter's mind but he resisted it. 'Yes,' he said, and added quickly, 'She seemed very moved.'

'Ah, good,' said Mrs Hennessy, who mouthed the words Very Moved to an eager Eileen. 'So we're getting along famously.'

'Um,' said Peter, thinking 'moved' was exactly right. Pamela was moved. She stood in her kitchen, moved enough to laugh her socks off, and to ask him if it was all some kind of test of her moral fibre. If she had said, *'Red* satin?' in that uncomprehending way one more

304

time, he might have told her what she could really do with it. As it was, he retained his dignity, suggested that she think about Dublin and Christmas, and departed.

True, she rang him up the following morning and apologized for being so insensitive, putting it down to the champagne, but by then he had lost the momentum. His knee hurt dreadfully and his head was not much better. Vaulting garden gates and launching himself upon moving taxicabs was not designed to help, and he felt extremely annoyed that it had been to no good purpose. Pamela, it seemed, was not to be wooed in a hurry. When she said, 'Why?' he just said, 'Why not?' very crisply, made some excuse and rang off. That, he thought, would teach her to be so obtuse.

'And Dublin?' said Mrs Hennessy. 'Will she go?'

'She's thinking about it,' said Peter.

'Excellent,' said Mrs Hennessy.

'Thinking about it,' he thought, was also exactly right. The other thing she said on the phone that morning was that she couldn't *stop* thinking about it. Before becoming overwhelmed with laughter and having to apologize again. Thinking about it certainly seemed to be as much as she was prepared to do. And then she bowled the googly that women so often bowl in such circumstances and said solemnly that she was glad they could be friends after all these years.

Friends didn't go with red satin, for which he felt both piqued and relieved.

He rubbed at his knee, removed his glasses and rubbed at his eyes. Truth was, he had been somewhat relieved at not having to stay the night after all. Late nights, heavy food and strong drink no longer encouraged the libido—if it ever had. Truth was, he would have been very happy to just get into the ruddy bed and *sleep* with her, red satin or not.

But you could hardly go saying that to a woman, now could you, and certainly not to an ex-wife.

He heard a whispering at the other end of the line and then Mrs Hennessy said, 'So you did not press home your advantage?'

She was obviously enjoying all this. He could tell from her voice. It contained a hint of conspiracy which must be due to the proximity of the Eileen woman.

'No,' he said, 'I did not.' This was perfectly truthful, of course, there being no advantage to be pressed.

'Well, that all sounds fine,' she said. 'Keep it up.'

He winced and rang off.

He was so irritated that he found himself, irrationally, blaming Pamela for everything, including the height of her gate. And he felt ambiguous. On the whole Dublin would probably prove to be a much easier experience

306

if he did not have to spend all his time looking after somebody else; on the other hand it was a golden opportunity to be on neutral territory and iron out their future. They had been very happy in Dublin years ago—from what he remembered. Walking about the town, visiting Trinity, sketching, talking about how they would change the world. Not an idle student dream for him. He had. With Daniel grown up and gone, they could be like that again. He would have said so if she had given him half a chance. But her reaction to the suggestion about Christmas was as nothing to her reaction when he said he wanted them to work on the Rosen commission together.

'Together?' she said. 'What way together?'

He told her. Basically he needed a helpmate. 'And some advice about sensualizing the interior.'

'Sensualizing?' she said. 'I see.'

'Well?' he asked.

'I'll let you know the answer,' she said, 'soon.'

'And Christmas?'

'The answer to *both*, soon.'

He felt reasonably confident. After all, as Mrs Hennessy said, and this he did agree with, it would make perfect sense. A very neat tying up of ends.

He looked around the chequer-board room and saw the white oblong lying on its black background. He limped over, picked it up, and, slipping on his glasses, checked the contents for the umpteenth time. Two seats for the noon flight from Stansted next week. He repositioned the telephone, also on a black square of paper, and sat back with a very weak vodka and tonic. He thought about ringing his son, but, then, he thought, Daniel could always ring him.

*   *   *

Douglas ran his hands along the perfect folds of curtaining and, despite himself, he smiled. The peacocks which had looked, as peacocks will, silly but decorative in the book of samples, looked absurd hanging here amid all this high-tech steel and glass. Sometimes you could marry the old and the new and get away with it—the Italians were always good at that—but this . . . He felt a frisson of guilt. Too late now. Anyway, Zoe would probably change it again in a year or two. Her boredom level was even lower than his.

Beyond the window barges went up river, a few little boats bobbed about, a police launch slid lazily by. The satisfyingly ordinary scene exactly framed by these absurd, posturing birds. He should not have let Zoe do it—and yet, she was really pleased. The emperor's new clothes? Or had they all stumbled on the next style revolution? He might put that to Pamela when he spoke to her. She would laugh. Him,

308

too. Somehow—he smoothed them again—somehow he did not think they had found the new Bauhaus.

'Well,' said Zoe, 'what do you think?'

He shrugged.

'Don't be so modest,' she said, and handed him his drink. 'It was a brilliant choice. Very post-modern of you. I'll take you up to see Lionel's place after this. Do you know the only decent thing he's done in the whole apartment is the curtaining? The rest of it—well, you'll see for yourself.'

It was the game they played together all their adult lives. We are so much better than the rest, it was called, and it united them, so that they stayed invincible, strong—looking from high up and afar down on the unwashed non-cognoscenti. Whereas the stink was coming from them, he now realized. He had only just faced that. When he mentioned Zoe and her delight in her curtains to Pamela on the drive back, she said, 'There are worse delusions in life than vulgar curtaining, Douglas.' Very snappishly, breaking the mood. 'Like selfishness masquerading as love.'

'I'm sorry,' he had said. 'We both hurt each other.'

He touched the curtains again. He had promised himself he would not think about it. She went wild after he said that. Which he had not expected, given the way their evening had worked out. A real dam of accusation.

Sounding off in a way that he had never thought her capable of. 'Yes,' she said, 'you hurt me. You hurt us both. Why, why, why?' she yelled. 'Why did you put us both through all that shit, all that pain, all that suffering time apart? How could you possibly have wasted the love, wasted the pleasure, wasted our history—and now say you are sorry? It wasn't we, Douglas, it wasn't we. It was *you* . . .'

'I could not have coped with Daniel,' he said. At least that was truthful. .

'Stop telling yourself you can't cope, and get on with it. That's what most of the rest of us do. We don't sit around contemplating our damaged navels and hiding behind the skirts of our damaged siblings. We're too busy trying to bring up the next generation decently. How many people do you suppose there are out there in the world just *longing* to be loved and to love? To have the very thing you just threw away? Love is not something you cope with. It is something you desire. Love, Douglas, is good.'

'Yes,' he said. It was all he could think of in the blast.

She was picking at her stocking, shredding it, completing what the walk along that track and the brambles had begun. 'I've got a friend,' she said suddenly, 'who has struggled all her life to find what we had. She even gave up the chance of having children—which she really wanted—because she thought she had

310

found love. And now she's with some dickhead who can't make up his mind between his wife and his mistress. And you—*you* have the warped gall to just chuck it out because you can't cope with one *child?* And you don't know how to commit?'

'Yes,' he said quietly, thinking he had lost after all.

'And Douglas?'

'Yes,' he said, knowing what was coming.

'I love you very much.'

And being wrong.

As they travelled up in the lift, he thought about telling Zoe everything. Just making a complete, clean sweep of it all. And also telling her that he planned—or hoped—to be away over Christmas. She was going to stay in London for the first time—for the grand opening of her flat on the day itself and with a list of preferred parties and visits for them to attend. She assumed he would be there to support her, and she him, now that Mary was gone . . .

High up they might be, he thought, watching the light indicate each floor as they ascended, but the stench was still with him. He felt in his pocket. Crumpled up was Mary's letter. Begging to come back. Another one damaged. It had to stop somewhere, he decided. It had to stop somewhere. He told Pamela that. It was the last thing he said to her before she left, walked away from the car. She looked at him sceptically. 'I mean it,' he said. And he did.

He knew this hand, he thought, as Lionel showed him around. It might have been overseen by Jennifer, but this was Pamela's way. Or rather, it was what she had taught Jennifer, he supposed. In the bedroom Zoe nudged him and pulled a face. The walls were covered in hot Italian colours, cooled by raw silk blinds and a plain pearly silk bedspread. *Definitely* Pam, he thought. He remembered her sounding off at him about silk being both feminine and masculine—apparently delicate but strong; light to the touch but so densely woven it could keep you warm.

He said all that to Lionel, while Zoe looked on open-mouthed. 'I think it looks great,' he said.

'Do you?' said a perplexed Zoe.

And Lionel said, 'I wanted lemon chintz.'

*   *   *

Dean took the bus to Kensington High Street. It was the perfect solution—as if he had known it was there but needed to find the right key. And he had. He laughed aloud and punched the air, making the passing pedestrians stare as he walked up the hill towards Notting Hill Gate. Well, it *was* funny—the answer to everything in a dish of Irish stew. He was on his way for an interview to start training as a chef. For the last time, he promised himself, he had used his looks to schmooze a contact and get into one of the top places.

It was mid-morning, on a crisp, beautiful, late December day, and he felt happy. Christmas carols were mingling into one seasonal cacophony—Good King Wenceslas met the Babe in a Manger and Rudolph rang his bells. He smiled and felt no cynicism. It was the world. And he was about to step right into it up to his neck, at last. Once he was on track, all of Pamela's doubts could leave the room and turn the light off.

When something clicks into gear in your mind, he thought, when you suddenly *know* what it is you have been looking for, the world seems to do the same thing. The bus on the way here stopped at every set of lights? Of course it did. The old lady needed a seat? Of course she did. The pavements were crowded and he had to step in the gutter some of the time? Of course he did. It was all the world and it was beautiful. He held on to his empty Pepsi can until he found a rubbish bin. Of course he did. The world was beautiful. He must preserve it.

Pam knew the place he was going to, said it was really good, said, slightly embarrassed, that her husband had designed it. 'You'll like it,' she said. 'I'll keep my fingers crossed for you.' She would come to Dublin with him in the end, he knew she would. He stopped outside the glass-fronted restaurant, arranged his features into what he hoped was intelligent willingness, and went in.

'Why a chef?' said the pale, lanky man in check trousers and an odd white coat thing.

He did not look as old as Dean.

'Are you the owner?' asked Dean.

The pale, lanky man nodded.

'You don't look much different from me.'

The man said, 'Oh?'

'Doesn't that answer the question?'

He laughed and asked one of the minions to bring them both a cup of coffee.

It arrived in big white mugs, with a dish of biscuits that tasted like melting heaven.

'I want to do something creative but behind the scenes. So it is the product and not me who is judged.'

'Crap,' said the lanky man. 'Go on.'

So Dean told him. About the Irish stew. When he finished the lanky man looked him up and down. And then he drummed his fingers on the table. And then he sipped his coffee and stared out of the window. Dean saw the world outside as thin and insubstantial again, dirty and cold, the people grim-faced. He really wanted this. And for once his eyelashes were not going to be any help.

The pale lanky man stood up. 'OK,' he said. 'Speak to Genevieve. We'll give you a chance.'

'Jesus, thanks,' said Dean, standing up.

He tried to get hold of Pamela to tell her,

but she was unavailable. Busy, he guessed.

CHAPTER TWENTY-NINE

Ani Patel gazed bleakly past the stick-on holly and tinsel, out of the shop window, into the dark cold night. At least, she told herself, it had not snowed. The snow she found difficult to accept. So, she thought, with a slight quiver of humour, did the British. They were always surprised by it. Every year people came into the shop saying, Oh, what a surprise, and meaning it.

She noticed the card she had placed there for Miss Phoebe Glen. Out of date and, anyway, no more use for it. She reached up to take it down. Miss Phoebe Glen was now quite suited, thank you. So she said. Ani Patel was invited to a little gathering at the house tonight but she was not sure if she would go; she certainly did not feel up to it. If she did, she would take some Tropicana and a box of fudge. Not the bottle of wine Miss Phoebe suggested.

Pamela, hurrying swiftly along on the cold pavement outside, looked up and waved. Mrs Patel brightened and waved back. Pamela stopped.

'Are you OK?' she mouthed through the glass.

Mrs Patel opened the locked shop door.

'Did you want anything?' she asked.

'Why,' said Pamela, staring at her very hard, 'Mrs Patel, you look upset.'

Ani Patel shook her head as if to say it was nothing.

'And you,' she said, 'look very well.'

'I am,' said Pam. She had been on a sun-bed twice this week, despite its being carcinogenic Russian Roulette. But she liked the glow it gave her and what was the occasional risk?

'How is that son of yours?' asked Ani Patel, fiddling with the card in her hand.

'Fine, as far as I know,' said Pam.

'He is coming home for Christmas?'

'He is not coming home for Christmas.'

'I am so sorry,' said Ani Patel.

'Don't be. I'm going away.'

'Ah.'

'And you? Are you and Ari going back for Christmas?'

Ani Patel shook her head. Behind her glasses her eyes went watery.

Pamela came right into the shop and pushed the door closed behind her.

'Can I help?' she said.

Mrs Patel did not speak.

'Is it Ari?'

Mrs Patel nodded.

'Would you like to tell me about it?'

She shook her head. 'I have a little party to attend,' she said, 'and I must not be late. But thank you for asking.' She swallowed and blinked and then added in her usual neutral voice, 'Are you going somewhere nice?'

'Oh, yes,' said Pam.

Odd, thought Mrs Patel after her visitor had left, that she should look brown. She closed up, locked up, collected the Tropicana and the fudge, and set off for Miss Phoebe Glen's house with a heavy heart.

*   *   *

From her sideboard Miss Phoebe Glen took the bottle of sherry, unopened, good quality, Spanish. A cut above. She removed three glasses from the back of the shelf and dusted them on her sleeve. They reminded her of sitting with her mother in a far-off time, when the neighbours would call in at this time of year and sit and talk politely over port and lemon. Now her neighbours would not be seen dead in her house. The Baldwin man next door complained all the time. She put some cardboard where the plank came from and said, very firmly, that it was her fence, in deed if not in fact, and that the landlord would hear of his insults.

'Cardboard will not keep the cats out,' said the Baldwin man.

'My cardboard will,' she said triumphantly.

She felt on top of the world and there was no answer to that. Clearly. Because he went back indoors and said no more.

In the kitchen she put on one ring of the cooker. Just to take the chill off. It caused a little smoke and what not, since it had not been used for some time, but it was not unbearable. Out there in the cold would be unbearable. In here, in this house, she was warm and secure and she had her lodger. It would all be very jolly.

Miss Phoebe pulled the cork and helped herself to a little on account. It tasted delightful—delicate. She sipped it, having no need now to gulp it down in one go to feel the warmth from within. Phoebe Glen is coming home, she said to herself, borrowing a phrase from one of the tabloids.

The fat man arrived with a flourish. He had a small cardboard suitcase and a canvas bag of army origin. He brought these into the kitchen, since the front door was wide open, and even in this neck of the woods it might not be sensible to leave goods on show.

'Did you leave the plank off, Norman?' asked Miss Phoebe. 'I have asked Mrs Patel as our guest of honour, since she it was who brought us together in our trials.'

'Very fair,' said the fat man, who sat down on a red leatherette stool.

'I hope she gets here soon. That draught is fair whipping around my ankles.'

The fat man touched his beret reluctantly. It was chill, even with the kitchen door closed.

'You may keep it on in the house, you know. Being military,' said Miss Phoebe kindly.

'Thank you—' He could not bring himself to call her Your Ladyship, but he intended to when he had plucked up courage.

When Ani Patel arrived, looking pinched and tired and swathed in a number of shawls and scarves that gave her—as the fat man whispered to Miss Phoebe—a look of where she came from, Miss Phoebe nodded. She took the Tropicana and the fudge as if they were something quite disgusting, and said, 'Tonight, for a change, Mrs Patel, you will have something Spanish.'

'Spanish oranges,' said the fat man helpfully, reading the packet.

Miss Phoebe gave her friend a brimming glass while sending the fat man to close the plank. She was aware that she owed the shopkeeper a lot. Of course, she was also aware that the shopkeeper owed *her* a lot too, if not as an individual, then as the nation which she represented. How much they had taught them, and all those ship's halfpennies going into the jam jars at school every week, she thought, feeling a little hazy. Or were they for fishermen? Anyway. The sacrifice. As a girl she had made her sacrifice for the likes of Mrs Patel. In a way, Mrs Patel's help during her own crisis was no more than a repayment for getting her out of a grass hut all those years ago.

Ani Patel was not inclined to drink alcohol. Indeed, so far as she knew, except for a brandy when her husband died, none had passed her lips—but Ani-Vashtak was guiding her tonight, and she was among friends, so she thought she would. She took a sip. If she thought the British potty before, this just about confirmed it. Bad medicine, she thought, trying not to pull a face. How they could sit there and drink it for pleasure was beyond her. But then, so was *Coronation Street*. Nevertheless, she felt a warmth in her belly shortly afterwards, so she took another sizeable mouthful. It was like getting into a warm bath from inside. Perhaps the British were not so daft. She was certainly feeling better for it.

Miss Phoebe Glen stood up and raised her glass. The fat man gazed up at her admiringly. With the hat and the mittens and her bearing, she was every inch a lady. The Widow MacNamally drank Guinness only, and not without noises. He would serve Miss Phoebe Glen—as he had once served his mother, before her second marriage had sent him off to the Ford works at Dagenham, and never allowed him back.

'I give you a toast,' said Miss Phoebe. 'To Mrs Patel. Without whom . . .'

Mrs Patel, prone to something like a giggle, finished her drink. 'Oh, please,' She held up her hand in a gesture of modesty.

The chill of wintertime seemed to blow all

the harder. Despite the ring burning on the stove and the breath of the kitchen's inmates, something stirred the air around, bringing the ice of Siberia and the frosts of Norway into the room. Miss Phoebe paused. She was about to check if her plank was still in order when the kitchen door was flung back, apparently of its own accord.

In the entrance stood a girl with flaming hair, diamond eyes and the remnants of a very large bump on her forehead. She held up a plank.

'Your door is open to the elements,' she said. 'You are in need. You cannot stay here with the door flapping . . .'

She looked around her. Her voice trailed off.

'You!' hissed Miss Phoebe Glen, rising another inch on her toes. 'You!'

The fat man jumped and spilled a little of his drink.

But the girl with the flaming hair and the diamond eyes put her hand up to her bump and winced. This was all wrong. She had four single girls of under seventeen about to give birth, one of fifteen just confirmed up the spout by a schoolboy, three families at risk, and now this old trout, who was supposed to be easy and past it and on the register for Sunnybank Basic Unit, was entertaining a party of friends. Incapable of managing alone, it said on the form, and therefore not

321

supposed to be found sitting in a bloody kitchen full of good cheer.

'The door,' she said miserably, 'is swinging open.'

'My friend the repair man is just about to fix it,' said Miss Phoebe Glen, and she leaned over and touched the head of the fat man as he bent low over his bag.

'I have a man,' she said proudly.

At which the fat man froze.

And the girl with the flaming hair and the diamond eyes thought, peevishly, There's no arguing with that. She looked about her. The diamonds fell upon Ani Patel, and hardened. 'I am surprised at you,' she said. 'Out drinking at a time like this.'

'I have a screwdriver here,' said the fat man, riffling through his things, feeling, though not bringing out, various garments and tubes of ointment. 'Somewhere.'

'Always leave it to someone else to pick up the pieces,' said the girl to Ani Patel. 'Your sort.'

'A big screwdriver,' said the fat man firmly. But he skewed his head around to look at Mrs Patel. They all looked at Mrs Patel.

Mrs Patel looked back at them all in turn. An answer was required.

Very deliberately, she held up her empty glass to Miss Phoebe Glen, who immediately filled it.

She drank a little.

They waited.

Ani Patel drank a little more.

Ani Patel thought of her namesake and took courage. 'My son,' she said. 'Ari,' she said, 'is pregnant.'

There was a stunned silence.

Miss Phoebe Glen drank her own glass dry. And then, wiping her lips with the tips of her fingers, said, 'I don't think you mean that exactly, now do you? A little confusion with the syntax, I fancy?'

Ani Patel nodded. 'Thank you,' she said, 'for pointing that out. What I mean is, I am going to be a grandmother.'

'You've decided, then?' said the girl with the diamond eyes.

Mrs Patel shrugged. 'There was never,' she said with dignity, 'any question in my mind.'

'This calls for a celebration,' said Miss Phoebe Glen, refilling her glass.

That's what you think, thought Ani Patel, but she kept the consideration to herself.

The girl with the diamond eyes gave a low moan and backed out of the room. Sometimes these women just could not be persuaded. Old, young, foreign, they would dig in their heels and make everybody's life difficult. She went out, banging the door. Which promptly swung back open.

'Dregs,' she said to the night sky, which made her feel considerably better.

CHAPTER THIRTY

They closed the shop on the day before Christmas Eve. As Pamela said to Jennifer and the Amazon, they had all worked their feet off for the last six weeks and the tassel-bound cognoscenti could go hang until the New Year.

'Or drape,' said Jenny, sitting down and rubbing her feet. 'Or swag, or ruche, or pleat . . .'

The Amazon looked at them with eyes that bespoke postgraduate purity, eyes that believed their goal was to bring beauty out of chaos and raise the domestic into a fitting firmament for the gods. Interesting paint-finishes still interested her, thought Pam. Nevertheless, she, too, admitted that her feet ached and that if she saw the back end of yet another stencil brush this side of Christmas, she would self-combust.

What divides those two and me, thought Pam, is that whereas their state of mind, and tiredness of feet, is temporary, mine is nothing to do with the rigours of the season. I have come to the end of expediency. I want to go through the door that lies beyond.

She took them out to a very early dinner. Jenny looked at her a shade enviously. If there was one thing she could not do, she told Pam, as she emptied the till and so efficiently finalized everything, it was to persuade

324

Howard to go away anywhere for Christmas. One small fissure in the rock hard joys of marriage.

'Life after children,' Pam said firmly. 'It just seemed pointless with Daniel not coming home.'

'You're still not going to say where?'

Pamela shook her head.

'Like a honeymoon,' said Jenny. There was just a hint of disapproval.

'Yes,' said Pam.

'Hmm.' Jennifer pursed her lips.

Pamela remembered pursing her lips to her mother like that when she first moved into the Burlington. We disapprove of what we do not understand because it disturbs us, she thought. She was unable, then, to comprehend why her mother should abandon her life so cheerfully in exchange for the outer beigeness of the Burlington. Now she understood. Her mother did not want to play the role entitled 'the brave widow soldiers on'—just as now Pam had no intention of taking a starring role in 'the loneliness of the long distance mother'. There were always choices to be made, caskets to be opened, at every stage of your life. Dean had talked to her about Exit, euthanasia, as brightly as he might have talked about going to the dentist. It meant nothing to him now, but it would. Even approaching death, there were still choices to be made. And scarlet rooms, lemon chintz or peacock tapestry were yesterday's choices.

Even if Daniel and The Girlfriend had deigned to come and stay, she would not have seen her son's face on Christmas morning. That door was closed now, as it should be. The tousle-haired little boy with the wide eyes and the monster stocking creeping into her room before light no longer existed. The tousle-haired Daniel of now would probably have his face buried in The Girlfriend's pillow until lunchtime. It was his rite of passage and she had survived it.

She did not mention anything to Jenny and the Amazon until the cappuccino. Then she said, 'Are you happy doing what you are doing?' And they both said they were—very happy indeed. Which is when she dared to confess that she had become bored with it all herself. She saw the look that flitted across Jenny's face. Menopausal boredom. Well, let her think it, if it helped.

'I may not come back full-time in the New Year,' she said.

The Amazon looked completely relaxed at the suggestion. 'You're retiring, right?'

'No, I am not retiring,' Pamela snapped back, despite it being the forgiving season.

She'd have her in incontinence pads next. 'I want to do some more heavyweight stuff. Peter has asked me to work with him on the design of something quite different, and I might want to do it.'

Which made it sound a great deal more of a partnership than Peter proposed.

'Oh?' said Jenny, intrigued. 'What?'

'Can't tell you until the New Year.'

Which was true enough. It was all under wraps until then. And, of course, until she herself had made up her mind.

Peter had just said, 'Your coming in on the Rosen commission does not necessarily rest on the outcome of Dublin.'

She said, 'Thanks very much.' And wondered if it rested on wearing sketchy scarlet underwear.

She was looking to the future now, and there was quite a lot of it left, as her mother had so helpfully pointed out. This time nothing was going to detract from her talents, not gender, not cautiousness or age.

Jenny said, 'We can't possibly manage without you.' With about as much conviction as the latter-day Tories to Margaret Thatcher.

Jenny would be fine. A nice middle-class young woman, with husband and potential children and nanny, doing a nice middle-class job for the middle classes. It had served Pam well enough while Daniel was growing up. Now she wanted more. If it was to be Pryor and Pryor, it would have to mean it.

The Amazon looked at her employer and blinked her big brown eyes, but not before Pam registered the look in them. Kindly contempt. Pamela smiled at her. So you think you will change the shape of the world? she thought. The truth is, it is the world that will change the shape of you.

She ordered brandy. They drank to the future. Oh, to be young, she thought momentarily—and then, remembering Ani Patel's son and the baby, and Ani Patel's face as she told her, she quickly crossed her fingers. The journey the Patels were all about to make was long and difficult. She kept her fingers crossed and took everything straight back. I would not like to be young again, she said to the bottom of her glass, not for a million pounds. Just as well, said the reflection, sister to the mirror before her, because you are not.

She paid the bill. Half-past eight. The others left to get a taxi. She would walk. She gave the Amazon a set of keys, which seemed only right and proper. The Amazon took the gift in her amazingly long stride. Pamela felt the slightest frisson of regret as she ceded her territory. But she was moving on.

Tomorrow she was flying out. She set off for home through the crowded Christmas streets. Not a part of any of it any more. She carried a basket of flowers for Ani Patel. These days, in the name of service, she kept the shop open all hours. It gave her customers what they wanted, and probably took her mind off things. Ari hung around fondling his moustache, looking sulky, to hide his fear. Pretending not to need his mother, punishing her by not being helpful,

328

because he needed her so much. Thank God, thank God, it is not me, said Pam.

The shop was full. Pamela watched Ani Patel as she served and dipped and smiled, if a little wanly, at all her customers. Always helpful, always willing to tolerate any madness that her customers might bring. It would be like that for ever now. In the summer she would have a baby to play with, a baby in a carrycot in the shop, just as she remembered seeing Ari when she first came to live here. ' 'Tis all a chequerboard of nights and days,' she remembered from somewhere, 'Where Destiny with Men for pieces plays . . .' She certainly felt that when she was with Douglas all those years ago. 'Hither and thither moves, and mates, and slays, And one by one back in the closet lays . . .' Only you did not have to choose to remain in the cupboard for ever.

When Ani Patel first told Pam about the baby she said, 'Ah, but who will there be to care for me one day?' and her usually kind brown eyes showed a flash of anger—but only for a moment before apologizing. Then she fiddled with the Bounty bars and said, 'It is the fate of the coconut husk to float, for the stone to sink . . . My grandmother's saying.'

Pamela wanted to argue with it, but Ani Patel looked quite resolute and calm again. 'I have chosen,' she said. Which Pamela realized was ineluctable truth. And so have I, she thought.

The flowers were Pamela's way of saying thank you. Thank you, she thought grandly, on behalf of the world. For without its Ani Patels, it could not function. She had been lucky. She had escaped.

*   *   *

Margie was on the doorstep, cheerfully smoking.

'Oh, hell,' said Pam. 'I forgot.'

'Thanks, darling,' said Margie. She was surrounded by carrier bags, some of which Pam was astonished to see came from Harrods' Food Hall.

'You only said you might,' said Pam defensively, letting herself in. 'And it's not even nine.' No more guilt, she thought, no more guilt. 'I called in to take Ani Patel some flowers.'

'I always said she was a saint, that woman,' said Margie. 'But a *grandmother*? I suppose they wouldn't consider a—'

Pam shook her head. 'Pro-Life,' she said.

Margie shrugged. 'Except, perhaps, her own.'

In the kitchen Margie looked about her. 'No decorations,' she said wonderingly.

'Too busy doing everybody else's,' said Pam. And then she put her hands on her hips and said, 'That's not true. I just didn't want the bother. If you're going to be free, you may as

330

well be *really* free.'

'No baubles, no baggage?' said Margie. 'If only . . . Anyway, this is for us.' She put her hand into one of the Harrods bags and pulled out the statutory red wine. 'Don't worry. I'm not staying. I'll get the ten-fifty back. I know you've got to be up in the morning.' She gave Pam a sly little look. 'Packed yet?' she asked. 'Cheers.' She raised her glass and they chinked.

Pam laughed and reached forward. 'You should always make eye contact when you do that,' she said. 'Try again.'

They were silent for a moment. Then Pamela said, 'Why do we do it, Margie? Why?'

'Why do they do it? Why does anybody do it? You know your Dorothy Parker: Woman wants monogamy, Man wants novelty—'

'What happens when Woman wants novelty?'

'Trouble.'

'I want novelty.'

'I don't. I've had enough novelty to last a lifetime. It's called being on your own and doing everything for yourself and being perceived as liberated. But if you want novelty—' Margie waved her hands like a conjuror—'then have some, my dear . . . I'll settle for oppression and someone warm in my bed at night.'

It was like old times. Margie stretched out on the floor in the sitting room, Pam stretched out on the settee. She automatically felt the space beside her. 'Not even masculine old Piggins,' she said. 'I do miss all that, you know.'

'Ah, cats,' said Margie fondly.

'Not cats, men,' said Pam, a little sharply. 'Masculinity.'

'One day at a time,' said Margie. 'It's all psychological.'

Pam just laughed. Psychological, my foot, she thought. It's a great deal more physical than that, the stuff I'm talking about.

'I envy you,' said Margie, stretching. 'All this peace and control over your own life.'

Why do they always *say* that? thought Pam. While *doing* the opposite? But at least she could put her hand on her heart and say that she did not envy Margie. Whatever she was embarked upon was going to take a lot of energy. Ex-wives, current wives, ex-girlfriends, zealous mothers were the very devil and took a huge toll. And that was without all the energy the Beloved took as well. She stretched and yawned. No. She wasn't ready to expend that energy yet. One day maybe, but not yet . . .

'I still do that, you know,' she said, running her hand over the cushion next to her. 'I still feel for Piggins when I'm stretched out here.'

'Ah, Piggins,' said Margie, moved.

'Even he got it right,' said Pam, getting a little sentimental with the red wine and all. 'He just shuffled off this Feline Coil at the perfect

332

time. Right for him, decrepit old thing, and right for me—'

'Decrepit old thing.'

'Thank you.'

'Don't mention it.'

'I don't even have to worry about him any more. It's Christmas and I'm off out of it.' She sat up, suddenly anxious.

'And you—what will you be doing?'

Margie laughed. 'Cooking a fucking Christmas dinner with all the trimmings. Like what I have never done before. Should be interesting.'

'When in doubt, don't take it out . . .' said Pam, a little dreamily.

'Pardon?' said Margie, affecting the voice of an offended maiden aunt.

'It's what my mother used to say . . .'

Margie's eyes widened. She suddenly thought of old Mrs Hennessy in a very different light. 'She did? Raunchy old thing . . .'

'About the *turkey*,' said Pam.

'Oh', said Margie, disappointed.

Pam laughed. 'I'd like to be a fly on the wall in your Christmas kitchen. So you've managed to winkle him away from his wife for the day? That's positive.'

Margie picked at the carpet and said, 'He's coming to me on Christmas Eve. When I shall shag the daylights out of him. He is then going to spend the morning with me, and have Christmas dinner, and then, in the evening, he is going home. To eat another Christmas dinner. Only, if the plan works, he will be so tired, so full, and so brandied to his eyeballs, that he will just fall asleep.'

'And if I know Christmas,' said Pam, 'with all its precious and pressured delights—'

'She'll throw him out for good.'

Maybe, thought Pam.

'Ah, well,' said Margie. 'It keeps you young.'

*   *   *

After she had gone, Pam sat and opened her post. Among the cards was one from Danny. It said, 'Happy Christmas, Mum, from Danny and Lilian. See you in the New Year.' It was a cartoon of the Three Wise Men. The message, in its exactitude, was par for the course, she thought, putting it up in place of honour. See you in the New Year could mean any time between the coming 1 January and the following 31 December. Good old Daniel, why change the habits of a lifetime? As she picked up the envelope to throw it away, she noticed that he had written on the outside flap, in hurried scrawl, the extraordinary additional message, Dear Mum, I Miss You.

Maybe he felt he did not want The Girlfriend to know such things.

She rang, but the telephone was engaged. She could try the mobile, but the memory of his joy in it still rankled. Peter had it so easy.

334

The struggle had all been hers. And maybe all the joys, too. When she got far enough away from it, she might really believe that was true. She had ground to make up. Starting now. The number stayed engaged and she could no longer keep her eyes open. She would call him tomorrow.

And then, more or less packed, she went to bed. She still had her mother to see before the off.

CHAPTER THIRTY-ONE

Mrs Hennessy was staring out at the picturesque winter morning and smiling contentedly. We'll see about contentment, thought Pamela, as she hurried towards her mother. Never had the external manicuring of the Burlington shown to better advantage than under the coating of pristine snow.

Dreadful place, she thought. How could I have ever thought it tempting?

Neither Mrs Hennessy nor Eileen had seen her. Two sweet old ducks, thought Pam, or pretending to be. Of course, they were play-acting to some extent, and would continue to do so while they still had their marbles. They were laughing at Fate—being a bit mischievous with it; at the same time knowing that Fate was catching up on them. Pam felt like an admonishing headmistress bearing down. Nevertheless, it had to be done. A telephone call would not be enough. This was eyeball time.

She had spoken to her mother the day after her date with Peter and told her, in no uncertain terms, to leave well alone. If she was going to end her life restored to her former husband, it would be because she chose to. Mrs Hennessy was indignant. And unconvinced. Pam had gripped the phone, counted to five, and then said, 'If you want to interfere, then interfere with Kay . . .' A little sibling grudge, but why should she, Pamela, the eldest, shoulder the burden of being interfered with?

'Move that millpond of hers around if you like. But don't do it to me, please. I am quite capable of stirring up my own pond life when required . . .'

Mrs Hennessy insisted that she was only trying to help.

'No, you weren't. You were trying to get things tied up your way. And because, unlike settled old Kay, I'm still flapping about. Well, I like flapping about at present. So have a go at her next time. You're always saying, darkly, what will happen to poor Kay when the children leave home and Cormack suddenly dies. Why not give her a ring—now? Why not give her a ring and say, This is your mother, Kay, dear, and I just wanted to give you some advice on your impending widowhood.'

'Pamela, you are tempting fate.'

'Well, he won't, Mother, will he?' said Pam rather shortly.

'Your father did.'

'Yes, but there are no sodding roads up there for a ten-ton truck to come haring along and run him down.'

'It could happen with a horse and cart,' said Mrs Hennessy. 'He could fall off a bridge.'

'Mother,' said Pam. After all, she was still feeling quite raw from her experience with Peter. 'Mother, Cormack is not the sort of man to fall off a bridge—and if he did, he could swim.'

'Not if the bridge was over a road.'

Give me strength, thought Pam, but she held it back. She knew she would have to go there in person. 'Mother,' she said, 'I'll come and see you soon.' It sounded like a threat.

Good.

She arrived at the Burlington determined to be sweet. She gave her mother a kiss. And then, because it was Christmas, she gave one to Eileen, too. And a box, all wrapped up in pretty paper and ribbon. Eileen deserved something nice. She made a really excellent companion.

Eileen said, 'Thank you, dear,' and began to pull the ribbons apart.

Pamela handed her mother a smaller package, which she, too, began to untie.

She poured the coffee—as beige as its jug—and sat back, watching the two women open their gifts. She felt immensely relaxed. Her bags were in the back of the car, she could make a leisurely journey to the airport to catch the flight. She picked up a ginger-nut, dunked it, and sucked.

Mrs Hennessy was the first to get her parcel open. It contained a cashmere shawl. In what the friendly girl in the Scotch House called fudge.

'Lovely, dear,' said Mrs Hennessy, throwing it around her shoulders. There was also a small bottle of Dior. Pamela refused to let her mother go down the taupe path *entirely*—the woman in her was not all elderly. Mrs Hennessy opened it and smelled and, closing her eyes, said, 'Thank you. Most acceptable.'

'Dad's favourite.'

Mrs Hennessy nodded.

All was forgiven. In the end it is the duty of an elderly parent to become meek.

Eileen gave a squeak. When she finally broke through the ribbons and paper tissue that Pamela had so carefully rearranged, she brought out the red satin underwear, provenance of Peter.

Everybody's eyes met.

Nobody said anything.

Then, very gingerly at first, and gradually with a little more pleasure, Eileen began to hold its folds between her finger and thumb.

'It's very nice,' she said eventually. 'Lovely, in fact. I haven't had anything as lovely as this for a long time.' And, without meeting Pamela's eye, she gave her a kiss on the cheek and murmured, 'Most unsuitable.'

'You're a wicked girl,' whispered Mrs Hennessy, when Pamela got up to leave.

'I'll send you a postcard,' she said. And began to move off.

'Give my love to Peter,' said her mother.

Pamela gave her a look. The kind of look Mrs Hennessy used to give Pamela at times of schoolgirl transgression.

'When you see him,' added her mother, very innocently.

Later, sitting on their own again, Eileen smiled at Mrs Hennessy and Mrs Hennessy smiled at Eileen. They were very content. This morning they had watched the large pale turkey being carried in, and the tree (artificial, very sensibly) was dressed to gilded lily standards. They had both refused to be driven to church by the woman with a wart on her nose and a sunny smile, and were not on any of the lists for entertainments. Mistresses of their own destiny, they eyed their new gifts.

'Lovely shawl,' said Eileen.

'Lovely undies,' said Mrs Hennessy.

Eileen tapped the box. 'Shall I?' she asked.

Mrs Hennessy nodded. 'Oh, I think you must.'

And they both turned and beckoned to the

girl in the orange cardigan and brown pleats, who was busy taking requests for the carol service.

In the distance they could see Pamela's car driving up the gravel path, round the bend and out into the world. Just, thought her mother, as it should be, really.

CHAPTER THIRTY-TWO

Even though Peter Pryor was early for the noon flight, it was a long queue, there were many noisy children, his knee ached and he wanted to sit down. Worse, despite flying business class, he was forced to queue here. Security alert, they told him. And that was that. At least it was a pleasing environment to hang around in. Norman Foster had used the Stansted site well—better and more bravely, thought Peter, than he might have done. He would not have taken such risks. If he had a flaw, it was that he was too cautious, too restrained. When he saw the Gaudi in Barcelona, for example, he just felt sick. Cautious restraint was not what was required *fin de siècle*. Cautious restraint, *fin de siècle*, did not light up the sky. Cautious restraint, he thought sourly, was certainly not a concept embraced by his ex-wife. Very *fin de siècle* she was, *very* . . .

340

He stood there, looking around admiringly. It soothed the savage breast; made savage, he reminded himself, by Pam having turned him down. Looking back, he had been made a fool of. That *underwear*? He nearly bit his fist with the humiliation. We do not love each other, was the way she put it. We would both be unhappy all over again. He did not even bother to ask what *that* meant. After all, neither of them was a spring chicken.

He stared down the long, elegant lines of the building. Sir Norman might have got this commission, but he had not got Brigham. Peter straightened, despite his knee, feeling a little spurt of pride. And then the sourness descended again. *Pamela.* Pamela being wilful. Oh, she deigned to consider—only consider, mind you—coming on board for the Cambridge project—as a partner—but she was not prepared to consider coming on board in the manner of a wife. And he could not withdraw the Brigham College offer, because he needed her. It was all very frustrating and he found himself enjoyably imagining the sticking of pins into images of Mary Wollstonecraft and Sidney and Beatrice Webb.

How could he have let a couple of doddery old bats put him in the position? Fear, probably. Fear of ending up like them. Alone. He did not have Pam's touching faith in Daniel.

The queue moved up. He shuffled with it.

Going to Dublin—even alone—was better than staying in London. The hotel could take the strain. He was certainly glad to turn his back on those black and white squares. We do not love each other . . . how many people of their age did? He looked at his watch and tutted.

The man in front of him also looked at his watch, and also tutted. Even in the blur of failing eyesight, Peter saw it was a very special timepiece. Thin steel, almost not there, just the kind of thing he liked. The man noticed him looking. His taciturn expression lifted slightly to politeness. He also looked vaguely familiar.

'Swiss,' he said. And held out his wrist.

Embarrassed, Peter said, 'Very nice.' Then he indicated the people ahead of them. 'Interminable.'

They both scrutinized each other for a moment.

'I'm sure I—' they both began.

And then Peter remembered. This was the man who came with his sister to Pamela's shop.

'We met briefly. Your sister was looking for curtaining?'

Douglas remembered. Oddball. Dressed like a refugee from the thirties' Riviera. He looked considerably more civilized today. 'Oh, yes,' he said. 'Sorry. I was a bit caught up. Didn't recognize you without the roses . . .' He

342

did his best to sound bright.

Peter ignored the joke.

They both stared at the roof space, searching for something more to say.

Peter was not going to break the silence. Following on from thoughts of satin underwear, the memory of playing pass the parcel with the roses was the more raw.

Eventually Douglas said, as airily as he could, 'I believe she's rather good.'

'Who?'

'The woman who runs it.'

'Pamela,' said Peter.

'That's it. My sister was very pleased.'

'Not my sort of thing.'

'Nor mine,' said Douglas.

There was another silence.

Eventually Peter said, 'They were just to say thank you.'

'Ah,' said Douglas, thinking, What were?

'The roses,' added Peter. And then he gave a nonchalant shrug. 'You know women. They like that sort of thing.'

Douglas had the briefest suspicion. 'Have you known her long?'

Peter nodded. 'Years. She's a useful contact. And you?'

Douglas said, 'Quite a long time. Off and on.'

'Well?' asked Peter as lightly as he could. He, too, harboured a suspicion.

Douglas shrugged. 'Not really, no.' He

paused, thinking that was bloody true. 'She's more my sister's friend really.' He enjoyed saying that. It was a tiny, harmless revenge for the hurt she caused him.

'Ah, yes,' said Peter, implying the two of them probably constituted a coven.

They both laughed. The queue moved on.

'I'm hoping she'll do a little job for me, you see,' said Peter.

Douglas nodded.

'And she's being difficult. Hence the roses.'

'She is difficult,' said Douglas. 'Very.'

'Very.' Peter nodded as the queue moved up. 'You use her, too, then?'

'Occasionally,' said Douglas.

Peter was about to ask more when a child came running between their legs and round their luggage, diverting them both. Peter sent her away and glared at her parents.

'I'm business class,' said Douglas, 'but they seem to have lumped us all together.'

'Me too.'

Peter looked about him, at the piles of bags and suitcases ahead, the harassed parents, the running, shrieking children, and the general air of confusion.

'I'm not sure,' he said feelingly, 'that I wouldn't prefer to risk being blown up.'

Douglas nodded. 'No discipline. It's the kids first every time.'

He said this so vehemently that Peter was startled. 'My son never behaved like that,' he

344

said quickly. 'Or at least, not when he was with me. What he did when he was with his mother, of course, I couldn't say.'

'My girlfriend has dumped me for her son this Christmas.' Oh, shit, thought Douglas, it was out before he could stop himself. Why, oh why, did I open my mouth?

Peter gave a little half-smile and looked away. 'Oh,' he said.

Disturbed by the sudden intimacy, they lapsed into silence.

Peter realized something was required. He went for neutral. 'How old is the boy?' he asked. 'Makes a difference.'

Douglas gave a derisive snort. 'He's twenty-two and she's *still* putting him first.'

'My ex wouldn't do that. She's the complete opposite,' said Peter. 'Can't shrug off the family quick enough. Booted me out when she'd had enough. And now our son's left home, she doesn't want anything more to do with me.' He laughed bitterly. 'Or very little. Different when the maintenance was paid. Got no lever with her now. She always put her career above us.'

'Mine just let hers go. As soon as the boy came along. Ended up working in a shop.'

'Something to be said for knowing your limitations,' said Peter. 'Women must learn to walk before they can run.'

'I could do with a drink,' said Douglas.

'So could I,' said Peter.

The queue went slowly on.

Peter said, 'She was supposed to come on this trip. I *thought* we were trying for a reconciliation, but she changed her mind. Let me down at the last moment. No explanation to speak of—something about love. Love . . .' He shrugged. 'Whatever *that* is.'

'You've been dumped, too, then?' Douglas felt a sense of relief.

'And how. Tickets, hotel—the lot.'

The ensuing silence was uncomfortable.

'They're an odd bunch,' said Peter.

'I don't think they know what they really want,' said Douglas. 'One minute they're throwing themselves at you—the next you say something harmless, and they're off . . . Fickle? Or what?

'Unpredictable. One minute you think you know where you are, the next they've shot off without so much as a by your leave.'

'I don't even know where mine is.' Douglas tapped the side of his bag with his heel. 'She didn't even bother to tell me that.'

'Nor do I,' said Peter. '*And* she hasn't told her mother—who is frail and elderly in an old folk's home—' He paused to let this sink in. 'And she hasn't told our son . . . Completely irresponsible. Just gone off.'

'Sounds the exact opposite of mine. *She'd* probably bring the son *and* the mother along on her honeymoon.' He gave a bitter laugh.

Peter felt himself growing hotter and hotter

with rage as he thought of Pamela out there, somewhere, careless of his needs. Free. Independent. And, what was worse, healthier than he was. 'Just fucked off. Nearly fifty and acting like a juvenile.'

'I don't think age has got anything to do with it,' said Douglas. 'Mine's not young.' He paused, and then added, 'I think that was part of the problem. If she'd been younger—' he was almost talking to himself—'then she wouldn't have been so rigid. No wonder most of my colleagues have gone for the younger model. They're easier.'

'Don't you believe it,' said Peter. 'I had a younger one. Wouldn't have sex for a month because I didn't take her to the Academy Dinner.' He closed his eyes at the memory. 'Half her hair was green, for God's sake.'

There was a suitable pause for the grossness.

'I mean,' said Peter, with feeling, 'how could she think she looked appealing with green hair?' He shook his head. 'And boots,' he added faintly. '*Boots!*'

'A friend of mine has just married a Filipino,' said Douglas.

'I can understand why,' said Peter. 'A proper wife would be very nice for a change. Indian women are very beautiful.' He looked around thoughtfully. There were several Indian women doing menial chores.

They became silent again, aware of the

347

depth of the confidences they now shared, and needing to retreat a little.

Douglas was relieved at the silence. What he really wanted was to get drunk, very quietly, on the plane, fall into the hotel, and sleep the Season away. There was no point in trying to call her. She was not there. He stopped at the house on the way here and a neighbour, looking like something out of a New York police series, shook his head and glowered until he backed off down the path. He had never felt so disappointed. And the disappointment led to humiliation, which in turn led to a very real anger. He could not believe any of it. Why, when it was all still so good? Everything he planned for that first night went so perfectly. And then her note arrived saying no, and he was dumbfounded. He did not understand. You separate, you come back together and find each other again. And then you separate again? When the very barrier to happiness in the past has been removed? Daniel. He said all that when he finally managed to see her. And she said, Leopards never change their spots, which applied to them both. And was clear as mud. She would not see him again after that.

He could not even tell Zoe. He was too humiliated. I do not want your fucking son, he had yelled across the crowded pavement at her, I just want you. She turned her back and she walked away.

He wanted some peace. It was only thanks to Lionel that he got away on his own. Lionel, lamb to the slaughter, filled the breach. Zoe just said, 'Oh, go on, then, I'll have to make do with him.' Zoe and he would continue to move in and out of Lionels and girls in red suits for the rest of their lives. Well—it was a better prospect than feeling helpless and angry like this. If that was love, you could keep it. Douglas said to her that he thought love, as she called it, was supposed to be accommodating. She just kept on walking, didn't turn round. And he realized that her talk of independence and liberation was just a cover for selfishness.

Peter eyed the queue ahead of them. 'Only a few more to go. Looks like the flight's going to be full. Not surprised. Christmas in London.' He shrugged.

'I know,' said Douglas. 'I'm usually in Barbados.'

They both stared around—up at the roof; down at the floor; over to where the cleaners and baggage staff made their slow, gladiatorial progress in chariots; across to the wide glass windows of the real world beyond. Then Douglas said, as casually as he could, 'Where do you stay? In Dublin.'

'At the Sheldonian.'

'Ah.'

'And you?'

'The   Old   Judge's   House.   They've

refurbished it.'

Peter said, without thinking, 'That's where we honeymooned.'

'Really?' said Douglas politely.

Peter nodded. 'It used to be a really nice old Georgian building.'

'I think they've done it carefully.'

'Might come and have a look.'

'Do,' said Douglas. 'Come and have a drink.'

'You might even be in the same room.'

They laughed.

'It's where our son was conceived,' said Peter.

Douglas said, 'Oh, really?' Politely.

'She was very different in those days,' said Peter. 'You know—cared about what I did. No question then about who should work and who should stay at home.'

'They soon change,' said Douglas.

'They do,' Peter agreed.

Eventually they reached the desk without much more talking between them. Peter's seat was dealt with first. For some reason, largely to do with neither of them quite knowing how to gainsay it, they were given seats next to each other.

'Terrific,' said Douglas firmly, as they wandered away together.

'Yes,' said Peter faintly.

A young man was causing some trouble at one of the other desks. An Irish accent and insisting that he must have a seat, although he was late for check-in. The flight was full.

'Then I'll have an upgrade,' he said.

The two of them stood watching, for something to do, and were both of the opinion it was a bit thick to see that the youngster got his upgrade to business class. It was easy to see why—which was even more irritating. The girl on the desk just stared up at the persuasive young man, and he leaned forward and dropped his voice low. His eyelashes almost swept the floor and he had the sparkling white smile of a toothpaste advertisement. Within a few seconds he was whistling on his way. Well, not exactly whistling, Peter was pleased to see—looking somewhat dejected.

Par for the course, thought Peter. Why not? It was bloody Christmas. Miserable time of year. Upgrade. Damn cheek, really, considering how much he and the rest of them had paid for the full price of a ticket.

Douglas agreed.

The drama over, and nothing left to do but walk across to departures together, they passed through security, each one feeling uncomfortable, and then Douglas saved the day by saying, 'Just going to have a look round,' and escaping.

'Fuck, fuck and more fuck,' he said under his breath. He supposed he could get the seat changed but that would look churlish. He was stuck with sitting next to the man and probably chatting all the way.

He spent the next hour wandering aimlessly around the shops, pretending to study the transient, peripheral items on display—handbags, scarves, perfumes, watches—and thinking that if she were here with him he would like to buy her something. And then thinking, again, how she had hurt him, and feeling the emptiness in his heart once more. Zoe had a point. Get them before they got you.

When the flight was called, he went to the back of the queue. It was only a short flight. That was a blessing.

*　　　*　　　*

Peter Pryor sat pretending to read the newspaper, relieved that his new-found seat companion had gone to the Duty Free. He was not looking forward to the flight and having to talk. And then, to crown it all, the young Irishman, the upgrade, sat down opposite him in the departure lounge and began reading. Peter peered, screwed up his eyes, tried to focus on the book's title. It was the same with someone else's newspaper—overpowering curiosity. Irritatingly, the youngster noticed, leaned forward, and said, sorrowfully more than rudely, 'It's called *In Praise of Older Women*,' and went back to reading again, deeply engrossed.

Peter felt himself go bright red. To cover it, he said jokily, 'I should stick to your own age if I were you. They get worse as they get older.'

The young man looked at him coldly. 'Maybe,' he said. And went back to the book.

* * *

Dean put the book aside. There was only one older woman he felt like praising at the moment and that was his mother. At least she never let him down. She was waiting there with all the family—ready to reward him with her affection. Real affection. Not like Pamela the last time he saw her. When he went to plead with her she stroked his hair and touched his cheek and showed him tears (real, were they?) as she said that no, she would not come. That he must find someone of his own age, that she had been wrong to even think they could take up again. Not acting responsibly, was what she said of herself, acting crazily; it could not be.

He said, 'That is what life is about: impulse, follow your heart, all that.'

And she said, 'You forget that I have a son, and I would not want him to bring me home. I would not wish this on him, and I will not bring it on you now.'

'Come with me,' he shouted.

And then Pamela also got angry. 'To arrive in your mother's kitchen and present myself as your girlfriend? The one who needs cookery lessons? Can you imagine that scene, Dean Close? To come to your flat and meet your friends? Can you see me there? At parties?'

'You should never have started it, then.'

'I know.'

He waited for her to say that he had started it. To throw that back at him. But she did not. She just sat there looking down at her hands. They were both in tears. And she said, 'Better now than in ten years' time. You will want to leave me eventually. I will never feel secure. It will not work. Ten years between us, fifteen years, maybe. But not twenty. No.'

'You cannot know that.'

'It was always for the moment.'

'But you came back.'

'I just took a drive,' she said. 'And I am sorry.'

'Men do it,' he said defiantly. 'My oldest brother married a girl from Wicklow and she's younger than me. They've a dozen years between them.'

'It is different.'

'It is no different.'

'It is called biology. We are arranged to protect it. And it is different.'

'I've no interest in babies,' he said. 'I want you.'

'Dean,' she said, 'if you were my great passion, if I felt I could not live without you, then I would let the world talk and go hang, and be with you. But it is not like that. And it only feels that it is like that for you, for now.'

'For always.'

'No. One day you will want all those other things. You will.'

'And anyway, there are ways. If I ever did.'

'Dean,' she said, suddenly the schoolmarm. 'I do not want any more babies. I do not want to be a mother again. I don't even want to have responsibilities. I want my freedom.'

'That is so selfish.'

'It's reality.'

'Then you don't love me?'

'I loved our time together. I am sadder at losing you than I am at losing anyone.' She held him. 'Dean,' she said, 'you were the best and the most generous in love. Don't lose that, because it's the future.'

'Piss on the future,' he said.

'You won't,' she said. 'You mustn't.'

And then she called a cab for him. His last act, done with dignity, was to refuse to let her pay the cab driver in advance. He was driven off into the night and he did not look behind again, once. Fuck the world.

At the restaurant they were pleased with him. He learned and he was quick and he did it all in defiance of the pain. If he was beating eggs, he would beat them as if they were Pamela, beat, beat, beat. But he knew he did not mean it. Not really. Somewhere inside himself he felt he was growing. The job felt good. They had a few good sessions after the

355

restaurant closed. He flirted with one of the girls in the kitchen. He began to have the shadowiest feeling that Pamela might have been right. As Christmas approached and he thought about seeing his family again, he was aware that he would have dreaded their response. Nevertheless, he would have done it. He was proud of being with her, proud of how much she knew, proud of the things he had learned with her. You wouldn't get that with the girl in the kitchen.

He said that to Deirdre, who drove him to the airport. He knew he would never love again and he said that, too. You might, she said. That was all. In his pocket was a small parcel she gave him as he said goodbye. He opened it now, shielding it from the nosy bloke opposite—Dean did not see why he should share the opening of the box with him as well. So he turned away to lift its lid and out tumbled a silver crucifix on a chain. He sighed. A good, kind, Catholic girl. Well—not that good. But his mother would approve. Not that he had any intention of giving her the chance. Never again, he vowed, dangling the chain. Nevertheless, he put it carefully back in its box.

And then the flight was called.

Thank God, thought each of the three men.

CHAPTER THIRTY-THREE

At a different airport, Pamela made her slow way towards Terminal Four. She thought of the three of them. It was too weird to contemplate. But maybe they would not go through with it? Dean would go home, of course. But Peter and Douglas could just as easily cancel the trip and stay in London. She decided that they would go home. At best, if she saw them in her mind's eye getting on the plane together, she saw them sitting miles apart. What she refused to see was them sitting in a chummy row and discussing her. They would not, of course. Margie—to whom she had finally confided—said, 'Best test of all. Ask yourself: if the plane blew up, which one would you want to be saved?'

'Daniel's father, of course,' she said. But inside she thought, And Douglas and Dean, for they were all important parts of the jigsaw that was her.

What was an easy choice for her mother at Brighton came at the beginning of her life, and in another part of history. You had to be a particular kind of person, from a particular piece of time, to settle arbitrarily like that. It was probably just as brave to do it her mother's way as to do what she was doing now: embracing the void. She shivered and hurried towards the desk, anxious to be gone.

*   *   *

If it was not enough, the young Irishman with the upgrade was the third member in their row of seats. He gave Peter a broad smile and Peter thought, Just don't speak to me, *don't* . . .

He was still feeling irritated. By Pamela, by his knee, by the niggling thought that he was going to have to talk all the way. He sat down. You could hardly feel alone in this particular situation, he thought, as Douglas shifted a little to acknowledge his arrival.

Douglas gave Dean a tight little smile that was more designed to freeze him out than be friendly. Little fucker, he thought. Pushing his way in like that. An oik. He gave Peter a look that made his view clear.

'Bloody ridiculous,' said Douglas.

'Bloody ridiculous,' agreed Peter.

Dean said, 'Bloody ridiculous,' too, thinking they were talking about the delay.

They eyed him. He smiled back.

For some reason the oik had got the window.

Peter stared ahead.

Douglas stared ahead.

Dean stared ahead, but he was staring ahead smugly. You could get anything if you used your charm.

Once airborne, Douglas immediately ordered a large whisky. Peter followed suit. God knew what it would do to his knee, but it could not be worse after all that stuff with Pamela. Dean joined in, realizing, suddenly, that the drinks were free.

Irish bloody upgrade, thought Douglas, taking the whisky gratefully. And the Irish upgrade smiled. Peter took his and rolled his eyes at the presumption. Then, since it was Christmas, or nearly, and because they were stuck with each other, Peter and Douglas raised their glasses very slightly to indicate bonhomie. Dean did too. The other two continued to look ahead, so Dean said, 'You should always look in the other person's eyes when you do that.'

They both turned their heads and looked at him as if he had arrived on the sole of their shoe. He leaned across, chinked both their glasses and said, 'Cheers.'

They sat there, motionless, both knowing that there was no way out. 'Cheers,' they said faintly. And knocked it back.

'Deirdre told me that,' said Dean.

Silence.

He peered at them both. They looked totally uptight.

'You have family in Dublin?' he said, suddenly, out of nowhere.

359

Both men said no. And clamped their mouths shut, opening them only to consume their drinks, which were finished very quickly, Dean noted. He signalled the passing stewardess and, with a gesture of flamboyant generosity, ordered three more. 'Might as well get stinking,' he said cheerfully. 'It's free.'

'Thank you,' said Peter.

'Yes,' said Douglas.

The drinks appeared and were taken and were begun.

Peter closed his eyes for a moment and leaned back. He did not want to communicate any more. He just wanted to relax.

Douglas caught Dean's eye, which was a mistake.

'Have you been to Ireland before?' Dean asked.

'Yes,' said Douglas shortly. 'But not for some time.' He also closed his eyes, but it was too late.

The voice beside him said, 'I wanted to bring my girlfriend, but she wouldn't come.'

Peter kept his eyes closed very tightly and muttered, 'Not another one.'

'Pardon?' said Dean, leaning across.

Douglas felt obliged to open his eyes. 'Ah,' he said. And then he felt a welling of something—maybe the warmth of the drink on his empty stomach, maybe an innate need to communicate, maybe a slow spreading self-pity—who could say. But he found himself giving a slight chuckle. 'We're all in the same boat,' he said. 'Or plane.'

'Oh?' said Dean.

'My girlfriend wouldn't come.' He jerked a thumb at Peter. 'And neither would his.'

Peter opened his eyes wearily.

'What can it be about Dublin?' he asked rhetorically. 'I think I'm going mad.'

Dean looked at him with interest.

There was something about the youngster's clear expression and unlined brow that offended him. 'Oh, let's have another,' he said, rubbing his eyes.

Douglas said, surprised at how funny he found it, 'Perhaps it's the second coming? Any stars out there?'

Dean peered, taking it literally, and Douglas and Peter exchanged amused glances that implied youth was wasted on the young.

'Don't know what it is about Dublin,' said Dean thoughtfully. 'Hard to say when you live in a place. My girlfriend liked it when she went with her dickhead husband years ago. I thought she'd want to come again . . .' He took another swig of his drink, feeling a warmth and fondness suffuse him. 'My girlfriend is a woman,' said Dean proudly.

Douglas, well into his third glass, snorted. 'Well, what else would she be? A kangaroo?' Which he found even more funny than the stars. And surprising, since he had no idea that he had kangaroos on his mind. But Peter

361

snorted, too, so that was all right.

'I mean,' said Dean with dignity, 'an *older* woman.' He leaned round to eyeball Peter. 'Hence the book.'

'Ah,' said Peter. 'I had a very young girlfriend once.'

'Did you?' said Dean excitedly, nearly spilling Douglas' drink as he leaned forward. 'How was it?'

'Bloody nightmare,' said Peter. 'Bloody nightmare. They're all a bloody nightmare.'

'This one was grand.'

'Till she dumped you.'

'They're all grand—until they dump you,' said Douglas.

'She was sexy,' said Dean. 'I think older women are sexier than young ones.'

Peter said, 'My ex-wife was an older woman and she wasn't sexy. Too busy getting herself fulfilled, or whatever it was she called it. Looking after our son *and* doing her own thing. Talk about having her cake and eating it. If she'd been a bit more of a support to me, we'd have been very comfortable together now. She's a romantic. There's no meddling with a romantic.'

'Mine wasn't. I organized something *very* romantic and she just turned her back on it,' said Douglas glumly.

'This is slipping down,' said Peter, looking at his depleted glass in surprise.

'I've gone off intelligent women,' said

Douglas. 'They're always trouble. If they're young, they want to settle down; if they are older, they won't. And if they are older and they *do* want to settle down, they get boring. You can't win.'

'Say that again,' said Peter. 'That's definite. And goodbye sex life.'

'I never had that problem,' said Douglas, giving a little smile as though remembering. 'We had great sex. All the time. Everywhere. Had her in a field by moonlight last time . . .'

'Dumped you, though, didn't she?' said Peter, quite maliciously.

'We've all been dumped,' said Douglas, indicating that more drinks were required. 'All I said was that I wanted her to myself. I'd have thought she'd have been flattered. But no. She said it was selfish. What the hell is love if it's not selfish? You find someone and you want to possess them. You don't want to *share* them, for God's sake. In that respect it has to be selfish.'

'I'd have shared. Love is a compromise. She told me that,' said Dean.

They ignored him.

'My ex-wife is a terrible woman,' said Peter. 'An interior designer of very dubious quality.' He took the new drink from the anxious-looking stewardess. 'Whereas I am a designer in the broadest possible sense. I deal with issues.'

'She dumped me,' said Dean, 'because she

363

was afraid of what my friends would say about her age. Being mature.'

'How old was she?' asked Douglas.

'Forty-eight.'

'Same age as mine.'

'And mine,' said Peter calculating. 'I think.'

'The trouble with mine was she had an old fart of a husband,' said Douglas, 'who let her down badly. Damaged her for life. That's what my sister said.' He attempted the word 'remarkable', failed and substituted 'intelligent'. 'Intelligent woman, my sister. Never catch her with a rug over her eyes.'

Douglas was not quite sure what he meant by this, and neither were the others, but they accepted it.

'And now she's at the wrong end of forty . . .'

'Who, your sister?' said Peter, a little lost.

'No,' said Douglas. 'Her. Her with the son and no ambition.'

'They don't like getting old,' said Peter. 'It affects them.'

'Mine didn't mind being old,' said Dean. 'She quite liked it—so she said anyway. She was great . . .'

They nodded at him impatiently.

Peter said, 'The trouble with mine was she was jealous of my success. And she never managed to get another man after me. Well, not one that did much for her—if you know what I mean. I think that turned her, really.'

'They do get neurotic,' agreed Douglas.

364

'She was definitely strange. I took her out to dinner recently and she wore something orange and cried a lot.'

'Well, you would if you were wearing orange,' said Douglas.

The two of them laughed.

'Mine did everything brilliantly,' said Dean. 'She was a great cook, great in bed, a good mother, did up people's houses, knew all about films and things—great . . .'

They looked at him sourly. 'Those sort of women don't exist,' said Douglas. Peter nodded.

'She did. She said, *Somebody* has to stay at home and keep the fire stoked, Dean. Her husband could only concentrate on one thing at a time. Great designer, she said, lousy husband.' He looked at Peter. 'He was a designer too—'

Peter said, 'Really?' politely. Anyone this oik knew could not be in the same league.

'And she said the one before me was a lot less mature than I was. She said he was jealous of her son. Can you imagine that? I mean—I didn't like it, but I'd have got on with him if she'd let me. He wanted to send the son to boarding school. Selfish bastard. So she left him.'

Douglas said miserably, 'She was right. I went to boarding school. Loathed it.'

Dean gave them another sublime smile and said, 'We are having a good time, aren't we?'

They said no word.

'Here's to Pamela Pryor, then,' said Dean. 'Wherever she is.'

If he had expected a response, it was not the colossal response he received. The man in the glasses went rigid in his seat, staring straight ahead. 'Pamela Pryor?' he said faintly.

And then his voice went right up high.

'My wife was called Pamela Pryor.'

'Really?' said Dean politely. 'Helluva coincidence.'

Dickhead, Peter was thinking, dickhead . . .

But it was the other man who let off a real rocket.

'What name did you say?' he roared. 'WHAT NAME?'

And Dean, mellowed by love and not caring a fig for anyone, repeated it.

'Pamela Pryor,' he said. 'My lover. My older woman.'

The roaring man now went a very bright colour. In Dean's opinion he was over-reacting. They both were. Each of them was staring at him as if he had grown at least two heads. Fuck them, thought Dean cheerfully, he had done nothing wrong.

'Say it once more,' said the man with glasses.

'Pamela Pryor,' he said very loudly, considering them drunk, unlike himself. 'PAMELA PRYOR . . .'

They neither of them looked too happy.

A tiny sliver of clarity peeped into Dean's mind. 'Why?' he said cautiously. 'Do you think you know her?'

The bright-faced man was nodding very slowly.

The other one had gone very pale. He was nodding, too.

'What,' they both began, 'was her son's name?'

'Daniel,' said Dean easily. 'Danny Pryor. Not much younger than me. He nearly caught us on the job once.' He laughed. 'I suppose it was quite funny, really, though I didn't think it was then. She was great in bed, just great . . .'

'Christ Almighty,' said Douglas.

Peter Pryor continued to sit rigid in his seat, staring straight ahead, giving a slight acknowledgement by bending his neck towards Dean. He said faintly, 'Pam?'

Pinch me, he thought, for I must be dreaming. The whisky, the air pressure—something. And he thought that for a man who only knew the woman in question slightly, and in the matter of sisters and soft furnishings, the other man was reacting very strangely. 'It's my ex-wife he's talking about. Think about that.'

Douglas gave a very defined picture of a man thinking very hard about that.

'*You* are Peter?' said Dean. 'The dickhead?'

Peter had never considered hitting anyone before, but he came close, he came very close.

The moment was engulfed by a cry of

singing disrapture from Douglas.

'She?' he said, looking at Dean. 'And you?'

Dean nodded. 'Yes, she and me. Why not?' He bridled a little.

Then Peter also had a sudden and very dreadful prick point of clarity.

He stared at Douglas and he said, hoping not for the expected answer, 'Can I ask . . .' He swallowed. 'Can I ask—what is your name?'

'Douglas Brown,' said Douglas quite mechanically. 'Your ex-wife and I were . . .'

'I bloody know what you were,' said Peter.

'Seat-belts on,' reminded the stewardess, scooping up their glasses thankfully. They were lost, quite suddenly, in their own private hell of whisky and bad dreams.

'Excuse me,' said Dean, trying to point not very successfully, 'are you telling me that you are her . . .' He indicated Peter.

'Old fart?' he said acidly. 'Yes, that's right . . .'

Dean's finger wobbled slightly. He aimed it at Douglas. 'And are you saying you are the . . .'

'Selfish bastard?'

'That's the one,' said Dean with spirit.

'Good God,' said Peter, putting his hands over his eyes and rubbing them into a roseate blur. 'Did she do this?'

'Fuck knows,' said Douglas. 'But I wouldn't put anything past her.'

'Fuck,' said Peter Pryor in wonder. And his knee began to throb like the beating of a drum.

368

The anxious stewardess returning gave them each a look. Possibly there was going to be trouble. 'Sssh, gentlemen, language,' she said, pointing at a Japanese couple across the way.

Peter looked up at them and said, 'Ying Tong Iddle I Po,' before smiling graciously at the stewardess.

Douglas, despite himself, laughed.

They both relaxed. What the hell. That's life. Lucky escape.

Only Dean was left to muse on how Pamela Pryor could have got involved with either of them.

'Six—eight years?' said Douglas. 'And we never met.'

'Nearly thirty and, no, we didn't.'

'Douglas Brown,' said Peter Pryor. 'I heard all about you. Mr Super Stud . . .'

'Is that what she called me?' Douglas looked down at his hands to conceal his smile.

'No,' said Peter. 'I did.'

Still Douglas smiled.

'Well, how about Mr Small Dick?' said Dean aggressively. But neither paid him any attention.

The three of them sat in spectacular silence. The plane seemed to be going around and around.

'Just like us,' said Douglas after a while.

Eventually the stewardess fussed up to them and said that the security alert was over. They had clearance to land. 'No bombs,' she said brightly, 'after all.'

'I wouldn't say that,' said Peter Pryor.

'Imagine how she'd miss us if we were blown away,' said Douglas with a touch of pathos.

Even Dean was bound to admit it was a thought.

Douglas said, 'Just think, we're all sitting here and we all knew the same woman.' He did not sound entirely convinced.

'Yes,' said Peter. 'We did.' He did not sound entirely convinced either.

Dean Close said, with complete conviction, 'I don't think either of you knew her at all . . .'

Little upgraded oik, they both thought. What does he know?

The silence sat heavily as they waited to land.

Peter Pryor, in all the waiting, felt a sudden expansion in his heart. After all, they had all been through quite a lot together. Douglas Brown was looking pale now, his jaw set rigid like a cockle-shell. Dean Close was scowling at the view from the window and tearing bits off his sick bag.

Bonhomie among fellow men, thought Peter Pryor, and he leaned back in his seat.

'Helluva journey coming down,' he said to Douglas. 'Bloody M25 as usual. I really think they should do something . . .'

Douglas unbent a little. 'Damn silly,' he said. 'Build a road and then you can't use it.'

'Quite,' said Peter.

370

Dean went on picking at his bag. They ignored him.

Peter Pryor relaxed more. He was comfortable with this.

'What do you drive?' he asked.

'Saab for out of town and long journeys. Otherwise a TX 70.'

In the seat beside him there was a sudden lurch. Dean Close sat forward excitedly. 'Wow,' he said. 'Is that the GTI?'

'No,' said Douglas. 'The GTI is only in the LX range. I've got the Turbo.'

'Wow,' said Dean again.

'But not the automatic. I like to feel the gears.'

'I want a car like that,' said Dean.

'Well, they keep their value.'

'I'm just changing to an automatic,' said Peter Pryor. He did not say his knee made it necessary. 'Smoother.'

'Sure,' said Douglas, taking it very seriously. 'Horses for courses.'

They each nodded at the wisdom.

'Pam drove a little Citroën. Not new,' said Dean.

'She was a bit odd that way,' said Douglas.

'Funny woman,' agreed Peter. 'Odd sense of style. Probably why she never made it to the top like me.'

'Yes,' said Douglas.

Dean's thoughts were roaming free. One day he would have a beautiful car. He suddenly had quite a hunger for it. You are the future, she said, and she was wise. He had so much to come. So much pleasure. He suddenly realized that. A great life. And she was right about his mother. She would have been terribly upset if he had brought Pamela home. He said softly, 'She's best left to get on with it.'

Which was more or less what the other two were thinking. 'Great cars,' said Dean softly. 'Both of them.'

'Easy to handle,' said Peter and Douglas.

The inference being that not everything was.

At the airport they went their separate ways.

'Merry Christmas,' they said in turn. Each one thinking that he never wanted to see the other again. 'And a happy New Year.'

And out they went into the cold, dark night.

CHAPTER THIRTY-FOUR

On a felucca floating down the Nile, Pamela Pryor sat staring out at the fertile greenery that clung like a slash of life to the banks of the river. Well, she had been quite wrong about Daniel needing her—at Christmas or at any other time. And she had been quite wrong about a lot of other things—three in particular. But not wrong about coming here where it was lovely—quite, quite lovely.

Green, fertile, growing. Beyond lay dry desert, dead land. She had not ventured into it; she liked it here, on the water, with the smells and the dampness and the light. Such light.

In the distance behind them rose the mighty shape of the Temple of Philae, the only temple dedicated to a single goddess, Isis. What fantastical magical powers they told of her. Earlier, in the cool of the morning, Pamela stood amid those ruins, enraptured and amused as the guide told her how Isis brought back to life her husband Osiris, and how her spells saved her son Horus from death.

They were good to their menfolk in those days, she thought, returning to the boat. But who could compete with a goddess?

Now she watched the gleeful splashing of the children on the banks, the bright white smiles of the passing boatmen and their happy calls. Heard the quintessential sound of Egypt, cradle of civilization, in the slapping of the water as they cut along. She felt better and happier as each mile slipped by, and it was no loss to be alone. Nike did not belong here. These gods were more ancient than her. And if she did succeed in making Pam groan out loud once in a while, well—maybe it was the price you paid. And not necessarily for ever . . .

She stretched out her bare arms to the wonderful evening heat. She had always wanted to come here, and she had. She had not expected it to be solo, but it was. And that was enough. It felt good. Bury the past. Build on its foundations. The evidence of the good sense of this was all around her. Karnak, Luxor, Memphis, names to conjure with. Ancient wonders that made the traveller feel very small, made her feel that her time on earth was infinitesimal. That she must use it before she, too, was blown away like a grain of sand. She had wondered, all the way by coach from Cairo, all the way by felucca from Luxor to Aswan, if she had done the right thing. How could you know? How could you ever know?

It came to pass. All things would pass. To worry and speculate was a waste of one small lifetime's store of energy. Action was what counted. One day she would get it right, perhaps. That mixture of obligation and fulfilment. Until then you did what you could. You made your bed. She smiled. And the figs, oh, the figs, were very ripe. She peeled one and thought it was no effort at all.

Of course there were regrets, moments when she wanted to turn to Peter, or Douglas, or Dean, and say, Such splendours. How could one woman create such marvels? She felt it when she saw the great tomb of Queen Hatshepsut. Peter would talk of the engineering stresses and strains, Douglas would kiss her and say something about the young queen using her feminine wiles, and Dean would probably say, You could do that . . . With alarming admiration. Impossible to live

374

up to.

But she knew its true limits. One woman could create these marvels because she invented a divine birth for herself, usurped her nephew's throne, and adorned herself with the golden beard of kings and the dress of a male heir to show that she was fearless and unbound by their ancient gender beliefs. A woman in a man's world and accordingly frail.

Hatshepsut survived untrammelled because the nephew she usurped was happy to be sent away to make pottery amongst the people in a different part of the valley. He found contentment in becoming a skilful artist, and for a while he no longer wished for power. So she built great temples, massive obelisks, superb columns with a hundred stories inscribed to her powerful successes. She almost thought she had made it. But no. One day, when her nephew finished with his pots and wished for a return to his former glory, he came back and wiped her out. Erasing her memory from almost every particle of her stones.

Pam peeled herself another fig, sighing for the destruction. No false beard could save her. Only her tomb could not be destroyed, because it carried the name of the God. Clever Hatshepsut. Feminine. Brain not brawn. But the rest of her was ground into oblivion. It was ever thus, Pam thought. A few steps forward, a few steps back. With luck and determination, maybe the former would outstrip the latter. It was to be hoped before the protesting maternal organs made themselves permanently barren in the attempt.

In Cairo, looking at the queen's mummified remains, Pam was astonished to see that she was still beautiful. Proud, long neck, high cheeks, cascade of hair—unquestionably female. To win the power game she hid all that femininity behind a false golden beard. Crazy times. So what's new? Yes, and the smiling keeper smiled all the more at her, as one will smile beneficently upon foolishness, when she bent towards the glass casket and whispered in those shrivelled ears, We'll get there one day. Maybe.

Now she smiled at the thick brown water rolling by. It would happen when seventeen angels could dance upon a pin. But, like the existence of those dancing angels, it would never happen at all if you did not hold fast and believe that it could. Yet another small conundrum in the battle of life.

Cattle were being brought down to the water for their evening drink. She waved and the boys leading them waved back. Then they dived in, one by one, and splashed about, full of delight. The girls hung back watching them . . . When seventeen angels could dance on a pin.

Tomorrow she flew home. A New Year, a life beginning anew. She had bought only two souvenirs. One for herself and one for Margie. Carved figurines of Amnenshekat, the goddess of deceived women.

'Deceived by their lovers or deceived by themselves?' she asked the seller.

'Yes,' he said obsequiously, nodding and smiling through his cracked and broken teeth. 'Yes, yes, yes.'

She laughed then and did not haggle.

She chose the goddesses carefully from the serried lines on offer. The two she chose were carved looking up at the sky.

*　　*　　*

Daniel Pryor let himself into the house. He was glad to get home a day before his mother to sort out his thoughts a bit. He knew he would not go back to Liverpool, and he knew that he did not want to see Lilian ever again. She felt exactly the same.

She saw him off on the train and they agreed. He wanted a bit more from life than diving into other people's technology. And the sex had gone right off. Strange that. It was great for ages and then—over. Long evenings with nothing to say except, You are a long time dead, which Lilian said often. So he came home.

He dumped his bag in the hall, picked up the post and took it into the dining room. It all looked very neat and clean. And—he sniffed—

it smelled of home. He was really glad to be back. On the other side of the room, still leaning against the piano, was his old guitar. He picked it up and played a chord. It felt really good. That was what he wanted. He would call up Rick later and get him over for a session. A few beers and some old stuff—like it used to be.

But first he would sleep. They had been fighting all night. Neither had slept. And he was tired. He was also hungry. He looked in the kitchen but there was no food. Which was surprising. Not like his mother. He had never known this kitchen without food in it. Not even a loaf. The fridge, when he looked in, had an end of cheese, a couple of apples and butter. He found some biscuits and ate them with the cheese and the fruit as he wandered about, trying to feel his way back.

He never wanted to see Lilian again. He had been crazy to leave here for her. She even moaned if he left his socks on the floor.

Bits of biscuit dropped from his hands; he watched them fall absently, and walked over them. When he had finished he mounted the stairs to his room. Thank God for home.

When he opened the door and walked in, he found nothing. A pure white cube. 'What the fuck is going on here?' he said out loud.

EPILOGUE

Pamela Pryor, mother of Daniel, ran down the stairs. The June morning was still cool, despite the sun that poured into the hallway. It blinded her for a moment. She stumbled. Her leg made contact with an object that lay at the bottom of the stairs. Something rasped and she felt a tearing beneath her knee. She looked down. Then, taking a deep breath, she yelled up the stairs in the direction of what she still thought of as the spare room, 'Daniel Pryor. Will you come down here this minute and put this bloody guitar somewhere safe?'

No answer.

'And while you are about it,' she called, 'your washing is about to start crawling out of the basket of its own accord. And your father is expecting you to pick him up from the station in less than an hour.'

'Oh, Mum,' came the sleepy answer.

'Daniel.'

'All right. All right . . .'

'Pryor and Pryor. That's you, now, remember. And I've got to go or I shall be late. Now up!'

She looked down, cursing under her breath. There was the beginning of a hole in the nylon. Damn, and damn, she thought. And then she heard laughter. Coming from the top of the stairs. She looked up. Daniel stood there, grinning. In his arms he held a precarious mound of washing. But behind it, and the sight nearly required a lie down, she could see that he was fully and properly dressed, with what appeared to be shower-wet hair. He even had his shoes on. Proper shoes.

'Danny?' she said faintly. He advanced down the stairs, a sock or two dropping on the way.

But what was a sock or two . . .?

'You'd better go,' he said, as he passed her by, heading for the kitchen. 'Or you'll be late.'

He had the air about him of one whom it is all beneath.

Oh, Danny, she said under her breath, and, grabbing her keys, she fled.

Down the path, running and running, more like the White Rabbit than a woman of the world, along the street, round the corner, flying in the direction of Ani Patel's shop.

As she neared it, she looked up and could see the studious head of Ari Patel, bent over his books. He still wore the moustache, although now it gave him a ponderous, more serious expression. He was in the middle of his exams, so she did not call up or wave to him.

In she went.

The shop was crowded. Ani Patel was standing by the counter holding the new baby in her arms. Her face was radiant with pride and she jiggled the infant, even though it was soundly asleep. He had blonde curls and cheeks like russet apples. Everyone agreed he was the handsomest baby ever. Surrounding her was the strange woman with the ragged white hair and the fat man in his beret. They were—no other word for it—adoring the child.

Pamela came forward and looked.

He was scrumpled into sleep, contented, sweet, perfect . . .

And somebody else's, thought Pam, thankfully.

'Ah,' said the assembled. 'Ah,' as he moved a little in his sleep.

'My grandson,' said Ani Patel happily. 'My grandson.'

Arms reached out. Ani Patel came forward and placed the child in Miss Phoebe Glen's open arms.

Just for a moment.

She held the child to her chest, where it murmured contentedly.

'Ah,' they all went again. 'Ah.'

Pamela said, 'He is growing.'

Ani Patel said, 'They do.'

'Tell me about it,' said Pam.

Ani Patel thought this was yet another strange linguistic quirk of the English. They said it, but did not mean it.

'Can I help?' she said.

'Stockings,' said Pam. 'I have a hole in mine. And I'm late.'

'Alas, I only have tights,' said Mrs Patel.

381

For the barest moment Pamela hesitated. Then she smiled. 'Oh, well, tights, then.'

She slipped them on behind Ani Patel's door and threw the stockings away. Then she tiptoed up, stroked the russet cheeks once more, before running out into the bright sunny day.

Must not be late, she told herself happily. Must not be late. For a very, very important date.

And Ani Patel, taking the baby back, held him to her as if he was the most precious thing on earth.

Which was a fact.